LET SLEEPING AFGHANS LIE

Michael Thall

Walker & Co.
New York

DEDICATION

This book is dedicated to Dr. Moms.

ACKNOWLEDGEMENT

I wish to thank Richard C. Digon, Attorney at Law, Ypselanti, Michigan, for the many courtesies he extended while introducing me to the procedures and personnel of the Washtenaw County 14th District Court and the 22nd Circuit Court. Mr. Digon acted in good faith and is, of course, entirely guiltless of what I subsequently made of this information.

Copyright © 1990 by Michael Thall
All rights reserved. No part of this book may be reproduced or transmitted in any form or by any means, electronic or mechanical, including photocopying, recording, or by any information storage and retrieval system, without permission in writing of the Publisher.
All the characters and events portrayed in this work are fictitious.
First published in the United States of America in 1990 by Walker Publishing Company, Inc.
Published simultaneously in Canada by Thomas Allen & Son Canada, Limited, Markham, Ontario
Library of Congress Cataloging-in-Publication Data
Thall, Michael
Let Sleeping Afghans Lie / Michael Thall
ISBN 0-8027-5755-3
I. Title.
PS3570.H318L48   1990
813'.54—dc20   89-28944
CIP

Printed in the United States of America
2 4 6 8 10 9 7 5 3 1

1

THE MORNING OF THE Tuesday I learned my ex-wife was a murder suspect, I woke up to discover someone had crocheted my Afghan hound to my afghan rug.

I'm a night person, so I consider eleven or twelve the civilized hour for greeting the world. It was the crash and tinkle-tinkle of breakables being broken that woke me. Natasha—the dog, not the rug—was waddling happily around my sixth-floor condo, dragging my afghan rug like a cape. There were leftover hors d'oeuvres scattered around and sour cream dip on her nose. Groggy from last night's party, I collared her and discovered that the ends of her long silky hair had been cunningly interwoven with the woolen rug.

Afghan hounds are supposed to be aristocratic creatures. Natasha is a fat, stupidly amiable beast who would rather eat than sleep, and would rather sleep than anything else. She must have lolled placidly in the living room all night while the deed was done. Natasha was a parting shot from my ex-wife in our divorce settlement. The rug I got on my own. Now both had scythed my home.

Keeping a grip on Natasha, I punched a number on the phone. One ring. Natasha slurped my left ear. "Down, girl,"

I muttered. Two rings. Another slurp. "Natasha, down, down."

On the tenth ring a diabolically languid voice answered.

"Very funny, Biswanger!" I said in a mild shout.

"Why, George! Whatever are you doing up at this hour?"

"You're not fooling anyone, Biswanger. Only you would stoop so low."

"Emily." Biswanger was calling to his wife. "Emily. It's George. Yes, George. I know it's only eight o'clock. Perhaps he's turned over a new leaf. Have you, George?"

I could feel my temple begin to throb. "How do I separate them?"

"Separate whom, George? I hope you aren't contemplating breaking up someone else's marriage. You did a thorough enough job on your own."

"You know whom... who. Natasha."

"Separate Natasha?" Biswanger feigned a puzzled pause, then he exclaimed, "Oh, George, you're breeding her! Emily, there's going to be a litter of little Natashas. But George..." Back to me in a low, confiding voice. "... I hope you've checked the sire's papers."

"From my rug," I hollered.

"Oh, that..."

"Yes, that. Any suggestions?"

"Then we won't have the first pick of the litter?"

"There isn't going to be a litter. Not while Natasha is Siamese twins with my rug."

"Timmy will be disappointed, George. No furry yapping bundles of joy to play with."

With superhuman control I said, "How do I get her separated?"

"Well, Natasha has been due for a trim."

"Trim? What about my rug? We're talking ten thousand

dollars of irreplaceable Caucasus mountain art. Pre-Russian invasion."

Biswanger made a yawning sound. "I imagine any good reweaver... although in this case, I suppose one would have to call it unweaving."

"I'll get you for this, Biswanger."

"Now, George, it's obvious you haven't had your coffee yet, so there is no point in pursuing this banal conversation. By the by, don't forget our one o'clock lunch with Irene. I've booked a table at Cicero's."

I groaned. A business meeting with Irene. My former wife. I'm a toy designer. We have joint interest in board games I invented when the bloom was still on the rose. One is called *Matrimonial Monkeyshines*, but our big seller is *Hotel Rompé*. Actually, Irene still has a lot of bloom on her. When the light hits her a certain way.... Oh, well. Water under the bridge.

"I heard that groan, George. I expect you to assume a human personality by lunchtime. I'll tell Emily you send your love."

"And kiss the kiddywink for his Uncle George," I said sourly.

"See you at one, George."

While I hunted in vain for a pair of scissors, I continued my slow burn. Back when Biswanger and I were college roommates at the University of Michigan, we'd started this idiotic tradition of playing practical jokes on each other. Mine are of the gentle sort, mature and never causing more than a transitory mental sting. Biswanger's jokes, on the other hand, still carry the reek of unresolved adolescent hostility. More often than not, they cross the line of good taste. Biswanger is now my lawyer. For an overly generous ten percent of my meager earnings, he sees to it that the corporate sharks don't steal my licenses.

I had to use my toenail clippers. While Natasha lapped at my scowling face, I made hundreds of minute snips to separate her from the afghan. I stood back to survey the results.

I had an Afghan dog with a crew cut and an afghan rug with a new fringe.

I showered, shaved, dressed, and took Natasha to Liberty Plaza for her walk. Like most university towns, Ann Arbor has its share of franchised weirdos, so Natasha didn't draw a second glance. She entangled her leash around a lady walking a Pomeranian. A hoody-looking guy in a designer leather jacket, the type of guy who sells little packets out of his designer pockets, got up from the bench, walked over and introduced himself, first to Natasha and then to me. I figured he'd set up shop, or else he had a thing for feeding sparrows. He was taken with Natasha's new "fab haircut." With her unerring canine instinct, Natasha returned his overture by deciding to make friends with him. After some pleasantries—his name was Delmore—he said he'd always had a thing for doggies, and would I consider trading Natasha for a quantity of his special stuff? Deducing that he wasn't there for the sparrows, I politely declined his offer, whereupon he turned up the heat of his winning shark smile.

Reaching into his pocket he said, "I like the look of you, my man," and withdrew a business card. "In case you change your mind."

His card was beautifully engraved on expensive vellum stock. It said *Delmore Black Personal Services* with two phone numbers. Just another enterprising, third-economy businessman. I thanked Delmore and conspicuously put the card in my wallet.

My head still needed clearing, so I walked down State

Street and joined the teaming student throng as I crossed the old campus diag, a combination pedestrian highway and Hyde Park for the political protest of the day. The old University of Michigan campus is bounded on four sides by East University, South University, North University, and State streets, which shows the practical-mindedness of the founders. That was long ago. Ego-enhancing endowments have turned the University of Michigan into a Minotaur's maze of institutes, schools, and labs. A nondescript Greek revival frame house might house an offshoot of the psychology department, although recently there's been a trend to leviathan construction projects. The dental school is a mega-complex on North University, sort of a prelude to the biomedical complex surrounding the U of M hospital to the northeast—an area fondly called pill hill. Further northeast, past the golf course and playing fields, is the North Campus where Gerald Ford got his tax write-off in the form of the Gerald R. Ford Library. It sits on the edge of oaks and greensward, across from the engineering department's research nuclear reactor. If anything unites the U of M potpourri, it is an ecumenical hatred of the Ann Arbor parking ticket.

I exited under the engineering arch onto South U. Since I'm always on the lookout for clues to the new direction, I browsed the clothing, fast food, and book stores that service the academic multitude. I decided against breakfast at the Brown Jug, and instead popped into the Bagel Factory for a raisin bagel. Natasha prefers onion bagels, but since she'd already snaffled last night's onion dip, and since I must live with her breath, this morning she had to be satisfied with pumpernickel.

When I got back to my lobby at noon, to my surprise Biswanger was waiting for me. His sleek, overfed face was grim.

"Where were you?" he demanded. "My office has been phoning you all morning."

"Out walking Natasha."

"All morning?" He sounded suspicious. Peculiar.

"It's a long story." I didn't feel like explaining Delmore.

"Hey, what's wrong? Did Irene cancel?"

"She was arrested this morning. Someone killed Miles Dixon last night after he got home from your party."

Biswanger drove us east on I 94 toward District Court 14B at the Ypsilanti Civic Center. I had bundled Natasha into the back seat of Biswanger's waiting Continental, and there she now sat with her snout out the half-opened right rear window, watching Ford Lake go by, while Biswanger filled me in.

Irene had already had her first arraignment before the magistrate that morning and was now back in lockup. Biswanger told me it was merely a reading of the initial charges, with an automatic not-guilty plea entered. Thanks to the twelve-day rule, Irene's probable-cause hearing would be within twelve days, when her bail could be discussed. As it stood now, the magistrate had set her bail at "seven hundred-fifty thousand dollars, ten percent," which meant I had to come up with seventy-five thou, or else Irene would stay in jail.

"Last night the police got an anonymous phone call," Biswanger said. "Apparently from one of Miles's neighbors in Huron Towers, about a loud fight going on in his apartment. When they arrived to investigate, they found him stabbed to death through the throat with a pair of scissors."

I swallowed. "Why arrest Irene? The scissors could belong to anyone."

"The scissors had her antitheft serial plate on them."

I groaned. When Irene and I were still together, Irene had

joined a neighborhood crime watch. She had put metal identification plates on our valuables. But her scissors?

I said, "Irene didn't have anything against Miles. What could anyone have against Miles? Unless it was that he could bore them to death," I added, thinking of his many victims laid low from spiritual exhaustion whenever he got on the subject of foreign policy.

"I'm afraid there's more," said Biswanger. "One of the investigating officers said there's evidence Irene was a... not infrequent visitor... to Miles's apartment."

I was totaled. In the aftermath of the silent explosion, I flung my head back against the headrest, eyes closed to the leather-scented luxury of Biswanger's car, while my thoughts wobbled through the detritus of my shattered emotions.

Miles and Irene. Irene and Miles. How long had they been fooling around behind my back? I tried to recall those telltale signs of double-dealing the advice columnists warn you about, only to realize how devious Miles and Irene had been. *My* Irene. Oh, perfidy!

"Stop moaning, George."

Unable to open my eyes and face the world, I said, "All the time during our breakup, I actually thought maybe I was to blame."

"You know perfectly well you were."

I opened my eyes. Natasha's upside-down face was gazing down at mine. Seized by a maniacal hatred of Miles Dixon, I straightened up.

"I'll kill him."

Biswanger glanced over at me. "He's already dead."

"Then I'll resurrect him and kill him again," I snarled.

"You're a long way from walking on water. Now listen to me, George. You mustn't say anything like that within earshot of the police. When we get there, you behave yourself. Irene is not your wife any more."

2

THE YPSI CIVIC CENTER was on a golf green sitting out in the middle of nowhere. We drove by a pond with a fountain jet and with big white swans paddling around, on to a building complex. In front of the main building was a terra cotta sign: *District Court 14B and Police Facility*. Irene was in there somewhere.

It was like entering a sociologist's dream of enlightened criminal justice. Clean bright hallways with lots of glass, helpful signs, and neutrally hued offices. No crummy linoleum. No battered coffee makers with tight knots of cynics gathered round, talking tough big-city slang. At the information counter opposite the magistrate's office, a clerk was explaining arraignment procedures to a leather-jacketed young man whose metal studs, tabs, zips, and boot rings were belied by his despondent, stumbling questions. She gave him a sheet with his legal rights printed on it, and he clumped off. I asked the clerk where the jail was. She cheerfully handed me a building map and gave directions.

The cops were crisp and polite as Biswanger and I were patted down and buzzed with a metal detector before being ushered into the visitor's room, where we waited at a large table under a telecamera. Irene was brought in by a policewoman who resembled a school-crossing guard, and who remained to stand watch over us.

Normally, when Irene smiles no one can help but smile back. She looked drawn and tired and, I had to admit, very lovely. Her face had become fragile over delicate bones, her tawny hair darker. Maybe it was the fluorescent lights. She sat at the table opposite Biswanger and me, crossing her legs and tilting her head to regard me from her shoulder.

I tried not to think about Miles Dixon. "Hello, Irene."

"Hello, Georgie."

"Are they treating you well?" I asked, still trying not to think of Miles Dixon.

She pushed her hair back and gave a weary smile, revealing her left dimple that still had the power to captivate me. "The arresting officers were very polite about it. Everyone here is very polite."

"Did you do it?" It was a dumb thing for me to say, but it popped out by itself.

Her grey eyes flashed. "Is that why you came here? To insult me?"

"No," I snapped. "To worship you."

"That was always your trouble, Georgie. You idealized me."

"Most women wouldn't see that as trouble."

"No woman could possibly live up to your ideal. You set me up to disappoint you."

"That's not true," I cried. "I was never disappointed. You were dazzling then, you're transcendently lovely now, and you damn well know it. And lest we forget, you were not above calling me 'cute.'"

"You *are* cute," she snapped back. "Like a klutzy Cary Grant."

"Oh, I see. When you do it, you're not idealizing me?"

"I know the difference," she said airily.

"You're still infuriating."

"Just like old times, Georgie."

"I just want to ask you something."

"You already asked me if I did it."

"What did you see in Miles?" I asked, and paused, but saw neither guilt nor remorse flit across Irene's features. "The police said you went regularly to his apartment."

"I'm not accountable to you," she replied with maddening calm.

"My God," I said. "You and Miles. The notion is absurd."

"That's right, Georgie. Boorish and absurd."

"What did you see in him?"

"There you go again, comparing yourself like it's a contest. You've never understood mature relationships."

At that moment, I could have cheerfully throttled the life out of Miles Dixon in full view of the security camera. But as Biswanger had pointed out, Miles was already dead. I said, "Come on, Irene. Even at his best, Miles was magnum of chloroform."

"Miles was very sensitive and caring."

"I'll bet."

"O-o-oh, what a dirty mind. This is so typical of you, George."

I was plain George again. I said, "I'd appreciate it if you'd explain that remark."

She pushed up her sleeve and flipped back her hair again. "You're using my crisis as an excuse to take control. I didn't ask you to come here."

"You know what's typical?" I retorted. "Putting your serial number on a pair of scissors."

"For your information, those scissors are a valuable heirloom. Silver-chased handles. My grandmother brought them over from England."

I knew it was contemptible of me, but Irene had pushed all my buttons, so I said it anyway. "I'm sure Miles appreciated that."

At this point, Biswanger interrupted. "George! May I remind you, Irene is here on open murder. May I also remind you, she couldn't have done it, because when Miles was killed, she was at your apartment with Natasha and the rug."

We all took a breather. I noticed the policewoman had a contrived air of disinterest, which meant she was savoring every juicy detail.

"How do I come up with the seventy-five thousand?" Irene asked Biswanger.

Biswanger opened his briefcase and took out papers. "I've arranged to put up your *Hotel Rompé* licenses as collateral."

My heart skipped a beat. Currently, my share of the royalties from our *Hotel Rompé* board game was paying the mortgage while I cast around for another winning idea. Since Irene had gone, my creative muse seemed to have taken a leave of absence.

Biswanger cast a sharp look in my direction. "I'll need *both* your signatures."

I was miffed. Did Biswanger really believe Irene's accusation that I would caddishly exploit her situation? Me, the wronged party?

With gallant cool, I took the pen and signed. Rather like Cary Grant, I thought.

Irene was out on bail, but since my visit at the jail had been less than joyful, we stayed out of each other's way until her hearing ten days later. I decided to forgive her about Miles Dixon.

Five minutes before nine o'clock on Tuesday morning,

LET SLEEPING AFGHANS LIE 13

Biswanger and I arrived at District Court 14B. Irene and her trial lawyer weren't there yet. No one was there yet, because the courtroom was pitch black inside, and I wondered if it was the right day. I checked the docket sheet posted on the wall by the courtroom door. Irene was scheduled for ten. We were early. Other people started arriving. We all stood around in the hallway like people waiting at a VD clinic.

It was a quarter after nine when a stocky attorney carrying a briefcase hurried through the crowd, opened the courtroom doors, saw it was dark inside and muttered, "They never start on time," before going inside. There was a dull banging sound, followed by a muttered curse. The fluorescent lights flickered on. He stood by a light switch, rubbing his shin where he'd cracked it on a chair.

Biswanger and I looked at each other. I said, "why didn't *you* think of turning on the lights?"

"I'm not a trial lawyer," he replied.

We filed in with the crowd.

District Court 14B had soothing gray-green carpet and matching gray-green, cloth-padded chairs for the spectators. There were no windows. Under the soft fluorescent lighting, isolated from the outside world, there was a pervasive, oppressive sense of "Time to put up or shut up."

Up at the judge's empty bench was a large name plate: *Hon. John B. Cole*. High on the wall behind the bench was a State of Michigan seal. The court officer had a gunbelt, a yellow badge, and just so there couldn't be any doubt, a large arm patch on his white shirt that said *Michigan District Court Officer*. For a moment, I wondered if we'd all be issued name tags.

Irene arrived, dressed for a funeral. We exchanged civil hellos. In low, dulcet tones that went nowhere, Biswanger introduced me to Irene's defense attorney, Mr. Grunion, from the firm of Grunion, Grunion, Littlefield and Grunion. He was Grunion the youngest.

To me, Grunion looked like a corn-fed kid who'd gotten by because of his frat house test files. His expression was fresh and eager, without the duplicity and guile I expect from a defense attorney. Why hadn't Biswanger insisted on a senior Grunion? Still, first impressions could be deceptive.

"How does it look?" I asked in a low, level voice.

Grunion said, "Wusthof is prosecuting..."

"Mack the Knife?" Biswanger said in an intense whisper. "Oh, shit."

"But that's good for us," Grunion whispered back.

Biswanger looked doubtful.

"Why is that good?" I whispered to Grunion.

"Because Wusthof's got a big ego," Grunion whispered to me. "He pursues weak authorizations. And this is a lousy authorization. He's going for premeditation."

"Murder one?" Biswanger exclaimed, his whisper rising a full octave.

Apparently this was news to him. I was still trying to come to grips with Mack the Knife.

Grunion said, "If Wusthof had any sense of proportion, he'd allow it was mitigated by passion and be satisfied with manslaughter. But, no-o-o, not Wusthof. I'm going to build a transcript and ram it down his throat at the trial. When I'm done, Wusthof will know who he's tangled with."

I said, "Excuse me, but I thought the purpose of this hearing is to determine *whether* Irene should be bound over to circuit court."

"Ri-i-ight," Grunion said softly.

I looked over at Irene. She was doing her relaxation exercises—slow breaths in and out, in and out.

A nervous thrill rippled through the room. Prosecutor

Wusthof marched in with an accordion folder of case files. Wusthof had a hundred-dollar haircut and European-tailored suit to go with his lean and hungry look. He took his place at the prosecutor's table.

The side door from the judge's chambers opened. A blonde came out, carrying files and a water carafe to the judge's bench. She wore a clinging gray fuzzy sweater with a large matching bow in front. She bent over, arranging the files, and all talk ceased while the large bow swung from her bosom.

The court officer ordered us to rise. We stood, and Judge Cole entered. He sat, and we were declared in session.

Charles Finch came into the courtroom. I knew Charles since he had sold Natasha to Irene and me. He was still Natasha's veterinarian and he shared my interest in collectibles, which included my afghan rug. With an apologetic look Charles whispered, "I was subpoenaed by the prosecutor's office."

Charles a prosecution witness? He'd been at my party the night Miles was killed.

Charles shrugged. "You know as much as I do."

I looked at Irene, and she shrugged.

I looked at Grunion. He returned a blank look.

There were a few cases scheduled on the docket before Irene's hearing.

Two of the cases were robberies of Stop and Go convenience stores. I had long been of the opinion that Stop and Go's were created expressly to give bread and butter business to defense attorneys. The first case was iffy whether it was armed or not, there being a serious question whether the gun had in fact been only the top of a whiskey bottle protruding from the accused's vinyl bag. In the second robbery the guy had walked in, talked with the clerk, then grabbed some cigarettes and run out. He claimed he'd been elsewhere at the time, but it was no go. He was the ne'er-do-well brother of the Stop and Go clerk, who had since lost his job there. What kind of fool robs a store where his own brother is working, and with a video camera going? I thought the charges should have included gross stupidity.

Wusthof had the hapless clerk in the witness chair, forcing him to testify against his brother. It went on a long time. I felt sorry for the clerk. Apparently, Wusthof was a devotee of the nuclear warfare concept of overkill. The carton of cigarettes was there merely to mark target zero.

It was when Wusthof referred to the accused robber as the clerk's younger brother that the clerk balked. "*I'm* the younger brother. We're twins."

I looked from the brother on the witness stand to the brother at the defense table. Clearly fraternal twins, not identical.

"If you're twins," Wusthof asked, "how can you be his younger brother?"

"I was born thirty-five minutes after him."

On such small victories do the poor bastards of the world get through the day.

Irene's hearing was next. My palms were sweating.

Irene's arresting officer spelled her name for the court: F-r-e-i-d-a-y.

Detective Nancy Freiday looked a bit frazzled, as though maybe she could have done with six more hours of sleep, but her testimony was professional and to the point.

I followed along with a copy of the police report that Grunion had. Responding to a 2 AM call about a possible domestic disturbance, she and her partner, Detective Sergeant Clancy, had gone to Apartment 18 at Riverside Towers. The door was ajar. They announced themselves and, not hearing a peep from inside, they entered. In the living room they found Miles Dixon fallen sideways on the sofa, with the handles of a pair of scissors protruding from his throat. Two drinks were nearby.

Besides the scissors, other items in the apartment had identification plates with Irene Spinoza's registration number. On her initial interview Ms. Spinoza did not deny they were hers. Other items of a more personal nature were traced to Ms. Spinoza; she did not deny they were hers, but professed ignorance as to how they had gotten there.

Wusthof called Charlie Finch to the stand.

Grunion had his pen ready to take notes.

"What is your name?" Wusthof began.

"Charles Croyden Finch."

"Mr. Finch, where do you work?"

"I am head veterinarian of the Northside Animal Hospital, and a partner in Cuddly-Wuddles, Incorporated."

"What kind of enterprise is Cuddly-Wuddles?"

"A purebred dog service."

"Do you know the defendant?"

"Yes."

"How long have you know the defendant?"

"About two years."

"How did you first meet her?"

"She and her husband were looking for a puppy."

"By her husband, you mean George Spinoza?"

"Yes. Sorry, I should have said her former husband. They were married then."

"After that initial meeting at Cuddley-Wuddles, did you continue to see them?"

"Yes. Many times. We became friends."

"And since the Spinozas' divorce, have you remained on

friendly terms with both the defendant and her former spouse?"

"Yes."

"You've continued to see them socially?"

"Yes."

"Did you continue to see them with their old friends?"

"Yes."

"At parties, and other social occasions?"

"Yes."

"With Miles Dixon?"

Grunion said, "Objection, your Honor."

"I'll rephrase. When Irene went to these parties, was she accompanied?"

Charles looked as uncomfortable as the Stop and Go clerk had. "Sometimes."

"Was she ever accompanied by Miles Dixon?"

"Yes," he said reluctantly.

"Did you see the defendant and the decedent together at other social occasions?"

Grunion piped, "Objection, your Honor."

"Your Honor, I am establishing that there was a personal relationship between the defendant and the decedent."

"Overruled."

"Mr. Finch," Wusthof continued, "when you saw Miles Dixon with Irene, did you ever see them quarrel?"

"No."

"You're sure of that. You never saw them arguing."

"On the contrary. They were always on the friendliest of terms."

Wusthof turned to look at some papers, and I saw a nasty gleam in his eye. "Were you a guest at a party held at George Spinoza's home this past May 17th?"

Charlie said, "Yes, I was."

What was Wusthof getting at? That party last month had been to celebrate the sale of our millionth *Hotel Rompé* game, but Miles was killed only a week and a half ago.

Wusthof said, "Did you see Irene Spinoza at Mr. Spinoza's party?"

"Yes," said Charles.

"Did you see Miles Dixon at the party?"

"Yes."

"Did you see Miles Dixon and Irene Spinoza talk with each other?"

"Sure. It was a party."

"What time did Miles arrive at the party?"

"I'd say about two hours after I arrived."

"Would it be accurate to say he arrived when the party was well under way?"

"Yes."

"About what time did he leave the party?"

"I don't know."

"When you say you don't know, Mr. Finch, do you mean you forgot?"

"Yes."

"The night of the party I know you can't give me the exact time because you forgot. But since you were at the party, did Mr. Dixon leave the party before you or after you? You can tell the court that, can't you?"

"He left before I did."

"How long did you stay at the party, Mr. Finch?"

"About three hours."

"Then you were at the party three hours, and you forgot that Miles arrived two hours after you arrived, and you forgot that he left within an hour after he arrived. Is that accurate?"

"Yes."

"I know you can't remember exact times, but can you tell

us, did Irene Spinoza leave before or after you left the party?"

"Before."

"So, you remember that you forgot that both Irene and Miles left the party before you."

I glanced over at Irene. She refused to meet my eye.

Wusthof was saying, "You remember that you forgot that both Irene and Miles left within the remaining hour before you departed. Is that a fair summary?"

"Yes."

"Now within the one-hour period that you forgot they both left the party. Did Ms. Spinoza leave before Miles Dixon?"

"Not exactly."

"Do you mean that as a no?"

"Yes. I mean no, she didn't."

"Did she leave the party *after* Miles Dixon?"

"Not exactly. I mean, no."

"Well, then, did they leave around at the same time?"

"Yes."

"Mr. Finch," Wusthof said, "did you see Miles Dixon and Irene Spinoza leave the party together?"

Long pause. "Yes."

I was distraught. Miles had dropped by that May 17th party to pick up Irene.

I couldn't believe it. Grunion was putting Irene on the stand, his reasoning being that her statements to the police had to be explained. But that meant she'd be open to cross examination. Either Grunion was blessed with the consummate artistry that conceals legal technique, or else, as I suspected, he had a tad too much rasa on his tabula.

"Can't you do something?" I asked Biswanger.

"He's her counsel of choice."

"You mean *your* choice."

Irene spelled her name for the court, gave her address, and I thought, Maybe it'll be okay.
Grunion said, "Ms. Spinoza, what is your marital status?"
"I'm divorced from George Spinoza. Amicably," she added.
Hah, I thought.
"What was your relationship with Miles Dixon?"
"We were friends."
"Nothing more?"
"We weren't intimate, if that's what you mean."
"Did you ever visit his apartment?"
"Sure. And sometimes he came over to mine. Sometimes with friends."
"Did you ever lend Mr. Dixon anything?"
"Yes. A blender. Books. Once some tools—he had a leaky faucet."
"Would it be accurate to say you lent Miles Dixon things for the household?"
"Yes."
"Did he return everything you lent him?"
"Eventually."
"Then if those things he hadn't returned were found in his apartment, you wouldn't be surprised?"
"I'd be surprised if they weren't."
Grunion said, "Ms. Spinoza, did you visit Miles Dixon's apartment any time June 9th?"
"No."
"Did you go there after midnight?"
"No."
"Please tell the court where you were the night of June 9th."
"From eight o'clock until about eleven thirty I was at home."
"And where were you after eleven thirty?"

"I went to my ex-husband's apartment."

"And how long did you stay there?"

"Until three in the morning."

Prosecutor Wusthof snapped, "Your Honor, is counsel alleging infidelity with Ms. Spinoza's former husband as a basis for a defense against killing her former lover?"

Judge Cole said, "That question will be stricken. Mr. Wusthof, put your question to the court in proper form."

Wusthof withdrew the question, but I saw its effect on Irene; then I realized he had said it to rattle her.

Grunion said, "So you were alone with Mr. Spinoza in his apartment between eleven thirty PM and three AM?"

"Not exactly *with* him. I was busy with Natasha and the afghan."

Judge Cole's interest picked up, along with that of the rest of those in the courtroom. Aside from Irene, the only discernible sounds in the courtroom were heavy breathing.

"He was in bed at the time," Irene explained.

"The Afghan?" Grunion asked.

"No, George. Natasha had gotten into the champagne and was zonked out on top of the afghan in the living room, and she couldn't have cared less. . . "

Prosecutor Wusthof said, "Objection. Hearsay. Defense is attempting to introduce into the record the unsworn declarations of an out-of-court witness."

Grunion said, "Your Honor, no such third-party statements have been made."

Wusthof shot back, "Then I strongly object on the basis of relevance."

Grunion said, "Is Mr. Wusthof objecting to my client's explaining the statement to the arresting officer, which Mr. Wusthof himself introduced and which the court has admitted into the record?"

Wusthof said, "In which, I remind counsel, your client admits the murder weapon was hers. The fact that she represented in her statement that the Afghans were witnesses should not allow it to be used by the defendant to manufacture her own evidence. Let this Natasha and the other unnamed Afghan be sworn in."

Grunion said, "Your Honor, we are establishing that my client was not with the decedent during the critical hours. My client should have the opportunity to explain her statements to the police."

Judge Cole said, "Which is it, Mr. Wusthof? Hearsay, or relevance?"

"Uh, hearsay, your Honor."

"Overruled. You may continue, Ms. Spinoza."

Irene said, "What was the question?"

Grunion seemed to have forgotten, too. He said, "Now, Ms. Spinoza, returning to the June 9th party where you were a guest along with Natasha and the other Afghan..."

"Not exactly. Natasha *lives* there. George and I had reached an agreement about that."

Grunion was a picture in frustration. "Ms. Spinoza, after your husband invited you to his party..."

"George didn't invite me. His business manager called me at eleven thirty."

"Mr. Biswanger?"

"Objection," Wusthof interrupted. "Counsel is leading."

Judge Cole looked at Grunion. "Counselor?"

"I will rephrase. Ms. Spinoza, please tell the court the name of the person who called you at eleven thirty on June 9."

Irene looked coolly at Wusthof. "Biswanger. Spelled B-i-s-w-a-n-g-e-r."

"What did Mr. Biswanger say?"

"He told me Natasha had gotten into the champagne, and he wanted me to come over with my knitting basket."

Grunion hesitated. "What did you do then?"

"I got there a little after twelve o'clock. And sure enough, Natasha was zonked out on top of the afghan. So I knotted them together."

You could hear a pin drop in the courtroom. Good God, I thought. They think I'm running a pervert's nest—orgiastic parties until three o'clock in the morning with guests tied together on the floor. They'll think we had a kinky menage à cinque: Miles, Natasha, Irene, me, and an unnamed Afghan.

Irene gave an embarrassed shrug. "It was a silly idea."

Biswanger leaned over and hissed into my ear, "Silly? It was a brilliant idea."

Grunion was making a show of looking through Irene's police statement. "Then the night of June 9th, you were at Mr. Spinoza's apartment and stayed there into the early hours of the following morning with Natasha and the Afghan."

"Yes. That's when I noticed my scissors were missing from my knitting basket."

Those wretched scissors, I thought.

"Was that because you intended to use them to knot Natasha and the Afghan together?" Grunion asked helpfully.

Wusthof again objected that Grunion was leading the witness, but Judge Cole, who clearly was fascinated, overruled.

"Yes," Irene answered.

"Obviously, Natasha couldn't have taken them," Grunion said in a jocular voice.

"Objection," Wusthof shot out. "Counsel is asking the witness to draw a conclusion."

Irene said hotly to Wusthof, "I ought to know since Natasha was right there."

Judge Cole said, "Ms. Spinoza, just a moment please. We're going to interrupt the hearing. Counsel, please approach the bench."

Wusthof and Grunion conferred with Judge Cole.

I wondered where in hell it was all leading.

Their bench conference was over. Grunion had a final question for Irene: "Ms. Spinoza, did you stab Miles Dixon with a pair of scissors?"

"No."

It was Wusthof's turn.

Wusthof said, "Ms. Spinoza, you state that June 9th you went to a late-night party at your ex-husband's apartment. You further state your husband didn't invite you. Will you tell us what your husband was doing when you arrived at his residence?"

"George was already in bed, asleep."

Wusthof looked at her in exaggerated puzzlement. "Now let me get this straight. When you arrived, Mr. Spinoza was already in bed."

"Passed out cold. The party had broken up."

"But if the party had broken up, and Mr. Spinoza was in bed, who answered the door?"

"Mr. Biswanger."

"You told Mr. Grunion you stayed at the apartment approximately three hours. Was Mr. Biswanger with you those three hours?"

"No. He left about five minutes after I arrived."

"Then after Mr. Biswanger departed," Wusthof said, counting on his fingers, "those who remained were you. . . and Natasha on top of the Afghan, zonked out. . . and your former husband, who was asleep in bed. Is that correct?"

"Yes."

"So it would be accurate to say that for those three hours, you were the only person in the apartment who was conscious?"

"Yes."

Wusthof paused significantly, as if a jury were listening, instead of the clerk taking it all down. "Thank you, Ms. Spinoza."

Irene was excused.

I leaned over to Biswanger and said, "That sure cleared things up."

3

Biswanger and I sat at one of the tables with the lunch crowd outside Zingerman's Delicatessen at the corner of East Kingsley and Detroit streets. Natasha was leashed to a tree, chewing on a boiled bone that the counter girl had given us with our order. Irene was not with us, having stayed in Ypsilanti with Grunion "for a working lunch to discuss further aspects of strategy." The strain of not seizing Grunion by his corn-fed neck upon the conclusion of Irene's hearing had left my battered soul in a profound melancholy, which only Zingerman's could assuage.

"We're getting Irene another lawyer," I announced to Biswanger.

"Out of the question," said Biswanger. Both his hands firmly gripped his Pat and Dick's Honeymooner: *No. 27: smoked turkey breast and Muenster with Mucky Duck mustard, grilled on thick slices of challah.* "Grunion, Grunion, Littlefield and Grunion is one of the top firms. They represent many state legislators on drunk-driving arrests. They're very well thought of. And any change would have to be Irene's decision."

"Why did we get stuck with the third Grunion?"

"Our Grunion isn't the third Grunion. Good Lord!"

Biswanger admonished, wagging his head. "You didn't think he was already a *partner*?"

"You mean he doesn't even rate a listing on their stationery?"

"If he applies himself he'll make it. He's got a lot going for him."

"Like what?"

"He's the favorite nephew of Grunion Senior."

"He's a nincompoop."

"I won't stand for that kind of talk about a member of my profession, George, especially when it's true. Grunion Senior and Grunion Junior and Grunion the Third are keeping an eye on Irene's case."

"You've spoken with them?"

"Not directly, but our Grunion assures me."

Despair clamped on my already gloomy heart. It was a crisis and Biswanger was driving me over the edge. "We went to the U of M together," I said, appealing to his youthful ideals. "Right here in this town. Beer busts and football games in the autumn," I reminded him, tears welling up in my eyes. "Remember how it was? Remember the Wave?" I asked, referring to the practice at home games, now banned, of passing a girl over jam-packed stadium seats on a conveyer belt of willing male hands to spare her the chore of clambering to her place. "Remember the time we passed along that girl, the one with the fantastic bod, and I struck gold? Don't those memories mean something to you? I'm appealing to you. Use your influence to get Irene's case transferred to another Grunion. At least Grunion number three."

Biswanger paused in his chewing. "If you are referring to the October game when Michigan State had a seven-to-nothing lead in the first period and then Leach hit White on a twelve-yard touchdown pass, and Willner booted a fifty-yard field so at half-time we led ten to seven, then my answer is no, you weren't in that Wave. God, she had a great ass." Biswanger was lost for a moment in fond remembrance. "Even through those jeans, mmm-hmmm!"

My head reeled. How could he be so insensitive? "You bastard, I was in the seat right next to you."

"You didn't even cop a feel of her shoe, George. Are you going to eat your pickle?"

Hunching defensively over my pickle, at the ready for surreptitious attempts at theft, I said, "And you made up that stuff about the plays and the half-time score."

"Go look it up."

"That's an evasion."

"You want to bet your pickle that I'm wrong?"

"Go to hell. So what are we going to do about Wusthof?"

"Oh, Wusthof's not interested in Irene, per se," Biswanger declared matter-of-factly.

Mystified, I studied Biswanger's face. With his cheeks stuffed like a chipmunk's, all I discerned was refulgent gluttony. I said, "It's a murder case; what *else* could Wusthof be interested in? He was very convincing at the hearing."

"The grapevine has it that Miles was mixed up in drug money."

"I don't believe it."

"Wusthof does. He has his eye on running for the U.S. Senate. If he can pull off a major drug case, it will springboard him into a campaign. His strategy is to use this murder charge to pressure Irene into revealing what she knows about Miles. Then he'll do a deal with Grunion."

"Irene wouldn't knowingly get mixed up with that kind of thing," I said. "What if she doesn't know anything to reveal?"

"Then in the interest of justice, Wusthof will pursue a full and vigorous prosecution."

"But Irene didn't kill Miles."

"Justice is a process, not a result," Biswanger said gravely, and popped another Sicilian olive.

"Talk like a human being," I threatened, "or I won't have lunch with you."

"You still want that pickle?"

"Go inside and get one."

"Sometimes you leave yours, and it's thrown away."

"All right. Here. Take it."

"You're sure?"

"Take the goddamned pickle!"

"If you insist," Biswanger said, and deftly performed a two-finger snatch of the pickle from the table straight into his mouth. "You're having second thoughts. I can tell by your twitch."

I said, "We should hire a detective."

"You mean a private investigator. I'll ask around for someone experienced," Biswanger said, crunching away. "By the way. Now that your *Hotel Rompé* licenses are in hock, as your business manager I must advise you to come up with another best seller."

After lunch with Biswanger, I trudged home along Kingsley. Irene was facing a murder trial, I was facing penury, and I had heartburn. My head felt as if a wet towel had been threaded into my left ear and was slowly being pulled out the right side. Natasha pranced along, blissfully insensible to my tristesse.

We turned south onto State Street, and a familiar voice said, "How you doing?"

It was Delmore; I remembered I still had his card in my wallet. He was elegant in a European leisure ensemble that cost more than most people's yearly clothing budgets. He ruffled Natasha behind her ears and she returned a slurp. He twitched his nose and said, "Zingerman's?"

"Zingerman's," I said.

"Sorry to hear about your lady."

Sympathy is much more touching when it comes from an unexpected quarter. I sighed. "Word travels fast."

"The word is," said Delmore, "that Wusthof wants to run for the U.S. Senate. If he succeeds with a big drug case, it will help his campaign. His strategy is to use this murder charge to pressure Irene into revealing what she knows about Miles. Then he'll do a deal with Irene's lawyer."

"No kidding?" I said, wondering if Delmore's and Biswanger's mysterious sources were one and the same, when I had an inspired idea. If Miles had been involved with drugs, who better to investigate than Delmore? He seemed to be extremely well connected, although to what I wasn't exactly sure, but that knowledge would come in time. He clearly had a knack for creating opportunities—hadn't he given me his business card on our first meeting? And he liked Natasha. Biswanger might object to the idea as reckless, but fuck him. He knew damned well I had been a full participant in that Wave. I said, "Delmore, I'm looking for a private investigator."

Without missing a beat, Delmore replied, "I'm a real fan of your *Hotel Rompé* and I like Wusthof less than you do. It would be my pleasure to help get Irene off."

"For the standard rate," I said. I made a mental note to ask Biswanger what the standard rate was. "And Irene is innocent."

"Hey, you don't have to lie to your P.I." His smile was so ingratiating that the sun glinted off the gold in his molars.

"No, really. She wasn't anywhere near Miles Dixon's apartment that night. She was in mine."

Unlike Wusthof, Delmore had the grace to let lie the obvious implication. "Do you have a theory as to who did kill him?"

"Frankly," I confided, "aside from Wusthof's drug theory, which I think is utter bullshit, I can't think of a single reason why anyone would want to."

Delmore whipped out a small leather-bound notebook, and began jotting with a gold Cross pen. I saw him write *Wusthof theory bullshit.*

"Describe your relationship vis-à-vis Mr. Dixon," he said, his accent becoming crisper, almost British, as he submerged himself into the role.

"I met Miles about a year and a half ago through a rug dealer."

Delmore raised his eyebrows. "You were in the Middle East?"

"Ann Arbor. Marderosian's World of Oriental Ruggery, on Liberty and Fourth. I was looking for a rug for my workroom, when our vet suggested that since we already had Natasha, why not get an afghan rug, too. Irene thought it was a cute idea. Then about a week after I got the rug, Mr. Marderosian called and said another customer was interested in afghans, and would I mind if he sent him over to see the one I'd just bought, since it was a particularly fine example. That's how we met Miles Dixon," I concluded. "Any ideas where to start?"

Delmore finished his note-taking. "Marderosian's Ruggery."

"That trail is cold by now," I protested.

"Who's the P.I. here? Call Marderosian and set up an appointment for us."

"Us? You're the P.I. You call him."

"He knows you. Tell him I'm looking for an afghan rug."

I glanced at Delmore's notebook. The last thing he had written was *Rug = dog (vet), cute idea (Irene)*.

I returned home with Natasha and my tristesse in full resurgence. I put a silver-framed photo of Irene on my vacant worktable and sat in my swivel chair.

As usual, Natasha sat in the chair with me. She started sharing my swivel chair as a puppy (Irene thought it was cute), and I've been unable to break her of the habit. When she grew big, it was necessary to get a more capacious swivel chair to accommodate us both. She climbs up and lowers her doggy butt in beside mine and sits erect with her forelegs planted like tree trunks on the front edge of the seat; and there we sit, shoulder to shoulder, as it were, she silently staring at the table at whatever I'm working on. She is content to remain in this temple-guardian posture for hours, sometimes dozing. I have never heard of a dog behaving this way. It is useless to shove her off. She waits until I become engrossed in whatever I'm doing, then she puts a paw up beside my left leg, then both paws, and patiently wedges me aside with her long snout and climbs back up; after awhile I become aware that a second pair of eyes are critiquing my work. Her other ploy is to wait until I get up to go to the refrigerator or the bathroom. When I return, there she sits in the chair, perusing my drawings with what the dog breeders call a "piercing warlike stare" that's supposed to freeze the advance of strangers. According to Charles Finch, Natasha has aristocratic parentage: *Ch. Daoud's Royal Blue of Kandahar ex. Ch. Tadjik's Natasha of Faizabad*. What it comes down to is that I've been stuck with a long-haired, overbred critic.

Now I was stuck with a ghastly situation. Irene was a pawn in the political game plan of a politically ambitious prosecutor. Romantic memories aside, our fortunes were linked through our *Hotel Rompé* licenses and the legal meter was ticking away. Biswanger was right. It was in my interest to get Irene extricated as rapidly as possible.

Biswanger was also right about my income and the necessity of coming up with a new game. With Grunion and Delmore to support, I needed to come up with a winner.

My phone rang. It was Charles Finch.

"I want to apologize for what happened on the stand this morning," he blurted. "I had no idea that bastard Wusthof was going to do what he did. The relationship between Miles and Irene was purely platonic."

"There was nothing you could do," I said lamely.

"I want to make it up to you and Irene."

"It's okay," I said. "I've hired a private investigator."

"I'll help with the legwork."

"Sure."

"I mean it, George. When is the next time you're seeing him?"

"Well, we'll be going to Marderosian's Ruggery."

"I want to go, too."

"I appreciate the offer, Charles, but you really don't have to."

"He might want to ask me questions, and three heads are better than two."

"I still have to set it up."

"Phone me."

"What if you're operating on a cat?"

"I'm an executive. I've got associates and assistants for that stuff."

I was touched. "I'll get back to you," I promised.

After Finch hung up I thought, What a world, what a world. If only my business manager were half as supportive as my veterinarian. Oh, Biswanger, you rotten, condescending bastard. I was best man at your wedding to Emily, I am godfather to your child, Timmy, I give you my dill pickles, and you treat me like crap. It's a good thing for you that I'm your best friend.

Natasha was looking at my desk calendar. Biswanger's son's eleventh birthday was coming up. The kid had hinted with varying degrees of subtlety that he wanted a guitar. I had to call Marderosian, but first things first. Cackling like one of Macbeth's doomsayers, I reached across Natasha for the yellow pages and thumbed to *Musical Instruments*.

"Me and my girl are crazy about your *Hotel Rompé*," the salesman gushed, after I identified myself and told him I was looking for an electric guitar setup. He assured me I was speaking to the right guy. He was a graduate of G.I.T.

"G.I.T.?" I asked.

"The Guitar Institute of Technology." He reeled off the names of several models, then said, "This one has two custom humbuckers, a five-way pickup selector, with a tremolo, and Sperzel tuners. They're a little more expensive. . ."

"But they're worth it!" I chimed in. "Tell me more."

There were preamps and amps, sustainers and effects loops, and foot-switching capabilities.

"The foot switch can adjust stereo chorus/delay for flanging effects."

"What's a delay without flanging," I said gaily. "What else?"

"A trio of Rocktron XDC Deluxe Hush IIB Signal Processors," the salesman cried, "will add spice to any onstage and studio sound. May I suggest the model 310?"

"I'll take it," I said.

The salesman could scarcely contain himself. "Wise choice, sir. The Model 310 has a fully automatic compressor/limiter/leveler for keeping signal levels under control. It employs logarithmic compression and program-dependent ratio attack and release with selectable compression or leveling modes."

Attack. The word was music to my ears.

"The XDC Deluxe guitar preamp contains a user-adjustable distortion unit," he babbled on, "and a psychoacoustic processor and exciter functions, plus two exciter channels."

"Sounds just right."

"Medusa speakers," he said breathlessly. "They have the ideal mix of tonal nuance and overdrive harmonics."

"You're sure there's enough overdrive?"

"All you need."

"You've sold me."

"It includes a ninety-day guarantee against defects in materials and workmanship," he shouted.

"I believe you. I want it all."

"Thank you, sir. We'll test it all out and have it to you by the end of the week."

"Oh, it's not for me," I said. "It's a birthday gift for my godson." I gave him Biswanger's address. "I want the card to say: Happy Birthday, Timmy. Uncle George."

"Bless you, Mr. Spinoza," the salesman choked, "for a kind and generous heart."

Home again, humming merrily, I fixed myself a Scotch. Biswanger, who would kill for a Cole Porter lyric, was doomed.

4

Grunion requested I meet with him and Irene to discuss those "further aspects of strategy." My translation of this was that after being devastated by Wusthof at the hearing, he was scrambling to apprise himself of things he should have asked about in the first place.

The Ann Arbor offices of Grunion, Grunion, Littlefield and Grunion were in the Liberty Building. Despite its architectural awards, it did not impress me so much with its edificial magnificence as its financial genesis. It had been built by a former mayor with generous financing from local banks because when he had been mayor, over strenuous objections from the city's assistant treasurer, he had generously allocated city monies to those banks for interest rates below market. The Liberty Building was proof that in public life, generosity and business acumen can be more than their own reward.

Grunion, Grunion, Littlefield and Grunion were on the fourteenth floor. The receptionist in the color-coordinated lobby informed me that nephew Grunion's office was one floor below.

Grunion's office was easy to find because most of the lower floor was unfinished. His office partitions stood like a lone shack in a junkyard of pipes, ducts, and bare lighting fixtures. The doorplate said *P. Grunion*. I knocked, waited, knocked louder, waited, then peeked inside.

His office was densely appointed in a style that would have better suited a larger space, like a Viking mead hall. A massive burled-walnut desk crowded the wingchairs against glass-fronted bookcases that lined the tweed-covered walls. There was room for Grunion to accommodate perhaps one ectomorphic client, as long as they both didn't exhale simultaneously. Neither Grunion nor Irene was within sight or hearing, nor was anyone else. I went back up to ask where Grunion was.

The receptionist further informed me that she hadn't the faintest idea.

The wisest thing the Duke of Windsor ever said, in my opinion, was that he never passed up an opportunity to relieve himself. Since the signs on the lower floor indicated the lavatories were in working order, I went back down, and upon entering the men's room I discovered baronial splendor.

Emerald marble streaked with black and flecks of gold; brass coat racks; three shoe-buffing machines for black or brown, cordovan or chestnut, tan or clear; neat stacks of fluffy towels by the marble basins. The urinals were the old-fashioned floor-length type that are a godsend to men of very short or very tall stature. The stalls had polished wooden doors and spot lighting for casual reading.

Grunion, unaware of my presence, was talking and gesturing to the mirrors.

"My client's life, liberty, and reputation are in the balance," he declaimed to his reflection. "I say to you, it could have been any of you who lent Miles Dixon a blender and a pair of scissors. If you had been Miles Dixon's friend, wouldn't you have acted in the same manner as Irene Spinoza? Or would you have told Miles he would have to forgo those domestic conveniences because you *would not* lend them to him?" Grunion let his hand fall dramatically.

I started to back out, but Grunion heard me and snapped his head in my direction. "What are you doing in here?"

Rejecting the obvious retort that sprang to mind, for he was still Irene's lawyer, I summoned up a credible amount of counterfeit warmth and said, "Hi there. I expect Irene is waiting in your office for her strategy session."

He was blushing furiously. "You don't have to pretend. You heard."

"It was impossible not to."

Grunion sidled over to a small chair by a requisites dispensing machine and sat down. "I practice speeches in here because of the acoustics."

"The acoustics are excellent," I agreed.

"I tried a tape recorder once, but it wasn't the same. How did Wusthof know about all that stuff?" he wondered aloud, switching trains of thought with a speed and an illogic that were awesome.

"I hope you won't ask rhetorical questions like that in Irene's presence," I cautioned him.

"No?"

"No. It might undermine her confidence."

"My Uncle tells me I've got a problem in that area," he said, chin on palm, gazing into the middle distance.

I've never been very good at divining the appropriate anodyne when strangers decide to bare their angst. "In what area?" I asked in a spirit of cautious curiosity, there being so many areas that seemed to apply.

"Inspiring confidence. He says it's more important than knowledge of the law. He says once I get it licked, I can write my own ticket. I've been thinking of some motions to make to Judge Cole on motion day."

"Motions sound like a good idea."

"So far I've thought of four. What do you think? Too many? I wouldn't want the judge to think I'm showing off."

"He wouldn't if they were good ones."

Grunion took out a pen and leather-bound notebook similar to Delmore's. "I'm open to ideas."

"How about you ask him to let us present new facts?"

"Great! What new facts?"

"I'm working on it."

"You'll let me know when you come up with something?"

"You're at the top of my list."

Grunion stood up, put his notebook back in his jacket pocket, straightened his tie, and tugged at his cuffs. "I want you to know you've made me feel really good about myself. Irene is going to get the best summation speech ever heard in the circuit court."

"Shouldn't we see Irene in your office first?" I suggested. "She's probably wondering where you are."

"Right you are. Let's go have one hell of a strategy session!"

"I'll catch up with you," I said, and headed for the floor-length porcelain.

"Ri-i-ight."

Grunion held his pen poised over a blank yellow pad, and his gaze shifted eagerly from Irene to me. "Now for my own information, I'd like your version of what happened that night."

"I was asleep at the time," I said, repeating what Irene had told Wusthof on the witness stand.

"Biswanger will vouch for that," Irene added.

"What time did you pass out?" Grunion asked inelegantly.

"I wasn't looking at my watch," I said. Already I was feeling peevish. Being careful not to undermine his confidence was becoming a strain.

"How about you ask him the last thing he remembers before he passed out?" Irene suggested.

"How about you ask her what she was doing leaving her lace teddy in Miles Dixon's apartment?" I replied icily?

"How about you ask him why he thinks it's any of his business" Irene retorted, her nose turning bright pink, "and how come he's so sure it was mine?"

"How about you inform her that I know it for a fact," I replied, "because me and my P.I. talked to Detectives Nancy Freiday and Thomas Clancy, who are the two investigating officers assigned to the case. It is fully described in their evidence list, along with some *other* intimate items."

"How about you ask him what he's doing hiring a P.I. without telling me, when I'm the one being charged, and I never brought anything like that to Miles's apartment, and if it was there then someone must have planted it."

"And how about you tell her that I didn't tell her about the P.I. yet because she hasn't spoken with me since I signed over our *Hotel Rompé* licenses for her bail."

Pausing to catch our breath, we stared at each other. Irene's pupils were dilated. Her perfume, heated to a flash point, came at me in seductive waves. I realized in the strongest possible terms that I had the hots for her. I could have humped her right there, but for the presence of idiot Grunion.

Grunion, who had been sitting tranquilly through this exchange, said, "I'd like to clear up a matter concerning your current residences. You're not living together since your divorce, are you?"

"Definitely not," said Irene, fingering her thin gold neck chain.

"Well, for some reason, you're down here as having the same address."

"That's easy to explain," I said. "We subdivided our condo after the divorce—it was easier keeping the mortgage that way."

"What?" said Grunion.

"It was a two-story condo," Irene explained. "We closed off the stairway at the top. Now I live in the upstairs part, and George lives in the downstairs part. Mail comes to the same address, but it's two different units."

"So when Biswanger called you the night of the June 9th party," Grunion said to Irene, "he was calling upstairs."

Irene nodded. "Now you've got it."

"That could be very significant," said Grunion, nodding back.

"How?" I ventured.

"I was hoping you could tell me."

Reaching deep within myself, I found the strength not to seize the bowling trophy beside the American flag penholder and use it to impact Grunion's pate. Instead I said, "The murderer took the scissors from your knitting basket. But he didn't know Biswanger would call you downstairs, which might have provided you with an alibi."

"If you'd been awake," Irene reminded me.

"Then you'd never have come down," I riposted. "After he stabbed Miles, he called the police to make sure Miles was found as soon as possible. The murderer knew you weren't at my party. So it could be anyone who was at the party."

Irene said, "Anyone who left the party *before* Biswanger called me."

"Which is just about everyone except me and Biswanger." Grunion waggled an admonitory finger. "You're forgetting Natasha and the Afghan."

I let him have it pointblank. "Natasha is a dog and the Afghan is a rug." And leaving him to sort out his confusion, I went through the guest list. "There was Biswanger, the Moores, Charlie Finch, Tanya Fassbender..."

"Is Tanya still the Women's Anti-Sexism, Consciousness-Raising, Rolfing Coordinator?" Irene interrupted.

"She switched to low-impact psychic mainstreaming. Morton Blue dropped by with his newest."

"Morton broke up with Tanya?"

"And he's left IMHUCR," I added, referring to the Institute for Mental Health and Universal Conflict Resolution. "He didn't get his grant for his model of Nineteenth-century Russian peasantry."

"No!" said Irene in a shocked voice.

"So he's going for a real estate license. Tanya's busy organizing a brown bag conference: The Female Experience in Transition—Networking for Survival Tactics. Or was it Survival Tactics for Networking? She still cooks up a mean tabbouleh with pine nuts. Everyone raved about it."

I rattled off a few more names, before Grunion interrupted me.

"Your dog was lying on a rug," he said with the pride of a chessmaster who has worked out a tricky practice problem.

I bestowed a look of approval on him. "Right-ee-oh. Perhaps we should be asking ourselves, How did Wusthof know to ask Charlie Finch those questions about Miles and Irene?"

Grunion said, "Of course you're asking that as a purely rhetorical question," and nervously glanced at Irene to see if her confidence was being undermined.

I said, "Someone snitched to Wusthof."

"You mean someone gave Wusthof misleading information to implicate me as having a motive to kill Miles," Irene said, looking me squarely in the eye.

"Wow!" said Grunion.

"It could be the same person who planted my lace teddy in Miles's apartment."

"The murderer?" Grunion asked.

"It had better be," I said, looking squarely right back at Irene.

"Someone is feeding Wusthof inside information about Irene and Miles," I said to Delmore as we strolled down Liberty past the Whole Earth Restaurant and Peace Coalition toward Marderosian's Ruggery. Since the meeting with Irene at Grunion's office, my suspicions had taken on a keen edge.

"One of your friends is a snitch," Delmore rephrased.

"It looks that way," I admitted. "And since you're supposed to be a buyer of fine carpets, you can drop that phoney Detroit Twelfth-Street accent. You're not Coleman Young, and you are obviously an educated man."

Without missing a beat Delmore said, "Yale, seventy-five, American history. And don't ask me how I got into this line of work." He spoke in an aristocratic cadence of the mid-South that reminded me of the actor Joseph Cotten.

I wasn't exactly sure what his line of work was. "I don't think your name is Delmore, either. You have preppie written all over you."

"Sir," he said, drawing himself up, "I am Reynolds Stuart Adams. . ."

The name fit.

". . . and I am a descendant of Thomas Jefferson."

Thomas Jefferson? The proud earnestness with which Delmore—or rather Reynolds Stuart Adams—delivered this statement warned me that he was dead serious. Oh, God, a genealogy snob! Just what I needed in a P.I. Sizing up his long-boned face and six-foot-four-plus height, I was put in mind of the story that Jefferson had fathered children by a black mistress at Monticello. So maybe Reynolds was descended from Jefferson. So what? Maybe I was descended from Benjamin Franklin. Both men certainly had the hots for plenty of women in their long lives. The best thing about genealogy is that it is so adaptable to the human psyche. I wanted Irene to meet Reynolds to see how she would scope him out.

We were at the door of Marderosian's Ruggery. I asked Reynolds, "Do you still want to be my P.I.?"

"I most assuredly do. After you, sir."

"Call me George, Reynolds."

The Ruggery ceiling was easily twenty feet high. Intricately patterned Beshirs, Bergamas, Turkestans, Oushaks, Soumaks, Hamadan's, Suiyans, Khorasans, Kashans and Kirmans hung from huge swinging arms so they could be turned like pages of a book. More carpets were stacked to the height of beds. Chased-brass lamps and cachepots with bedraggled palms were superfluous decoration. There was the odor of felt, wool, sandalwood, and tea.

"George-jan, my dear friend." Abdur Rahman came out from his office to greet us with a manicured hand over his silk-shirted heart, his coal eyes incandescent with anticipation of the bargaining ritual. It was a thousand pities his shop should be so unworthy of our presence.

"Abdur Rahman, I'd like you to meet Reynolds Stuart Adams."

After more greetings, we sat in Abdur Rahman's office,

where he had a silver plate of candied walnuts and rose jellies ready for us while he poured the tea.

When I had purchased my afghan rug, I had a very pleasant afternoon sipping strong tea and talking to Abdur Rahman. He was a Herati, which meant he had come from Herat, the western part of Afghanistan, bordering Iran. His family were scholars and merchants, trading through Iran. He had been a graduate student at the University of Michigan when the 1979 Russian invasion prompted him to sponsor as many of his clan out of Afghanistan as he could. Troop withdrawals and Mikhail Gorbachev's new style notwithstanding, Rahman had no tender feeling for the "Shouravi" invaders who had ravaged his beloved homeland.

Now the three of us chatted, preparing for the ostensible reason we had come, which was to look at rugs. To my surprise, Reynolds was up on the details of Afghanistan, from politics to mujahedeen strikes to Soviet troop withdrawals. He spoke admiringly of the mujahedeen blowing up pipelines in Jouzjan province that carried gas from northern Afghanistan into the U.S.S.R.

Abdur Rahman was very pessimistic. "The Shouravi pumped all Afghanistan's natural gas into the U.S.S.R.," he said, and his perpetually sad eyes became even sadder, "while my countrymen had only charcoal to get through the winters. The Shouravi paid but a fraction of the world cost, and even that was a cruel trick. They deducted the so-called payments from the puppet government's national debt to the U.S.S.R. Then they exported Siberian gas to Europe and charged the real-world rate. You see how they forced us to pay for our own destruction."

"A terrible thing," Reynolds agreed.

"They kidnapped our children and sent them into the U.S.S.R. for indoctrination in godless ways. They thought they would send them back as Shouravi-style bureaucrats to rule their own parents. One grows gray with the thought of it."

Reynolds shook his head in commiseration. "I have heard of other sources of money for weapons for the mujahedeen," he said. "Poppies grow in your homeland. Opium travels well on camel. It finds its way into Lebanon, and from there to the rest of the world. Is this not a fitting way to revenge the world for standing by while people of God are slaughtered by the godless?"

And a very clever way, I realized, to bring up the subject of drugs.

Abdur Rahman pursed his lips. "The Shouravi destroyed our houses, our crops, our livestock. They destroyed our irrigation and poisoned our wells. Only Stinger antiaircraft missiles were a match for their helicopter gunships. Despite the personal plea of Berhanuddin Rabbani himself, your president waited a long time before sending the mujahedeen missiles, and then only Soviet SAM-sevens, which are not as good as Stingers."

Reynolds nodded. "True. I am ashamed that my country took its own sweet time before it did what was right. And what choice did the landowners have? Either grow poppies and fight, or live in a Pakistan refugee camp while the iron claw of the Soviets committed more atrocities. I would have done the same."

Abdur Rahman quietly sipped his tea, turning Reynold's speech over in his mind. I was wondering if Reynolds himself was the drug connection. Did he have something to do with Miles Dixon's death? But why go through the elaborate charade of coming with me to the Ruggery, and arousing my suspicions? And how the hell had he been able to bone up so fast on Afghanistan? Whether there was a drug connection or not, it was clear that Reynolds Stuart Adams was no lightweight.

The bell over the door tinkled, and Charles Finch entered. He was spiffy in a Matka silk jacket, cream trousers, and tasseled Bally loafers. From his checkered cap, I knew he had driven his Jag to town. Once more I was reminded that Charles had done very well by his vet practice and his Cuddly-Wuddles pet farm, whereas I was scrounging for another game idea to keep the wolf from the door.

He stood there for a moment in the sunlight from the shop window, dust motes drifting around him, fingering his clipped mustache. "Oh, there you all are. Am I too late?"

"Hi, Charles," I said. "We haven't started the showing yet."

"And I haven't had the pleasure, Sir," said Reynolds.

While Charles stroked his mustache and Reynolds smiled blandly, I made the introductions. Abdur Rahman whipped out a fourth cup of tea for Charles, and then proceeded to show Reynolds his rugs.

"Ya-a-as, I was the one who put George onto rugs as an investment," Charles said to Reynolds as Abdur wrestled another rolled-up rug from a shelf. "I've got antiques, of course. But for my media room I got a twelve-by-fifteen, made to order in Pakistan. It took a year. You can't beat handwork. Oh, that's a real beauty!"

Abdur Rahman was laying out a breathtaking Chinese Turkestan. "Eighteenth-century Ch'ien Lung, seventy-two knots to the foot," he said, wheezing slightly. "You can see the Mongol influence."

Reynolds stared at the intricate pattern of stylized animal and human figures in indigo and cream on the rust background.

"I say, Reynolds," said Charles. "I wouldn't want to

influence you, but if you're not interested in this one, I'd like to pick it up."

Give it a rest, Charles, I thought. You've made your point. Now the whole world knows you're rich.

Abdur Rahman was watching Charles and Reynolds, enjoying the subterranean battle between aesthetics and avarice. He said, "Although this is Chinese, this most beautiful rug illustrates an old Afghan tale. You see the three men?" he asked pointing with a wooden yardstick at three figures.

By a stretch of the imagination they might have represented humans, or trees, or Shetland ponies.

"They are traveling over the mountains." He indicated a band of geometric shapes that sort of looked like mountains, or possibly dragons with bellyaches. "The man in the middle is a holy fool. Each of his two companions has told him that they are his friend. He does not know that they are enemies of each other, and would use him against the other. So, even though he bears neither of them ill will, he is in mortal danger."

"Excuse me," I interjected, "but why did the holy fool hook up with them in the first place?"

"They hooked up with the holy fool because neither can make the journey without him." Abdur smiled. "We have a saying: the enemy of my enemy is my friend."

As I absorbed this, I became uncomfortably aware that I was standing between Reynolds and Charles. "If both the holy fool's companions are using him as a pawn against the other," I said, working it out, "then they are both his enemies. But since both are also enemies of the other, they are also both his friends."

Abdur nodded. "You see the paradox. There is also the possibility that one of the holy fool's companions considers him to be less of a pawn than does the other companion." Abdur ran his hand over the pile of the rug. "Come," he said, "feel the quality."

Charles and Reynolds joined him. They expertly brushed the rug this way and that, admiring the lay of the tufts and the sheen. It was becoming a heavy petting session.

I, on the other hand, didn't feel like counting knots. "Abdur," I said, interrupting him in mid-purr, "How does the story end? Does the guy in the middle finish the journey?"

Abdur Rahman shrugged. "Perhaps. It is in the hands of God. A cautionary tale, wouldn't you agree?"

Perhaps it was my imagination, but it seemed Abdur Rahman meant me. Was I the guy in the middle? Did it have something to do with Irene's murder case? Or was he having a subtle Oriental joke by creating paranoia among me, Charlie and Reynolds?

Reynolds decided to buy the rug.

As we were leaving, I had to have a final word with Abdur Rahman. I adopted a facetious tone. "Abdur, about that little story. You wouldn't be playing me for a faribkhur, would you?" I asked, using one of the few Afghan-Persian words I had picked up from him.

"You, a sucker? Never, George-jan."

Which left me feeling even more paranoid.

5

AFTER OUR VISIT WITH Abdur Rahman, Reynolds Stuart Adams (a.k.a. Delmore Black) surprised me again when he phoned the next day.

"I've got bad news and good news," said Reynolds. "First, I can't find any tenant within earshot of Miles Dixon's apartment who called the police the night he was killed."

"That sounds bad, all right," I said.

"No, that's good. It confirms my theory that the murderer made the phone call, probably right from Miles's apartment after he killed him."

"What's the rest?" I asked, expecting the worst.

"Something the police missed. Miles Dixon had a secret lady friend. Her first name is Perdita and she works at the university."

"That's bad?"

"No, that was more of the good news."

"Any more good news?"

"No. The bad news is that's all I've got on her. Her first name."

Reynolds had learned about Perdita from the boy friend of a female tenant whose apartment adjoined Miles Dixon's. On several occasions the boy friend had overheard Miles and

Perdita. It seemed Perdita had been sneaking to Miles's apartment on Wednesday afternoons. The boy friend knew she was sneaking because once when he had gone up in the elevator with the two of them, they had pretended not to know each other and Perdita had gone on to another floor, then walked back down to Miles's apartment. He also told Reynolds (out of earshot of his girl friend) that Perdita impressed him as having hidden fires.

Wondering how Perdita's fires could be hidden if they were evident from a single elevator trip, I gave voice to my curiosity. "How did you find out this stuff when the police didn't?"

"You may have noticed that I am not without a certain aristocratic Southern charm."

Yes, I had noticed. Making allowances for physical and historical contradictions, I could picture Reynolds Stuart Adams dressed in a linen suit and lounging out on a veranda with a frosted glass, passing a hot afternoon in elegant badinage. And what other personae could this chameleon take on? I put the question aside from the more immediate consideration of Perdita. She had not come forward, even though Miles's murder and Irene's arrest had been reported in the Ann Arbor *News*, the *Free Press*, the Detroit *News*, the three Detroit TV affiliates, WAAM-AM and WUOM-FM, and town gossip. We had to find her.

"I was hoping you'd take it from here and find Perdita," said Reynolds, my P.I.

"*You* want *me* to find her?"

"Take it from one who knows," said Reynolds. "If anyone can, you can."

"I'll see what I can do."

"I have every confidence in you."

On that encouraging note, I called Morton Blue and asked him if he was still on good terms with a certain systems programmer at University Personnel.

"Maria the Rabbit? Yeah. I haven't seen her lately, though," he added with a sigh of fond remembrance.

"I always wondered why you two split up. You spoke so fondly of her."

"Frankly, I got too exhausted keeping up with her."

I was stunned that Mort would admit to such a thing.

"We went jogging together," Morton went on. "But then she got into marathon running. You want me to fix you up with her? How's your wind?"

I explained that I needed a computer file search for all university employees having the first name *Perdita*.

It turned out her name was Perdita Cunliffe. She was head librarian at the Transportation Research Institute, and she was married, which explained why she was sneaking on those Wednesday afternoons.

"Frankly, I didn't think Miles Dixon was the type to become involved with a married woman," I said to Reynolds, who had been very surprised when he answered the doorbell of the house he rented on Geddes and saw me standing on the porch. Since Morton was now into real estate, he'd also gotten me Reynolds's address. Reynolds and I now sat in the living room. It had been turned into an office, with a locked file cabinet, a personal computer, a copier, and a facsimile machine hooked up to the telephone.

"Still waters run deep," said Reynolds after mulling over my comment about Miles Dixon.

"You can say that again," I said. "According to the rental management company, you moved into this place three weeks ago. You're not a local undercover cop, because you wouldn't work out of a set-up like this. And I don't think you have an FBI personality. So what is your interest in this case?"

"I'm your P.I.," Reynolds replied smoothly, though without conviction.

"If you don't cut the crap," I warned him, "I won't let you be my P.I."

"I work for the State Department."

"Good-bye, Reynolds," I said, rising to leave. "I'd like to say it's been real, except it hasn't."

Reynolds sighed, and removed a laminated I.D. card from his wallet and gave it to me.

The card had his color photo and official-looking State Department stuff on it. "How do I know this is authentic?" I asked.

Reynolds unlocked the file cabinet and pulled out several official-looking State Department memoranda addressed to him about a drug investigation.

"Wow!" I said, backpedaling. "Then you're here because Miles *was* into drugs?"

"Miles Dixon was investigating an international drug money-transfer operation," Reynolds explained. "I came to Ann Arbor to be his backup."

"And I'm sure you would have been a great one," I said, "if only he'd lived long enough." Remembering our first meeting in Liberty Plaza the morning after Miles was killed, I said, "You thought I might have killed him."

Reynolds locked the file cabinet. "Jealousy is a powerful motive. I had to take up where Miles left off, and you seemed like a good way to begin. Can I still be your P.I.?"

"Only if you are really descended from Thomas Jefferson," I said facetiously.

"Sir," said Reynolds, with a resurgence of his old hauteur, "I am an Afro-Jeffersonian. I am in the direct line of descent from Sally Hemings's first son, who was born shortly after Sally returned from France, where she'd spent twenty-six months as servant to Jefferson's young daughter, Polly, whom he'd had by his wife, Martha, already deceased. Sally was seventeen and named the child Tom, and it was said that he bore a striking resemblance to Jefferson. As you can observe, I, too, bear that resemblance." Reynolds held his long-boned face at a Jeffersonian cant, as if posing for a currency engraving.

I didn't know what to say. My innocent jest had released an emotional catapult within Reynolds, launching him into unexpected socio-political terrain.

"Sally Hemings became Jefferson's intimate companion and emotional solace at Monticello," Reynolds added, apparently interpreting my stunned silence as deriving from a gap in my education that required remediation. "Other children followed, but Tom is the important one as far as I'm concerned. Jefferson's own grandson later admitted to Jefferson's biographer, Henry Randall, that, and I quote, 'at some distance or in the dusk the slave, dressed in the same way, might have been mistaken for Mr. Jefferson.'"

"Gosh," I said.

"Unquote," Reynolds said, nodding solemnly. "Times being what they were, Jefferson took the precaution of never listing Tom on the inventory, even though you will find him in the Monticello account books for clothing and such."

"Jefferson was a wise man," I said.

"Indeed. These facts explain some of my own proclivities."

"Toward inventories?"

"Toward not letting myself be defined by a State Department personnel file." Reynolds turned on his computer. A complicated tree diagram came up on the screen. "I keep my personal genealogical charts and records on tap in here," he said. His eyes were shining with the fanatical light of the hobbyist. "You will notice that Sally's other children were

Beverly, Eston, Madison, and Harriet. They were given their freedom at age twenty-one, per Jefferson's promise to Sally. Red herrings," Reynolds said with a sniff, "as far as my personal line is concerned." Reynolds was now in full gallop on his hobby horse. "For many years I labored under the false assumption that I was descended from a union between Jefferson and Abigail Adams. She was in France during the same period with her husband, John, you know, during his ambassadorial tenure."

"Jefferson got it on with the wife of John Adams?" I cried, shocked at the news.

"From Abigail, Jefferson got much advice on purchases of clothing, linen, and the hiring of French servants. They exchanged letters containing much implied passion."

"I see. I suppose France will do that," I said politely. Actually, I didn't see. As far as I knew, Abigail Adams had been quintessentially Anglo-Saxon. Perhaps Reynolds had discovered a relation who was an Abigail Adams descendent not mentioned in the Daughters of the American Revolution stud books. And perhaps Reynolds was a loon.

"Subsequent study," Reynolds continued, "showed that despite Jefferson's being taken by Abigail's wit and vivacity, she was too devoted to her husband and too much of a New England stickleback for this to be true. There are revisionists who would say that Sally Hemings's first-born was not Tom, and that he never existed, but I have unearthed much evidence to the contrary. For example, it is a known fact that Jefferson collected the bones of moose, elk, and mammoths. I, too, have an affinity for science and natural philosophy."

"Golly," I said.

"Am I still your P.I.?"

Face to face with genealogical certitude, I replied, "Let's pay Perdita Cunliffe a visit."

* * *

The Transportation Research Institute was located on the far eastern reaches of the university's North Campus, off Huron Parkway. Surrounded by oaks and crab apples on a hillock of greensward, the institute was three upended slabs of architectural concrete with windows. Across the road was the Industrial Technology Institute, three surrealistic, square layer cakes with curving corners and alternating horizontal bands of black glass and shiny chrome. With their air-conditioning units on top like bottle caps, they looked like designer aftershave. Reynolds seemed to be having similar thoughts; as we parked in the place marked for visitors, he shook his head and said, "What in hell has the school of architecture been up to?"

Perdita Cunliffe bade us come into her office, which was off the main reading room of the information center. She was in her early thirties, pretty and well tailored in a Betty Crockerish way, and spoke in a mellifluously constipated voice. She sat straight-backed and knee-welded, and for a moment I had a spooky feeling that she was the archetypal librarian of the type the school of library science has sought to eradicate from the profession. Like Betty Crocker, she might have been an invention, so cleverly conceived that she was believed by many to be a real person. Then she did something with her mouth, pursed it slightly as if in disapproval. The effect coupled with her slight overbite was to give off powerfully erotic vibes. Hidden fires, indeed. Given the right circumstances, she would turn into a real animal. Just the type Miles Dixon might unwind with. Brownies in the kitchen, then a feverish strumpet behind the locked door.

"You have a splendid library," Reynolds observed.

"We are an information resource-sharing facility," said Ms. Cunliffe. Her patient smile intimated that she had corrected many before us.

I looked out the open door at the rows and rows of books on the shelves. "Gee, it looks just like a library."

"What you see is our shelf collection. It is a node in a distribution network of on-line technical document files. Our virtual collection encompasses the Southeast Michigan Information Sharing Network. What sort of search were you gentlemen interested in?"

Impelled by a mischief-making devil that no forethought could stop, I said, "Then this isn't a real library?"

Her voice hardened. "We process incoming requests, we do keyword file searches, we access hard copy, and we interface with other information centers." She took an enormous three-carbon form from her desk and slid it toward me. "May I suggest it might expedite things if you made out a user-needs profile. If you need help, one of my assistants can assist you."

Reynolds bowed for both of us to the force majeure. "I think what Ms. Cunliffe is saying," he said to me, as if explaining to a child, "is that she is an information facilitator for the research community."

She nodded. "Precisely."

I said to her, "Then please facilitate our search by telling us about Miles Dixon."

Betty Crocker dropped her bowl of batter. She didn't acknowledge the mess at first. She merely stared at Reynolds and me. Finally, she blinked.

"I beg your pardon?"

"Miles Dixon," I said. "He was murdered in his apartment June 9th."

"Oh, yes, I believe I read something about that. Are you here in some official capacity... ?" she asked, letting the question hang a moment and, getting no response, she rose from her chair. "Then unless you want a literature search, I think both of you had better leave my office."

I picked up the phone.

"What are you doing?" she demanded.

"Dialing nine for an outside line."

"Whom are you calling?" she cried, innocent and unknowing, but taking the precaution of shutting the door. Her unspoken "my husband" was loud and clear.

I said, "Homicide Detectives Clancy and Freiday. They will be acting in an official capacity. Then I'll call the Ann Arbor *News* and facilitate a juicy tidbit about Wednesdays, Miles Dixon, and you."

"You are no gentleman," said Ms. Cunliffe. Then, perhaps sensing finer breeding in Reynolds, she appealed to him. "Have you no respect for the sanctity of the marital union?"

"Oh, I do. Truly," said Reynolds solicitously. "But his lady stands accused of killing Miles, and he will do anything to save her reputation."

"Even if it means ruining mine?"

I dislike being talked about in the third person. I said, "Ms. Cunliffe, if you don't tell us about Miles, you'll be facing recent journalism grads who can't spell, who are ignorant of history and propriety, and who are hell-bent on making their reputation in a competitive job market."

"You bastard!"

"I'm a desperate man."

She stiffened her upper lip over her overbite. "I didn't kill him."

"Dear Ms. Cunliffe," said Reynolds, "we are not saying you did. Nor is it our desire to incommode you."

What? I'd just threatened to throw her to the cops and the rabid press.

"Our only purpose in coming here," he continued in a voice dripping with sorghum and Spanish moss, "is to put an end to the unjust accusations against this distraught gentleman's lady."

Reynolds was talking about me in the third person again. But Perdita Cunliffe didn't mind. In fact, she seemed to have forgotten I was in the same room. Her eyes were bright and dilating. She inclined her head toward him and fingered her hair.

"I'm listening," she said.

"I speak of Irene Spinoza, a lady as liberated as yourself," Reynolds went on, gently rocking her in his Virginia cadence.

"Tell me more."

"Oh, dear Ms. Cunliffe, I entreat you to look at the anxiety that lies behind this gentleman's rash incivilities, and understand that it comes from the most tender feelings and gallant motivations."

Tender feelings? I was in hock for Irene's bail.

"Can you attune yourself with those tender feelings?" he asked.

"I think so. Yes, I'm definitely attuned," she sighed.

Caressed as she was by Reynolds's honeyed tones and buoyed on the sea swells of his languid diphthongs, she was near to swooning. Reynolds was better than the soundtrack of a French movie.

"Can you not imagine yourself in Irene's place, a woman living under the dark cloud of suspicion, cruelly accused in public hearings, your reputation sullied. Every day you face the world, brave on the outside but tormented inside because the world, jealous of your wit and your beauty, prefers to think the worst. It has no regard for the presumption of your innocence. Can you imagine this?"

She nodded dreamily. "Wit and beauty. Inner torment. Got it."

"You sustain yourself on black coffee and faith that your Lohengrin is swimming the deepest ocean, crossing the hottest desert, and climbing the highest mountain for his one and only. Shall I tell you how your Funny Valentine does these feats for you?"

"Tell me!" she cried.

"He does them with a glad heart. And shall I tell you why?"

"Tell me why!"

"Because within him burns an ardor so intense that he will not be satisfied until he possesses the true facts of your criminal case."

"Utterly and completely?"

"Body and soul, Ms. Cunliffe."

Perdita Cunliffe's eyes were heavy-lidded, her lips slightly parted.

"We asked your indulgence, Ms. Cunliffe. We solicit from you only such facts as will enable us to reconstruct the circumstances of Miles Dixon's tragic end. Even those which may seen so inconsequential as to be trivial."

Perdita Cunliffe gave a long, drawn-out sigh. After some moments she said in a husky voice, "Would you excuse me for a moment?" and left her office.

When she returned her makeup was freshened and her skin was fragrant from soap.

She said, "I'm not sure I know anything worth knowing."

Reynolds smiled away her modest disclaimer. "The night Miles Dixon was killed, June 9th, he had been invited to a party. Did he mention the party to you?"

"I knew he intended to go, but that's all."

"The week or so before June 9, did he say anything out of

the ordinary? Make any unusual request?"

Perdita blushed. "You said you wouldn't inquire about that. However," she added gamely, looking at him directly, "if you think it's relevant..."

"I meant about his work," said Reynolds, returning her direct stare. "Did he mention anyone he was going to see?"

"He didn't talk about his work. What was there to discuss about foreign student's visas? Though that last week, he was tense. Preoccupied. It made him very attentive," she said, and thought for a moment. "Miles asked me to find an out-of-print book from him. I remember because it was an unusual title. *Signs and Symbols in Oriental Rugs.*"

Bingo! I thought, careful not to show my excitement.

"Do you have the book?" Reynolds asked.

"I tracked down a copy in Chicago. I'll give it to you if you wish."

Reynolds looked deeply and sincerely into her eyes. "Thank you, Ms. Cunliffe."

"Call me Perdita."

"If you wish."

"I'd prefer you not call me at home. Why don't you give me *your* number?"

Reynolds obliged, and as she took the piece of paper I saw her fingers curl round his briefly.

If ever the Olympics held an event in bullshitting, Reynolds would have a shot at the gold.

We walked back to the car, and I said to him, "You must make out like crazy."

"I do all right."

6

It was Charles Finch's idea to give a brainstorming party. Everyone who had been at my June 9th party was invited to his place for next Saturday. We would put our heads together and reconstruct events to see if we could come up with anything to help Irene's case. Reynolds, my P.I., was invited. The more the merrier. So what if Reynolds was a secret agent of the U.S. State Department and nurtured fantasies about Eighteenth-century Virginia aristocracy? A little quirk like that shouldn't stand in the way of a good time. I suspected Reynolds was crazy and I was looking forward to a second opinion from Irene.

Friday, I met with Irene at Grunion, Grunion, Littlefield and Grunion to discuss developments. As before, Grunion was not in his office.

"I guess we're early," Irene said, looking absolutely stunning in a pearl-gray Ann Klein that rode agreeably up her knees when she sat down.

I checked my watch. In fact, we were a few minutes late. "What a coincidence, both of us getting here early. How've you been? Aside from the trial?"

"Is that supposed to be funny?"

"No, no," I said quickly. I felt as clumsy as a sweating

fourteen year-old, pondering how to maneuver the object of his affections into a receptive condition. "You're looking fantastic," I said, seizing upon the first safe inanity that presented itself. "You haven't worn your hair that way since. .. it's very becoming. How's your job?"

Irene took my question at face value. "My market report for Hudson's went over well."

"The one about teenage lock-step fads?"

"I called it, 'The beat of the different drummer and the eighty-percent markup.'"

"Catchy. Isn't it fortunate for the clothing industry that teenagers show their individuality by applying such inflexible fashion rules to one another."

"And that they can be persuaded to change them so often. Ethan thinks I've got a future in trend spotting."

"Ethan?"

"Oh, that's right. You haven't met. He's a V.P. at Hudson's. He says I have good marketing instincts and that I should develop them."

My hopes petrified in midair and plummeted. A rich, successful V.P. of a retail empire was telling Irene that she had good instincts. My agony over this development was unbearable. If I told Irene she had good instincts, she'd tilt her head and give me an amused, quizzical look. Why, oh, why do money and power anesthetize women's critical faculties?

"*He* says?" I said. "Who does he think he is telling you what to develop? You've always had the knack."

"Ethan was being complimentary. He's been very supportive since Miles was killed."

"I bet."

"What are you making such a fuss about?"

"I am not making a fuss," I said, wishing upon Ethan

plagues of boils, dropsy, scurvy, and multiple tax audits. I'm showing interest in your career. This is the first chance I've had to talk to you in a week."

"Oh, has it been that long?"

"Irene..."

"Where can Mr. Grunion be?"

"Let's not spoil the moment with Grunion."

Irene smiled tolerantly. "He *is* my lawyer."

"Lawyer? If your hearing in district court was anything to go by, you can look forward to a trial of irrelevant answers to misleading questions interrupted by stupid objections."

Irene murmured, "Lower your voice. He might be outside the door."

"Even when he's inside, he's out to lunch. Where have you been? I kept getting your answering machine."

"Are you checking up on me?" she said, sounding pleased that I was.

"Don't you return calls anymore?"

"I've become more selective."

"All right, all right," I said. "Listen, I found out that Miles Dixon was an undercover agent for the State Department."

"*Miles!* I don't believe it. How do you know?"

"From my P.I."

"How does he know?"

"Reynolds is from the State Department, too."

Irene raised an eyebrow. "The name of your P.I. who really works for the State Department is Reynolds?"

"No worse than Miles," I said. "Miles was investigating drug money. The week before he was killed, he had requested a backup. So, it looks like he was onto something more than he could handle alone."

Irene considered this. "I *knew* something was on his mind!"

"Of course, Reynolds couldn't tell me about this right away. He had to check us out first. Now he's on your side. He believes your stuff was planted in Miles's apartment to implicate you."

"When I told you that, you didn't believe me."

"I'm on your side. Why fight?"

Irene gave in to a sigh. "Poor Miles. He wasn't cut out for a job like that."

"Poor Miles," I echoed, secure in my knowledge of Perdita Cunliffe. Or had Miles played a double game with Perdita *and* Irene?

"Now aren't you sorry you didn't get to know him better?" Irene admonished me.

"What was there to know?"

"For one thing, that he was a State Department undercover agent." She peered toward the door. "Maybe the receptionist upstairs knows where Grunion is."

"I think I know," I said, and went to the men's room.

"Ladies and gentlemen," Grunion was intoning, his voice reverberating against the emerald marble. "I have great respect for Mr. Wusthof. He has done an admirable job of presenting the state's case against Ms. Spinoza. You may not know this, but it is a prosecutor's job, not to convict the accused, but to see that justice is done. And I think when we go over the evidence, it will become apparent that justice requires..."

"Hi there!" I said brightly.

"Oh, hello," said Grunion. "Fancy seeing you here again."

"Sorry to interrupt your summation, but Irene's waiting in your office."

Grunion's memory stirred and his eyes lit up. "Ri-i-i-ight. Our conference."

"I've got some news that may change your strategy. In

fact, it's possible we might be able to get Wusthof to drop the prosecution."

"Boy, that would be good news. Judge Cole rejected two of my motions."

"Sorry to hear that."

"And my conference with Wusthof didn't work out the way I thought it would. All in all, my week hasn't gone too well."

"How terrible for you," I said.

"I was a little depressed," Grunion admitted. "So I've channeled my energy into putting together a dynamite closing. It will take maximum advantage of the unique prejudices of the jury, whoever they may turn out to be."

"This will cheer you up," I said, and told him about Miles Dixon's secret mission.

Grunion's rapt face made me nervous.

"The State Department!" he exclaimed. "Holy smoke! Then a drug kingpin could have killed Mr. Dixon. You know something, Wusthof might drop prosecution."

Keeping my voice steady I said, "He just might do that."

Grunion had a wistful look. "If he does, I won't get a chance to give my dynamite closing to the jury."

"We can't have everything in life."

"It's not certain yet, about the drug kingpin?"

My frozen smile was becoming very burdensome. "Let's go see Irene."

"Did you get the meeting?" Irene asked as soon as Grunion and I had returned to the office.

Grunion went to his briefcase and removed a portable recorder. "Here it is."

"Here what is?" I asked.

"My conference with Wusthof," said Grunion, and pushed the rewind button.

Something wasn't right. "Wusthof agreed to let you record an off-the-record conference?"

"Tacitly."

My suspicions sharpened. "What does that mean?"

"He didn't say I couldn't."

"Because you didn't ask."

"If I'd asked, he'd have said no."

Horrific visions coursed through my mind, of outrage in the prosecutors' office over Grunion's conduct that would forever mark Irene's case. "Isn't it a violation of the legal canon of ethics?" I asked. "You could get into big trouble."

Grunion stopped fiddling with the recorder controls and weighed the possibility. "Not if he doesn't know about it. Besides, I was acting on instructions of my client."

I looked in stunned disbelief from Grunion to Irene. She seemed perfectly calm about the whole thing, and smiled sweetly back at me.

"What if Wusthof finds out?" I persisted.

Grunion glanced up at me in puzzlement. "Haven't you heard of attorney-client privilege? Unless instructed otherwise, I won't tell him."

"And I certainly won't," Irene added.

Their eyes bored in on me. "Hey, me neither."

Grunion started playing the tape.

First there were a series of sound effects: a rattling thud, presumably Grunion's briefcase being set down, then a loud click of the lock being opened, followed by about a minute of paper rustling that masked the two voices. When the rustling stopped, I could make out Wusthof's voice.

". . . sure you know we have been a leader in aggressive enforcement of the drug laws. Now we're really excited about the opportunity to bring big-time drug prosecution to the area. It's our number-one priority. That includes related cases, so our charging and plea policies apply in this instance to your client."

Grunion's voice came over as a blurred mumble. Apparently the directional mike had been aimed toward Wusthof. I could make out Grunion protesting that it wasn't how Irene was charged, then saying something about "a hypothetical trade situation."

There was more paper rustling, then I heard Wusthof replying.

". . . process more than twenty thousand cases a year. We have to target our time and energy. Your client isn't making things easier for us."

I realized Wusthof was referring to Irene's pleading innocent to killing Miles. So this was plea bargaining.

"In most cases," Wusthof went on, "a trial on the original charge could well end with the defendant found not guilty, or found guilty on a lesser charge, or given roughly the same sentence he gets by pleading guilty to a lesser charge. So by reducing the charges, we get the same results. But since your client insists on hanging tough. . ."

The tape played out in that threatening vein.

Wusthof's plea bargaining philosophy had my head spinning. I said, "Let me see if I got Wusthof straight. If Irene goes to trial on the original greater charge, she might be found guilty of a lesser charge, or—heaven forbid—found innocent. But if she makes a deal with Wusthof and pleads on a lesser charge, she'll be sure to get a lighter sentence, which she might get anyway if she went to trial."

"Wusthof believes in accountability," said Grunion, and put the tape on rewind.

"What if we show him that Miles worked for the State Department. . ." I began.

"That still doesn't get me off the hook," Irene said,

breaking her silence. "I'm a pawn in Wusthof's drug crusade. As far as he's concerned, Miles was into drugs and I was his main squeeze, so I either cooperate, or face prosecution on the full charge."

Even though you have nothing to cooperate with, I thought gloomily. Since when did being innocent become a handicap in dealing with the prosecution? I thought of Perdita Cunliffe. Could she have killed Miles? If Miles had told her about Irene, maybe she stabbed him in a jealous rage... but then how did Perdita get Irene's scissors, and how did she get Irene's clothing into the apartment? No, it had not been a crime of passion. It had been thought out in advance to frame Irene. There was someone else who had a lot at stake.

Saturday morning before Charles Finch's brainstorming party, I returned from walking Natasha in Liberty Plaza and discovered that a note had been slipped under my door. It was from my neighbor, Bob Compton. He had signed for a package, and would I be so kind as to take possession of my property as soon as possible.

Now Bob is an affable guy who manages one of the top clothing stores in Ann Arbor, and I'd been on good terms with the Comptons since we all moved into our condo building, so his brittle note was puzzling.

I went to their door and rang. Bob opened so quickly it was as if he had been waiting with his hand on the knob.

He greeted me with a peculiar, guilty look. "It broke open when the delivery man took it off the dolly,' he said nervously, indicating a large carton that could have held a refrigerator. The side was ripped and bulging, and apparently had been mended in great haste with a lot of tape. "We put it all back inside. Nothing's missing. Absolutely nothing."

"Accidents happen," I said, wondering what he was so agitated about. I tried lifting it, but it weighed a ton. It had wood reinforcements, like a refrigerator carton. "Could you give me a hand?" I asked.

"Okay. Just don't tell Mary."

What the hell was going on? Had Bob and Mary had a fight? Together we grunted and heaved and slid it over to my place.

We got it inside onto my landing. Bob remained standing outside my door, red-faced and wheezing violently as if undergoing a seizure. Between gasps, I asked him to come in for a beer, but he shook his head and gasped back, "No," though it seemed a gasp of great reluctance. Natasha came to the door and sniffed his shoes, then wagged her tail, adding her own invitation, but it was no go.

"Bob, is something wrong?"

"Hey, you know me. My motto is, Live and let live." He looked wistfully at the carton. "Mary's coming back from shopping soon. Maybe some other time."

And with that, he departed.

Bracing my back against the doorframe, I planted both feet against the carton and shoved it farther inside, sliding down the door frame onto my rump. I remained sitting there with my legs straight out, waiting for the pinpoint sparkles to fade from my vision and my pulse to descend from 160. Natasha helpfully slurped my face.

I got up and checked the shipping label. It was from The Thousand Happinesses Limited of Singapore, a company I'd never heard of. Impelled by volcanic curiosity, I got a screwdriver and had to stand on a stool to pry out the large staples fastening the top of the carton. I opened it.

The thud of my dropping jaw registered a solid five on the Richter. A six-pack of cherry-flavored nipple cream was staring up at me. It was nestled beside the Music Massager, "fully equipped with attachments for every mood." I lifted them out of the styrofoam packing pellets, and came upon Silver Lining Pheromone Spray, "packed with animal magnetism."

It was a shipment of sex toys. Now I understood Bob Compton's peculiar behavior. I grew dizzy imagining Mary Compton's reaction when the carton had burst open and disgorged some of the goodies.

In a trance, I slowly unpacked the cornucopia, as one might examine exotic objects from a flying saucer. The carton was chock-full of porno devices, gadgets, appliances, apparatuses, and whatnots. I laid them out on side tables, chairs, bookcases, and when I ran out of horizontal furniture, on my afghan rug. I did this with trepidation and some puzzlement, for quite frankly the activities that some of these things catered to were news to me.

There was every variety of erotic goody known to man. They promised to stimulate, enhance, delay, excite, and fulfill. They were manual, battery-powered, hydraulic-powered, vacuum-powered, inflatable, locksmithed, cream-whipped, articulated, lubricated, rubberized, vulcanized, and velcroed. There were "Hundred Pleasure Kits"—I supposed for people who couldn't make up their minds. And compact travel kits—for people on the go. And instruction manuals galore. Their thoroughness was encyclopedic, with how-to illustrations for the illiterate. The Southeast Asian entrepreneurs were living up to their reputation for attention to detail.

I marched back to the Comptons. Bob was surprised to see me again so soon. I politely asked him what the delivery man had looked like. As I expected, his description fit Biswanger perfectly.

Back in my living room amid the gadgetry, I did a slow

LET SLEEPING AFGHANS LIE 73

burn. Biswanger! The sneaky bastard had gotten the stuff from Thousand Happinesses Limited, then made the delivery to the Comptons when he knew I'd be out walking Natasha. There was no doubt in my mind that he had deliberately busted open the carton, ensuring me a lifetime of mortification and embarrassment from my neighbors. Already Mary Compton must have told twelve dozen of her nearest and dearest.

Biswanger had broken our Geneva convention. The electrical guitar setup for his son's birthday was nothing compared with what he had done, or with what he had coming. He deserved nuclear retaliation.

Natasha had nosed aside a six-pack of Motion Lotion and was gnawing on a gold Trimline vibrator. It was a deluxe model with five hypoallergenic attachments. I got it away from her, and then noticed a business envelope addressed to me. It contained a letter of transmittal from The Thousand Happinesses Limited, Sales and Distribution:

> Dear Mr. Spinoza:
> Your business representative has conveyed your interest about our "Thousand Heavenly Happinesses" product line, and we are flattered by an enquiry from someone of your international reputation.
> We should point out that whereas our line sells very well throughout the Pacific Basin, because of U.S. Customs barriers we presently have no stocklist within the United States. Therefore, we would welcome suggestions for design changes from someone with your vast experience. All manufacture for the United States would be made to your specifications.
> May we also propose as a solution to Customs barriers that final assembly of our components might be done in the United States.

We trust the above information is of help to you and thank you for your interest.
Yours very truly,
Ms. Linda Leung

There was a P.S. at the bottom, handwritten by Ms. Leung in graceful, flowing script.

P.S. I must tell you that I and the staff at our administrative offices and our manufacturing facilities are devoted players of *Hotel Rompé*.
L.L.

The warm personal addendum to Ms. Leung's letter touched me. I grew philosophical thinking of those factory workers playing *Hotel Rompé* during their leisure hours. It made sense. If one were surrounded by raw porn, day in and day out, one would yearn for the coyly suggestive, for naughtiness under the covers.

I had an hour before I had to leave for Charles Finch's brainstorming party. Just enough time to do something. I left The Thousand Happinesses Limited stuff where it was and sat in my swivel chair at my worktable. Natasha got up in the swivel chair beside me. She watched me tape down a sheet of the grid paper I use when I noodle around with ideas for toys or games. I made a list of "things to do":

Number one. Get Biswanger.
Number two. Sell a dynamite new game/toy.

It had to surpass even *Hotel Rompé*, making so much money that I'd be worryfree for the rest of my natural life, or at least enough to keep up my half of the mortgage. Actually, number two was already in the works. The past week, I had worked out a one-upmanship game that I was calling *Emotional Rollercoaster*. I'd roughed out a set of game cards. I decided to bring them to the brainstorming party for beta testing.

Number three. Really get Biswanger.

Number four. Find out more about Reynolds Stuart Adams.

How? Hiring another P.I. to find out about my first P.I. seemed redundant.

Number five. Convince Irene and Biswanger to replace Grunion.

Number six. Go to bed with Irene.

Having lined up my ducks in a row, and with my libido urging me on like a coxswain, I called upstairs to ask Irene whether she would like me to drive her to Charles's place, since we were both going there.

I got her answering machine.

In a snit, I put the leash on Natasha and off we went to Charles Finch's place.

7

CHARLES FINCH'S PLACE WAS a sybaritic time warp à la Hugh Hefner, built on two wooded acres overlooking where the Huron River is impounded and widens into Geddes Pond in Gallup Park. As a veterinarian, Charles could pass for human. As a rich veterinarian he'd become insufferable. Charles claimed that before he made his big bucks, he had the foresight to dump the buck-toothed giraffe he married when he was green and naive. Now he indulged in every toy: indoor pool with a motorized roof and wide panels that slid open for summer, exercise machine room, sauna room, billiards room (not pool, *billiards*), and a library and electronic media room. There seemed to be a special room for every bodily and mental function.

It was toward this San Simeon that I turned off Fuller and drove up the private gravel drive, with Natasha in the back seat and without Irene in the front. A van was at the service entrance of the main house. On its side was painted *Num-Nums On The Go: creative cuisine for the jaded*. I went past the four-car garage to the guest carport.

At the redwood portico, a bikinied girl greeted me with a breathy, Hi, I'm Terri—o-o-oh, wow! What's his na-a-a-ame?"

"I'm George," I replied. "And her name is Natasha."

The girl stroked Natasha's ears and crooned, "Well, hi there, Natasha. Hi there. How are you doing today? How are you doing? She's absolutely adorable!"

Natasha responded with uncustomary hauteur, perhaps because she sensed that Terri was competition.

Having exchanged amenities, the three of us trekked through the Mexican-tiled hallway, past the sunken living room with its bi-i-i-ig fireplace, and came upon a saturnine, pockmarked man whom Terri introduced as Rafael, one of Charles's business associates. Rafael regretted he couldn't join the party as he was flying out the next day and had calls to make. He excused himself and continued on his way, presumably into a special room for making telephone calls.

Terri and I continued out the back of the house to join the others gathered on the edge of the piney glade. Natasha romped into the glade.

I didn't see Irene anywhere. Tanya Fassbender and Morton Blue were dangling their feet in the pool, playing kissy face and feeding each other cheese puffs, so apparently they were back together again. I saw Gail and Toby Puffler. Toby is our town buffoon who writes for the arts section of the Ann Arbor News. There were a few others who had stopped at my party June 9th. They were strolling around, making a show of admiring the grounds. The real reason they were now here was that they didn't want to pass up the greatest opportunity at organized character assassination since a certain university official was discovered in the bell tower, stark naked and stone dead from a heart attack, with only the carillon as witness as to who else had been up there the night before.

I was met by Charles. Drink in hand, he was cool and unwrinkled in his safari suit and aviator shades. The girl, Terri, said, "Charles, this is George. I, uh, didn't get your last name."

"That's okay, Terri," I said. "I think it's much friendlier when total strangers start out on a first-name basis."

Charles murmured into Terri's ear. She giggled and went off. She was one of his everchanging house guests, one of many nubile "coeds" who apparently had never had their consciousness raised, nor attended classes. Charles exuded the smug satisfaction that comes with knowing you have it made and your friends don't.

"You seem a bit testy," said Charles. "Rough day, old boy?"

"You're looking spruce," I said, restraining Natasha from his designer khaki. "Bagged any rhino lately?"

"I'm always spruce, except when I'm grubby, and then I'm stylishly grubby." Charles shifted his gaze to the grocery bag I was carrying. "Picked up something from Kroger's fine selection of bulk vintages, have you? I'll have the caterers serve it with the Hostess Ho-Ho's."

"It's a game idea I've been tossing around."

"Jolly good," he said, giving his mustache a flick with the side of his knuckle. "If we get bored with saving Irene from the Prosecutor's axe, we'll toss it around, too."

"Go take a flying leap into the river, old boy."

"After you, George."

Biswanger was lounging in an Adirondack chair, refusing his wife Emily's invitation to join her in the pool. He claims he gets his exercise at his health club, but I know he goes there to play cards and take long naps. Upon seeing me, the treacherous bastard smiled and gave a friendly wave.

I was not going to give him the satisfaction of showing any reaction to the Thousand Happinesses Limited shipment. I put on a broad smile, renewed the vow of revenge I had made amid the scabrous litter of my living room, and walked over to him.

"Pull up a chair, George. By the way, that guitar equipment you sent Timmy..."

"Does he like it?" I asked innocently.

"He's crazy about it. He and his friends have formed a group. They practice every chance they get."

My cup was running over.

"The group keeps him out of the house and out of our hair," said Biswanger. "Days go by before I see him. The peace and quiet has been a godsend. Emily and I can't thank you enough."

"Have you seen Irene?" I asked in a strangled voice.

"She's with your P.I., What's-his-name, in the gazebo."

I looked over toward the gazebo in the pines and saw Irene, preternatural in the late afternoon light, talking with Reynolds.

"I must say, George, the man impresses me as being a little strange. We got into a *very* intense discussion about cultural self-determination, Jeffersonianism, and Afghanistan!"

"Reynolds is deep into international politics. Excuse me."

I made a beeline for the gazebo.

Irene was in a somber, preoccupied mood, though she looked splendid in a red-and-white striped pullover and jeans. The usually voluble Reynolds was gravely nursing a drink.

"I called, but you'd already left," I said to her. "Your car was still in the garage."

"Reynolds drove me."

Reynolds met my accusatory gaze with dignified innocence. He said, "I've been filling Irene in on the latest developments."

Suspicions multiplied around me like flies. First Ethan, the Hudson's V.P., now Reynolds my P.I.

Irene filled in the lull. "Reynolds has told me that Miles was married."

"No kidding!" I said. "How long?"

"For ten wonderful years," said Reynolds.

Thinking again of Perdita, I felt a savage joy, for here was yet another item of information that good old Miles hadn't thought to confide to Irene. I said, "He sure knew how to keep a secret."

"What I want to know," Irene wondered aloud, "is why she hasn't come here to make funeral arrangements."

"Mrs. Dixon does know he's dead?" I asked Reynolds, in case Irene and I had overlooked the obvious.

"She was notified at the appropriate time. The State Department tries not to keep important people in the dark too long."

I was quick to seize upon this scrap of information. "Mrs. Dixon is a VIP?"

"Miles was fortunate in that he married above his station into a very fine Maryland family with connections to high places in government."

"Was Miles on good terms with her?"

"The best," Reynolds assured me.

"It does seem strange that no one in the prosecutor's office has heard from her."

"I'm not sure I understand," said Reynolds with an earnestness that was devoid of any tincture of waggishness.

I had the stunning realization, like a dash of ice water down my back, that he did not find the silence of Mrs. Dixon to be at all odd.

"Does Mrs. Dixon acknowledge such things as death?" I asked.

"Not when it involves sensitive government business," said Reynolds. "Wheels within wheels. However, I am in a position to assure you that Mrs. Dixon is deeply concerned for her husband."

"But Miles is dead," I pointed out
"So you can appreciate how deep her concern is."
"How deep can it be," Irene demanded, "when she hasn't even assumed custody of her husband's remains?"
Reynolds looked puzzled. "I thought I explained. The operation is still in progress."
"The medical examiner did the autopsy weeks ago," Irene protested. "Officer Freiday told me Miles was cremated."
"Oh, is that what's worrying you? Let me put your mind at ease. The State Department is holding his ashes."
Despite the morbid turn of the conversation, my curiosity knew no bounds. "Why are they holding his ashes instead of giving them to Mrs. Dixon?"
"Because Miles is still on assignment. It would be a terrible mark on his record if he were taken off before the operation were resolved, and Mrs. Dixon wouldn't stand for that."
I was fascinated. "When will the department release his ashes?"
"As soon as he is off assignment."
"Which will be when this operation is over," I said, and thought, Poor Miles, stuck in an urn in bureaucratic limbo. I said, "Then we won't be hearing from Mrs. Dixon or her family."
"You can count on it," said Reynolds.
Charles's other guests were gathering at an enormous round white table that had been set up on the lawn. Irene, Reynolds, and I left the gazebo to join them. At last, I was going to hear what they remembered about Miles. Then I'd have some leads as to who actually killed him.

"George, there you are!" chirped Sandy Moore. "I thought I'd never get the chance. Now you sit right here and tell me what you've been up to." She pulled me down into the chair beside her. "Here, try some of these little hors d'oeuvrey things." Irene sat across the table between Reynolds and Toby Puffler.

Sandy Moore had been with the astronomy department her entire professional life, and was a big booster of the football team. In fact, she had a yen for football players and had a steady supply from her Astronomy 101 class, where they were sent for their science requirement. The joke went that her grading system was A for athlete, B for boy, and C for coed. Her tenuous reason for being at the brainstorming party was that she had stopped by my June 9th party for maybe ten minutes.

There were about a dozen of us. I was flanked on my left by Sandy and on my right by Emily, who had changed from her swimsuit into a light cotton wraparound dress. Biswanger sat one over from me on Emily's right. Gail and Toby Puffler filled out around Irene and Reynolds. Natasha stationed herself near Tanya and Morton to snaffle up fallen goodies.

We sat at the round table and watched the river several hundred yards below us turn gold from the dipping sun. The paddle boaters were churning back to the Gallup Park livery, and early evening joggers were out in force. Charles signaled the Num-Nums people to begin serving. King Arthur never had it so good.

"What is this?" I asked the white-jacketed guy who had set before me a greenish pancake decorated with miniature red marbles swimming in pink sauce.

"Zucchini galette with fish roe in rhubarb," he murmured.

On the strong likelihood that this was another of Biswanger's jokes, for which I was prepared to make a scene, I checked around. Incredibly, the same pancakes had been served to everyone.

"Why was Miles Dixon killed?" intoned Charles, the master of ceremonies. "That question is why we are gathered here. To mourn Miles's passing, to celebrate friendship, and to help Irene beat her murder rap."

Celebrate? I thought. The only thing you're celebrating is this villa to Mammon, you fatuous showoff.

I said, "Miles Dixon was invited June 9th to the party. Why didn't he show up?"

I waited, primed and ready to take mental notes. No one volunteered to answer.

I tried again. "When did you last see Miles?"

There was a chorus of murmurs: "Not at the party."

I felt my temple throb. Tanya suggested we go round robin.

"Good idea," said Morton.

'Capital!" said Charles.

"Super," said Sandy.

"Now we're getting somewhere," said Toby.

In the protracted lull that followed, I looked from face to face. They were under anesthesia from the lazy summer weather and Num-Num's first course. I caught Biswanger's eyes twinkling with amusement. Ignoring the smirking S.O.B., I reached into my paper bag and rummaged through the game pieces until I found the pad with questions I had written up about Miles. I pushed my zucchini aside and laid the pad before me on the table. "Now about Miles. . ."

"O-o-oh, what's in there?" Sandy Moore squealed, looking down into my bag.

"Just a game idea I've been tossing around. I've got a few questions here. . ."

"What's it called?"

"Its working title is *Emotional Roller Coaster*. Now about Miles. . ."

"Can we try it out?"

"Maybe later. About Miles..."

Sandy stood up. "Yoo-hoo, people! George has a new game."

Instantly, every face was alert with anticipation.

"Everybody who's for beta testing George's new game, say aye."

The ayes had it.

Bloody hell. I passed out game pieces from the bag and explained the rules.

Meanwhile, the Num-Nums people exchanged our plates with ones highly decorated with fruit cut into fanciful shapes surrounding gravid kiwi fruits. I flagged the waiter again.

"What is this?"

"Kiwi pousse, sir."

"Could you be more specific?"

"Certainly, sir. The chef cuts a cross in the top of the kiwi, scoops out the pulp, and divides it into two bowls. In one bowl he folds in crème-fraiche, grenadine, lime juice, and honey. In the second bowl he douses it with crème de menthe. Then ever so gently he spoons the two mixtures back into the kiwi skin in alternating layers, and the kiwi is none the wiser."

"Your chef didn't by any chance consult with Mr. Biswanger?"

"Mr. Biswanger?"

"The gentleman over there."

"I don't think I'm acquainted..."

I became aware of voices raised in discord.

"Wouldn't you be satisfied with Fatalistic Mockery?" Morton Blue was demanding of Tanya.

"Nope," she replied.

"I'll trade you one Abject Whimpering and two Stinging Retorts, okay?"

Tanya held her game pieces to her bosom like a Valkyrian shield. "It's Devastating Insight or nothing."

"You ever thought of going into loan sharking?" Morton snapped. "You've got an inborn talent for it."

"Look, smart guy. I've got the Devastating Insight card, not you. So either shut up or put up."

"Go stand on your head in an ashram."

"I will not be spoken to in that manner," Tanya cried. "I've got a Stinging Retort, so it's legal."

"I bet that's not what's printed on your card."

"Are you calling me a liar?"

"Then show me the back of your card."

I was appalled. All around the table strife was breaking out. My prototype was not the merry parlor game of psychobabble I'd intended. It was pure destruction.

I hurried round the table, grabbing the game pieces and stuffing them back into my Kroger's bag. "That's enough beta testing."

His eyes crinkled in sadistic merriment, Charles observed this while leaning back in his chair with Terri standing beside him. Keeping a hand covetously on her thigh, with his other hand he tweaked his mustache. "Interesting game concept."

I wanted nothing more than to drive my fist into his taunting smile. Natasha trotted up with a freshly killed rabbit in her mouth, and the moment passed.

Everyone wandered away. Biswanger and Emily went for another dip in the pool. Charles and Reynolds went off for a game of billiards. I finally got Irene alone in the gazebo.

"Charles Finch is the drug kingpin," I declared to her.

"Charles? Nonsense."

"Look around. He's living like one, for God's sake."

"You know perfectly well he can live like this because of

Cuddy-Wuddles and his animal hospital. Charles invited us here to help me. Not only are you jealous of his success, you're ungrateful."

"He set up this party as a joke on me."

"If you keep on like this, the joke *will* be on you."

"Irene, Irene," I pleaded, "can't you see? Charles has been laughing at us all during this brainwashing party."

"Brain*storming*. It's obvious the one who killed Miles is that State Department agent you hired."

"I hired Reynolds *after* Miles was dead. Reynolds was Miles's backup. What motive could he have?"

"Washington office politics. You know easily they knock each other off." Irene seemed to lose interest in her own argument.

"Let's not fight," I said.

"Who's fighting?"

"Irene, you know I care for you."

"I know."

"You looked so alone in that jail. Oh, Christ, my friends are a bunch of self-absorbed nitwits. What are we going to do?"

Perhaps it was the summery evening stealing upon us, the river below, the mellow season of ripeness and ripening. Irene and I were regarding each other with fresh interest.

"Georgie, take me home."

8

I DROVE IRENE AND Natasha home from the brainstorming party. The three of us were in a mellow mood. I parked in my reserved bay in the garage, and as I went around to open Irene's door I felt as if it were before our split and the subsequent bifurcation of our condo into separate residences.

Irene took my hand and stepped out of the car straight into my arms.

Agreeably amazed at the turn of events, I got in good and tight. Miracles were still possible. My planet had moved onto the cusp of Amorosa. I came up for air and moaned, "Irene, Irene."

"Oh, Georgie, I was hoping this would happen."

"So was I."

She blushed. "I know."

Buoyed on the marvelous prospect of our present hanky developing into full-blown panky, I said in a voice thick with passion, "There's never been anyone but you."

Irene gave no reply beyond a self-contained Mona Lisa expression, which I recognized to mean she found something terribly amusing. Curiosity overcoming prudence, I asked, "What's so funny?"

"You. Me. Us."

"What about you, me and us?" I asked.

"Well, me, for one thing. The night Miles was killed, there I was, one floor above you, hating you because you were having a good time at your party."

"No kidding?" I said. "And there I was, one floor down, missing you because you weren't at the party."

"No kidding?" she replied. "Why didn't you ask me down?"

"I thought you'd say no."

"I wouldn't have."

"Even though you were busy hating me."

"Only because you didn't ask me."

"You could have come down to the party any time," I insisted. "Why didn't you?"

"Because I didn't want to give you the satisfaction of knowing I wanted to."

"But you came down after the party for that stupid joke."

"That was different. I was jealous of you and Biswanger."

I was unprepared to have Biswanger brought into the picture. "He's patronizing and he insults me. What's there to be jealous about?"

"The practical jokes you two play on each other."

"Harassment and humiliation makes you jealous?"

"I've always felt left out."

"I had no idea," I said, surprised that she should covet what I found a strain.

"That's why I went along with his idea to knit Natasha to the rug."

Natasha, who had been sitting by the elevator like a patient Sphinx, gave no indication that she bore a grudge.

"Why didn't you ever tell me you felt that way?" I asked.

"I didn't want you to think I was jealous."

"To be honest," I said, "lately I've grown tired of the practical jokes."

"It's nice of you to say that."
"No, really."
"Irene's face brightened. "It's nice talking like this." She sighed. "I know there's been no one else."
"You sound awfully sure."
"I *know* you, Georgie."
I was given pause. "I see. I see."
"Georgie, what's wrong?"
"Nothing." I pushed the elevator button.
"Come on."
"You shouldn't have to ask. You *know* me."
"Georgie," she said, reclosing the gap, "you really must learn not to be your own worst enemy."

Inside the ascending elevator, Irene and I went into a second clinch. Irene murmured an invitation to come up to her place.

Though somewhat surprised at her usurping my prerogative by making the suggestion first, I realized it conferred an advantage; it took the pressure off. I eagerly assented. Everything was coming up roses.

"I just remember," she said. "My coffee maker is out being fixed. Let's go to your place."

Through the red haze of passion, I remember that my nest presented a riveting tableau of the entire product line of Thousand Heavenly Happinesses Limited! My hot blood transmuted into anxiety over how to prepare Irene for the initial shock. It happened to be the truth that Biswanger had ordered the shipment, but at this delicate juncture of our relationship, the fact that my living room looked like a knick-knack shop for erotomaniacs beggared explanation. I blindly groped for the elevator button for her floor.

"My cleaning service didn't come this week. My place is a mess—we'd better go to yours," I said, fervently cupping

Irene's face, and blocking her exit from the elevator as the doors slid open at my floor. "I don't want *coffee*," I added, giving her a confirmatory squeeze.

"That's strange," she said as the door closed. "We use the same service, and they did my place."

The crisis avoided, we disembarked on the next floor up. Irene unlocked her door.

"I've been robbed!" she cried.

I followed Irene inside. I hadn't been inside since we divided the two floors. I looked around for signs of mayhem, but instead saw an elegant sitting room in perfect order. Floral chintz sofa and chairs, gold-framed mirror over the mantle, ceiling mouldings, glazed walls. Everything was neat as a pin, from the celadon vase on the polished drop-leaf side table to the botanical prints hung over it. Nothing seemed out of place or missing. I knew she had remodeled after our split, but clearly an entire firm of interior decorators had gone hog wild.

Irene began to check the other rooms.

"This is incredible," I called to her, marveling at the disciplined opulence.

"Isn't it," she said bitterly. "This building is supposed to have twenty-four-hour security."

"I mean all the stuff. It's beautiful."

"Oh, you mean the remodeling."

"You must have spent a fortune."

"Not really. The plastering wasn't too hard, once I got the hang of it."

Plastering? Feelings of awe and admiration welled up in me.

"I got the rug on a clearance sale from Marderosian's," she said from the bedroom. "The kitchen was a problem. I contracted two carpenters for the cabinets and counters. You like the Mexican tile? I did a mud job rather than epoxy."

Knowing how hard it is to find a good nonunion tiler, my marveling deepened into adoring respect. "Incredible," I repeated.

Irene returned to the living room. "You think so?"

"You're incredible."

"I may have gone overboard in areas," she said, squinting hypercritically at her handiwork, "but I have to look like I'm a big success when I have clients over."

"I guess you'd better call the police," I said. "What did the burglar take?"

"I can't find anything missing yet."

"If nothing's missing, how can you tell someone's been in here?"

"I can tell. Things have been moved."

"What things?"

Irene colored slightly. "The bastard went through my underwear drawer."

I checked the outside lock on the door. "No scratches," I said. "No signs of forced entry."

"Dammit," she said. "I should have known."

"How could you know someone would break in?"

"Because I was burglarized before, when my stuff was planted in Miles's apartment. Whoever did it must have a duplicate of my key. I should have changed the lock."

"Call the two homicide detectives who are assigned to Miles Dixon's case," I advised. "Clancy and Freiday."

Irene went to the phone.

"Would you believe it?" she said. "They put me on hold."

I was wondering what reason the perpetrator had to break in a second time. Perhaps he had developed an underwear fetish. Which reminded me, I still had to deal with those land mines from Thousand Happinesses Limited.

"George, where are you going?"
"Downstairs to call a locksmith," I said.
"Don't leave me!"
"I'll be right downstairs. I'll make coffee," I added.

Natasha slipped out the door ahead of me. Rather than wait for the elevator, I turned into the fire stairway. Natasha raced down ahead of me.

Back in my living room, I began gathering up the Thousand Happinesses Limited merchandise and repacking it into the carton. Natasha thought it was a grand game of fetch. She raced around, scattering styro packing pellets. Precious minutes were wasted while she played tug of war with me over some latex items.

The door chimes rang.

I was perspiring. In the foyer mirror, I was the color of an embarrassed tomato. I couldn't let Irene in yet.

I opened the door.

Detectives Clancy and Freiday stood there. It was only about five minutes since I'd left Irene. Had they been in the area and gotten the message on their radio? Blocking their view of my premises, I held firmly onto the doorknob.

"Good evening, Mr. Spinoza," said Clancy. "We have a warrant to search the premises."

I was confused. What did they need a warrant for, when Irene had been burgled, even though nothing seemed to be missing? Also, they couldn't have gotten a warrant in five minutes. Then it dawned on me. They were at *my* front door. *My* premises. Biswanger! The S.O.B. had tipped off the cops that I was a purveyor of red-hot porn!

No galley slave, learning he'd been chosen for the Roman arena, experienced a more ghastly battering of the spirit than I did at that moment.

"Let me see the warrant," I croaked.

Clancy reached into his breast pocket. Coming up empty-handed, he tried the other pocket. Nothing. He looked at Officer Freiday, but she didn't have it either. From their battle of glances, I gathered there was a contretemps between them. Each seemed to be saying to the other, "I thought *you* brought the warrant!"

Detective Clancy fixed me with a warning look. "Tell Ms. Spinoza we'll be back."

Ms. Spinoza? Hope was reborn. "Excuse me," I said, "but I think there's been a mistake. If you had a warrant, where would it say you can search?"

Detective Clancy said, "The warrant, if we had it, specifies that we may enter and search the residence of Irene Spinoza."

"If you had the warrant," I explained, "you'd also see that you've come to the wrong residence. Ms. Spinoza lives one floor up."

Again, Detectives Freiday and Clancy exchanged looks. Hers seemed to be saying, "I told you so," while his said, "I don't want to discuss it here."

"It's an easy thing to get wrong," I said. "Someone got their signals crossed. Irene called your division because someone broke into her place this afternoon while she was out."

"That's burglary," said Freiday.

"We're homicide," said Clancy.

"I know," I said. "She thinks the break-in is related to her upcoming trial. Since you're here, how about I take you up?"

"Nice dog," Detective Freiday commented as the four of us ascended in the elevator.

"Purebred?" asked Detective Clancy."

"Purebred," I replied, falling into their clipped habit.

Irene appeared at the door with the phone. She was still

on hold. "That was fast! How did you get through, George? I'm still on hold."

Freiday and Clancy exchanged glances. Irene stood aside for them to enter, but they remained just outside the door.

"They forgot their search warrant," I explained.

"What do they need a warrant for?"

"Beats me," I said. I turned to Detective Freiday. "If you had your warrant, what did you expect to find?"

"We got a tip..." she began, then caught Detective Clancy's warning glance and stopped.

I said to Irene, "They're not here because I called."

Irene frowned and hung up the phone.

We were at an impasse.

"I don't suppose we could come in?" Detective Clancy asked, breaking the ice.

"Please do," said Irene.

While Natasha made her own reconnaissance, both officers began to look around from room to room, clearly impressed by Irene's taste in furnishings. Detective Freiday seemed particularly taken with the wall treatments. I still had to return downstairs to finish packing away the rest of the Thousand Happinesses Limited stuff.

Natasha began to bark furiously from the bathroom. We all converged there, to find her jumping up against the wall, pawing and biting at the light switch.

"What's the matter, girl?" I asked.

Officer Clancy smiled and ruffled her ears. "Good dog," he said. He withdrew a Swiss Army knife from his jacket. While Irene and I looked on, wondering what the hell was going on, he unfolded a screwdriver attachment and unscrewed the ceramic switchplate. He folded back the screwdriver and unfolded a tweezers attachment, which he used to lever the plate away from the wall.

A plastic bag of white powder fell out.

"That wasn't there when I redid the bathroom," Irene said.

Irene, Detective Freiday, and I trooped to the living room. Officer Clancy followed Natasha around for a while, but there were no more discoveries. Detective Freiday sat with Irene, who had started to shake as the implication hit her. She said to me, "I'm not spending another night here till the lock is changed."

"I'll go check the coffee," I said, and went back downstairs.

Quickly, I measured out coffee into the coffee maker, then went back to repacking the Thousand Happinesses Limited carton.

My door chimes rang again.

It was officer Clancy.

"Irene wanted me to tell you not to bother with the coffee. While we were going through her apartment, we found her old coffee maker."

"It's very thoughtful of you to come down and tell me, but wouldn't it have been easier to phone?"

"Detective Freiday is using Ms. Spinoza's phone."

"Thank you. Please tell Irene I'll be up as soon as I've finished tidying up."

"Will do."

I resumed my gleaning. I had the enormous cartons two thirds full when the door rang again.

It was Reynolds, holding the Kroger's paper bag with my ill-fated game pieces.

"You left this at the brainstorming party," he said.

"Reynolds, my man," I said, stepping swiftly outside and shutting my door against Natasha's greetings. "You've come at a propitious time. Irene is upstairs with the two homicide detectives. It seems her place was burglarized while we were at the party."

"What was taken?"

"Nothing seems to be missing, but the police made a very interesting discovery. How about you go up and have a word with them?"

Having sent off Reynolds, I went back to restoring my living rooms to a PG-13 rating. A few minutes later my doorbell rang.

It was Reynolds again. "Irene says go ahead with the coffee, since now there's so many people."

Reynolds departed. Natasha tired of playing with the goodies. She climbed up into my swivel chair, from which vantage point she gravely watched me race against time. I was vacuuming up the packing material when the doorbell rang again.

This time it was everybody: Reynolds, Detective Freiday, Irene with a steaming coffee carafe, and Detective Clancy, who had two Sara Lee coffee cakes, presumably from Irene's freezer. Natasha wagged a warm hello, her eyes bright and her conscience clear for having led Clancy and Freiday to the drugs planted in Irene's bathroom.

Irene had agreed to let police forensics go over her place. Detective Freiday had called, and the team would arrive within the hour.

"We can't disturb anything and we'd only be in the way when they come," Irene explained, "so I thought we might as well come down here."

"I hope you don't mind," said Detective Freiday.

Not three feet from me stood the Thousand Happinesses Limited carton. I gave her a jovial smile. "Think nothing of it," I said, and waved them all inside.

Detective Clancy shifted the frozen coffee cakes from one hand to another. "Do you have a microwave?"

"Be my guest."

His attention was caught by the Thousand Happinesses Limited carton next to the doorway. "New refrigerator?"

"Wrong model. It's going back," I said.

We all sat down to coffee in my living room. Natasha returned to my swivel chair, as regally sympathetic as an eighteenth-century aristocrat presiding over her salon, to give us her undivided attention.

"Does she usually sit there?" asked Detective Freiday.

"Most of the time," I replied.

Detective Clancy said to Reynolds, "We weren't informed that the State Department was interested in this case. Is their interest official?"

"Officially," said Reynolds, "the State Department has a long-standing commitment to vigorous and effective enforcement of the drug laws. We feel very strongly about that, and high-ranking State Department spokespersons have made public statements supporting that position, although I'm not at liberty to reveal their names, and if I did, they would have to deny it."

"What is their interest in *this* case?" Clancy asked.

"We share a community of interests," said Reynolds gravely.

"What do you see your role as in this case?"

"In this case," said Reynolds, "the State Department can bring its perspective to bear."

"But what specifically?" Clancy insisted.

"An international perspective," said Reynolds, serenely confident, his gaze clear and unswerving as that of a White House press secretary.

"Even when our government uses drug traffickers for arms shipments to Central America?" asked detective Freiday.

"It distresses me terribly," said Reynolds, shaking his head sadly, "when I hear the terrible slanders the national media make against the State Department and the CIA and the National Security Council."

"I'm a local homicide cop, so you'll excuse me if I see things from a local perspective," said Clancy, helping himself to a piece of walnut cake and getting crumbs on his sleeve. Detective Freiday reached over and brushed them from his sleeve onto her napkin in a manner so automatic and familiar, that upon noticing that I had noticed, she shyly lowered her eyes.

"Like when a U.S. attorney petitions the federal district court in Detroit," Clancy continued, "to dismiss an indictment against a drug trafficker who over ten years was the leader of a billion-dollar marijuana smuggling and distribution operation, and it turns out the trafficker was used by the CIA to run arms into Central America."

"It was a shocking revelation," Reynolds said. "People must believe their government would never do things like that and it will never do them again, until we have to."

"The U.S. attorney petitioned the judge to dismiss," Clancy went on, "because, he said, the trafficker had helped the feds in two drug stings. But it turns out the two stings were structured from the beginning by other branches of our government as bargaining chips to give Detroit feds something in exchange for dropping their indictment against the trafficker. They financed the sting with twenty thousand pounds of marijuana the trafficker flew up from Colombia into Northern Mexico with the active help of DEA personnel. And it also turns out the CIA supplied the drug trafficker with secret radio codes and passwords so he could get the twenty thousand pounds of marijuana by the U.S. Coast Guard patrols. What we have here is CIA and DEA personnel aiding and abetting a marijuana deal to save the ass of their drug-trafficking arms-supplier. So you'll understand if I get the impression that the left hand of the government doesn't know what the right hand is doing."

"How right you are," said Reynolds fervently. "Take Afghanistan. While freedom-loving Afghans fought the Soviets, and their families suffered in camps in Pakistan, we tried to curry favor with the Soviets by pretending to negotiate a coalition government that would include the Soviet puppets who the Afghans so bitterly hate."

Afghanistan again? I recalled Reynolds's impassioned speech to Abdur Rahman at Marderosian's Ruggery. Inexorably, I was coming to the conclusion that Reynolds really was crazy.

"May I speak frankly?" said Reynolds.

"That would be nice," said Clancy.

"Frankly," said Reynolds, "I think the tip that brought you to Ms. Spinoza's home is more than a little suspicious. The drug cache upstairs was hidden where any experienced investigator would find it. Obviously, someone who knew that Ms. Spinoza would be away all afternoon as a guest of Mr. Finch has tried to implicate her again, just as he did in Miles Dixon's murder. If we find that person, we'll have the murderer."

"Or else," said detective Clancy in a voice as dry as the Kalahari, "someone tipped off Ms. Spinoza about our tip, and she decided cooperation was the better part of valor."

In a voice that could have frosted the Bahamas, Irene said, "I was *not* tipped off about your tip. More coffee?"

My door chimes rang. I got up and answered the door. The forensics team had arrived.

"Reynolds Stuart Adams is off his rocker," Irene murmured, turning her head on the pillow toward me.

"Then he must feel right at home working for the U.S. Government," I said.

It was after one in the morning, many hours since the forensics team, Detectives Freiday and Clancy, and Reynolds had departed. Irene and I lay in my bed in afterglow. At the moment I was lazily engaged with her breast, and didn't give a damn about Reynolds or the State Department or the Afghan mujahedeen.

Irene said, "Reynolds could have killed Miles."

"If he did, I'll fire him. He'll be disappointed, but he's got his job at the State Department to fall back on."

"Don't fire him. As long as he's your P.I. we can keep track of him." She snuggled closer and whispered into my ear a request I hadn't heard for eons. "Make me one of your shakes."

My heart soared. In a flash I was out of bed, into my robe and puttering in the kitchen. Whistling a happy tune, I got out the Guittard chocolate, the Amaretto, malt powder, and ice cream. Some people go right to sleep afterward; some smoke; some eat chips and watch the late movie. Irene liked me to whip her up a brandied chocolate malted shake. Sometimes it was a caramel nut sundae, or waffles with apples flamed in Calvados. I'm very good with desserts when I have to be. Aside from Irene's murder rap, the future looked sanguine. But when I opened the storage cabinet for my Waring commercial drink mixer, I saw the shelf was bare. Then I remembered that after our divorce the sight of the Waring had evoked emotions so painful, I'd chucked it out along with a broken flashlight.

Barefooted, with a measuring spoon in one hand and a box of straws in the other, I cursed my past rashness. It was late. Discount appliance stores were closed. Elsewhere in the universe suns were exploding, galaxies were colliding, and quasars pulsating. I didn't care. At that moment, the only thing that mattered in all of creation was that I bring a brandied chocolate malted back to Irene, thus binding our relationship and ensuring our future happiness together.

While galaxies continued to collide, my mind went into its own whirl, fueled by frenetic desperation. I was a toy designer. An expert in creative gadgetry. What was a mixer, even one so exalted as a Waring commercial model, but another gadget with motorized parts? Like a flash from above the mountain, inspiration came to me. Irene would have her milk shake. Our future would be saved.

I hurried into the living room to the Thousand Happinesses Limited carton and rummaged around for what I needed. In my workroom I went to work making the necessary modifications to the Lotus Flex-a-Pleaser multispeed vibrating massager.

Back in the kitchen, I put in the ingredients into the soda glass and turned on my hybrid machine. There was a pleasant low-pitched hum. The ice cream within the glass began to gently swirl and froth with the chocolate and liqueur. After a minute or so, I taste tested. Not bad. Actually, it was rather good.

Irene had the television on when I returned. A late-night host was battering a guest with the one-note heavy sarcasm that had made him rich and famous. I casually handed Irene the shake.

"See if PBS has anything good," Irene requested.

I turned to Channel 56. They had another one of their interminable fund-raising auctions going. I turned off the TV and slipped back in beside Irene.

She took a sip of the shake, gave a tiny shudder, and made a long drawn-out sound that sounded like "Mmm-mmmph."

"Too cold?" I asked.

"This is the best chocolate mousse I've ever had."

"It's a shake. I just mixed it up, like I always did."

"This is fantastic mousse!" She greedily slurped some more. "You made it earlier, right? Kept it in the refrigerator in the hope... Oh, Georgie, you're as romantic as the first time!" With a blissful look, she finished the shake.

Much later, as I rolled over exhausted, Irene said, "I think I'm falling in love with you again."

"It's all in the mixing," I yawned.

9

IRENE HAD HER LOCKS changed. The police forensics people had found no unusual fingerprints on her bathroom light switch. Only dog saliva and claw marks. But they did find fingerprints inside her underwear drawer that did not match hers, mine, or the cleaning service people's. Also, another satin teddy was missing. That made two, the first having been planted in Miles Dixon's apartment. Apparently, the phantom drug-planter had a fetish for ladies' underwear. Four days after the break-in, I returned from walking Natasha to find Irene waiting for me in the living room—we had given each other copies of our keys—looking angry and upset.

"Someone's been messing with my car," she announced. "The seat was moved forward and the rearview mirror wasn't right."

We went down to the garage.

Since the doorlock hadn't simply been punched out, it was clear Irene wasn't supposed to know the car had been broken into. I checked the strips of rubber gasket around her car windows, and sure enough, on the passenger side I found telltale abrasions from either a bent coat hanger or, if it had been opened by a street professional, a thin strip of springy metal.

Irene unlocked the door. I peered inside, but I couldn't see anything out of the ordinary. I walked around the car, then knelt down and looked underneath. Just ancient oil stains on the concrete. I got up from the garage floor.

Irene said, "You've got a smudge on the left side of your nose." She took out a tissue, moistened it with spittle, and began to dab at the offending spot.

"Let's apply some logic here," I said. "Since the seat is forward from your usual position, that means someone shorter than you was in your car."

"Hold still."

"Or else someone taller who tried to readjust the seat back to where it was, but didn't get it exactly right. Therefore, we definitely know they aren't your exact height. Unless they had to move the seat for reasons other than to sit in it, in which case they could be your exact height."

Irene was less than enthusiastic about my impeccable analysis. "You're beginning to sound like Reynolds."

"I think you should notify Clancy and Freiday," I replied stiffly, "and we'll see if they can do better."

"If I call homicide about this, they'll think I'm a—what do you call someone who reports crimes all the time—like a hypochondriac?"

I saw her point. First a burglary, where drugs were planted and underwear stolen, then her car, where the seat was moved. It was my turn to call homicide.

I got Detective Clancy.

"More missing underwear?" he asked.

I got right to the point. "Someone tampered with Irene's car. I think you should take a look."

They found plastique explosive planted behind the dashboard, hooked up to the ignition. This time there were no fingerprints. Not even Irene's. The dash and steering wheel had been wiped clean.

I decided to get a sample of Reynolds's fingerprints to see if they matched those found on Irene's bureau drawer. Although he had driven Irene to Charles Finch's party and been a guest there, he could easily have planted the drugs some time earlier that Saturday when Irene was out, then come back to drive her.

I drove out to the two-story frame house that Reynolds was renting on Geddes. I rang and waited. If he wasn't in, I was prepared to climb in through a window and go through *his* bureau drawers. The summer air was muggy from the Huron River. After a time, Reynolds answered the door. Though it was three in the afternoon, he was clad only in a multi-colored wrap-around robe and looking distinctly disheveled, not his usual earnest self, from which I gathered he wasn't glad to see me.

He said, "I wish you'd called."

"I was in the neighborhood," I said. "I thought I'd fill you in on the latest development. I'd also like to see that book Miles Dixon asked Perdita Cunliffe to get for him."

"Come in, Mr. Spinoza," Perdita Cunliffe's voice called boldly from inside.

Reynolds stood aside and I entered.

Perdita was halfway down the stairs. She, too, wore a robe-de-chambre with designs that were vaguely familiar; I remembered seeing similar ones on Abdur Rahman's Afghan rugs. She continued down. "The book's in here," she said, and went into the living room-cum-U.S. State Department branch office.

Signs and Symbols in Oriental Rugs lay closed on a low coffee table among empty glasses and burnt-down candles.

"What do you think?" Perdita asked, pirouetting for me to see her costume, while Reynolds fixed drinks in the kitchen.

"Very exotic," I said.

She reclined on the sofa like a cat, curling her legs under her. "Reynolds has been raising my consciousness about the Afghan struggle."

Obviously, my arrival had interrupted their afternoon seminar.

"Miles was okay when it came to inside politics in the department," Perdita continued matter-of-factly—rather too matter-of-factly, I thought, with poor Miles hardly cold in his urn. "Reynolds on the other hand. . . " She gave a contented sigh. "For instance, I didn't know the Moslem border republics of the Soviet Union were ripe for Islamic revolution."

"I didn't either," I said politely.

"But they face such obstacles: people who are ideologically against their jihad, and their so-called friends who support them only because they are against the Russians."

"Sounds like you've been getting an education."

Throwing her head back, she said to the ceiling, "God, yes. I adore Afghan culture and politics."

I tried not to let my expression betray my thoughts. "Someone planted a bomb in Irene's car," I said as soon as Reynolds returned with the drinks.

"Did it go off?" Perdita asked, panic-stricken.

"No."

She relaxed back into her feline posture on the sofa.

Reynolds gave me a Bloody Mary and sat next to Perdita. His professional interest aroused, he said, "What kind of bomb was it?" as if inquiring about a gasket on a lawn mower's fuel line.

"The police said plastique. You State Department agents take special courses in bombs and terrorism, don't you?"

"We take lots of courses."

Perdita was looking at him with avid curiosity. "That's where you did your post-grad? At a special State Department school?"

"Camp Peary," Reynolds said with easy agreeability. "We call it The Farm."

I said, "I heard Camp Peary is for the CIA recruits."

"Ten thousand beautiful acres near Williamsburg, Virginia," he continued with an air of fond reminiscence. "They approached me in a student bar in Bologna. I passed the full field investigation by the Office of Security with flying colors: the lie detector, the psychological tests. The thing in my favor was that I was a natural at being crisp with authority. Our group was outstanding. It might be said we were the last of the thoroughbreds."

"Surely not," said Perdita.

"I'm afraid so. Nowadays they're trying to move away from hiring solely Ivy League." To my surprise, Reynolds's eyes were misting over. "I was first in my class in Flaps and Seals," he said.

"What are flaps and seals?" Perdita asked.

"Opening envelopes and resealing them. Those were the days. I ranked third in Picks and Locks. Fuses and Charges was rough, though I did rather well in American Urban Blackspeak. Afterward, my instructor told me he hadn't expected me to make it past Street Attitudes. He was the reason I decided not to pursue clandestine service, though I hold it in the highest regard."

"Why not?" I asked, disappointed at the abrupt end to what I thought was a prologue to confessions of a spy.

"Too much red tape and bureaucracy."

"Unlike the State Department," I said.

"It was a tough career decision. If I stayed with the CIA in some deep cover, I was afraid I might be pigeon-holed. A veteran warned me, if I ever went to a job outside the CIA, I couldn't say what I had done. They're an incredibly impressive bunch, and the public should be more appreciative of the sacrifices those people are making when they could command much higher prices in the private sector."

"What would the private sector pay them higher prices for?" I asked.

"For their great dedication and their love of their public policy role."

Especially when it isn't on their resumes, I thought. Was Reynolds a renegade, like that convicted felon Wilson who had sold tons of explosives to Qaddafi? As my P.I., Reynolds had a good cover for his State Department job; now I had to wonder if his State Department position was a cover for a CIA job, and if that were true what difference did it make? Since I still wasn't sure what Reynolds was accomplishing as my P.I., let alone as a State Department agent, I had to conclude it made no difference.

Wondering if he'd delivered some of those Stinger antiaircraft missiles to the mujahedeen, I asked, "How did you get so interested in Afghanistan?"

"I spent a summer sabbatical traveling through the country with a French buddy from the Sorbonne," Reynolds replied.

"The Sorbonne," Perdita sighed. "I knew it."

"There was a French connection?" I asked.

"The French had medical missions there, and it seemed like a fun idea. Back then, the Afghans just fought each other. The summer I toured, the Russians had only killed the American ambassador and installed their puppet government. The military invasion was still two years off. If you showed up at anyone's home, it was Afghan custom to put you up for the night. After dinner your host and his retinue asked you questions, and you told them your story. Since I was an educated Westerner from the outside, they assumed I was some kind of doctor." Reynolds was smiling. "I'll never forget those months, trekking and telling my life story over and over."

A version of it anyway, I thought. It explained why Reynolds was a such a well-practiced dissembler. "What did they think of you as an Afro-Jeffersonian?"

"They immediately saw the parallels between our own Revolutionary War and their thousand-year fight to remain independent from the successive invaders of their mountains. When they're not being murderous, they are very hospitable and courteous."

I departed with *Signs and Symbols in Oriental Rugs* under my arm, with Reynolds's glass with his fingerprints on it hidden in my pocket, and with my suspicions unallayed.

There is no substitute for patient, plodding investigation; however, I was in a hurry. I went straight to the horse's mouth, which, since it was lunchtime when I entered Marderosian's Ruggery, was grazing.

Instead of a roasted lamb and rose-water sherbet, Abdur Rahman had his jaws locked into a Stan's Canadian Hotfoot (Zingerman's No. 46: *Montréal smoked brisket, Switzerland swiss, sauerkraut, Russian dressing, spicy brown mustard, hot peppers, on rye*). A can of Faygo root beer was on his desk.

"George-jan," he exclaimed, putting down his sandwich with ill-disguised reluctance. "How kind of you once again to grace. . ." Perhaps it was my stern, determined cast, for in mid-exhalation he put the brakes on his flowery welcome. "Am I correct to intuit that something disturbs you?"

"Hah!" I said.

"Something *is* disturbing you."

I raised my arm in dramatic flourish. "I am beyond disturbed. I am manic. Also steamed, p.o.'d, and extremely disappointed."

A calculated look of hurt seized Abdur's features. "I crush my eyes if I am the object of your disappointment."

"Right in one, Abdur. Someone tried to kill Irene."

"Gracious heavens! God will punish the wicked person responsible."

"God would have to be crazy to get mixed up in this mess." I told him what had happened: the drugs planted in Irene's bathroom, her missing lace teddy, and then the bomb in her car.

Abdur rhythmically rocked back and forth in sympathy, muttering "Tch-tch's" in contrapunto to my tale. He opened a can of chilled root beer and offered it to me. "Can you describe the teddy?"

"Abdur!"

He shrugged apologetically and waggled his hand, dismissing his question. "Such horrendous developments. What have they to do with me?"

"Someone killed Miles and tried to frame Irene. Now they're trying to get her out of the way permanently because she knows something. She doesn't know what it is, but you do."

"Excuse me, George-jan, but what do you think I know?"

"You know what Irene doesn't know she knows."

"How do you know?"

"Come on, Abdur. I don't care what you have going on behind this rug shop. You know something about a drug operation that has Wusthof hot and the State Department interested. And I don't want to hear about two travelers going over mountains. What's going on?" In a flash of inspiration, I added, "Men shouldn't hide behind a woman's skirts."

Abdur flushed a deep magenta-purple that tended toward that of an eggplant. I had hit his cultural nerve point. He got up and went to the door of his shop, locked it, and put up the "Closed" sign.

"I swear to you, George-jan, upon the lives of my family," he said, returning to his desk, "I do not know which one of the travelers is a brother to our cause, nor which is the demon."

"You mean Reynolds and Charles Finch."

"One of them is the enemy who would steal a large amount of money that was collected to keep our resistance alive. Even now our people in Pakistan ask us, Where is the money? And we must tell them to wait a bit longer."

"Is the money lost?"

"Not precisely."

Abdur's habit of drifting into evasive indirection was making me peevish again. "Then is it so well hidden you can't find it.?"

"Temporarily. That is to say, we know where it is. Generally speaking."

"How generally?"

"It is in a bank in the Seychelles. We don't know the bank and we don't know the number of the account."

The money was lost.

"What does this have to do with Irene?" I asked.

"Our enemy—your enemy, too—seeks this bank account number."

Great, I thought. And Irene and I are caught in the middle. I thought of *Signs and Symbols of Oriental Rugs*. Was the account number encrypted, too? In rug code? Abdur had not answered my question.

"What does this have to do with Irene?" I repeated.

Abdur clasped his hands, and for a moment sat with his head bowed so the tip of his nose touched his knuckle.

"Hearing of that terrible bomb, I must hazard that Irene knows who the evil one is, and the evil one knows she knows."

"But Irene doesn't know," I protested.

He raised an admonitory finger. "She doesn't *know* what she knows that makes her a danger to him."

I took Abdur's point, since it had started out as my point. "Is it drug money in the missing bank account?"

"Shame on you. It is money for our resistance. If some of our people grow the poppy, it is to keep body and soul together in hard times."

"Is the murderer a drug dealer?"

"Not exactly."

"Abdur!"

"He washes their money."

"But not your money."

"You think we would trust outsiders?"

"Excuse me for even considering it," I said.

I already knew Miles Dixon had been looking into a drug-money launderer. Now the question was, Was it Charles, or was it Reynolds protecting his interest? "Let me get this straight," I said. "Your money and the money launderer's money go through the same bank."

"Yes."

"And the money launderer found out that the number to your account is lost."

"Misplaced. It is somewhere in town."

"How the hell do you lose a bank number? I mean, couldn't they send another copy?"

"The bank is very accustomed to secret accounts. Most

of their business is secret accounts. If you don't know the number, they don't know you. They are scrupulous."

With illegal monies from ruthless people, I supposed it was best to be scrupulous. "Then how did the drug-money launderer know about it?"

"That is a sad tale. You see, before we started doing our banking in the Seychelles, a brother fell to temptation and stole our money. He used it to build a condominium here in Ann Arbor."

A ghastly suspicion leapt into the forefront of my consciousness. I must have been staring oddly at Abdur.

"George-jan,' he inquired, "something else is disquieting you?"

"Uh, the condo that was built with the money stolen from your resistance, it wouldn't by chance be the one where Irene and I live?"

"The very one!"

"Abdur, *you* were the one who put us onto buying into the condo when it was still on the architect's drawing board."

"Of course. What are friends for if not to share one's good fortune with?"

"Are you saying that you stole the first batch of money?"

"Heavens to Betsy, no! How could you even think such an evil thing?"

"I've been under a lot of strain lately."

Abdur smiled his forgiveness.

"But Abdur, why did you ask us to buy into a condo that was built with money stolen from your resistance?"

"The miscreant was dealt with. . ."

I realized the miscreant was dead.

". . . and the profits from the enterprise were channeled back to our resistance. So calm yourself, George-jan. The guilt of the miscreant does not apply to you. You may continue to live in your lovely home with a clear conscience."

I was boggled. My domicile had been financed with Afghan poppies. Such were the intricacies of international finance.

"That is why we opened an account in the Seychelles," Abdur explained.

"The one that is temporarily misplaced."

"Yes. Only two of our most trusted brothers knew the number."

"Then why don't you ask one of them for the account number?"

"Unfortunately, they are both deceased."

Abdur's tale was getting awfully convoluted, with more dead bodies at every new turn. "Uh, how. . . ?"

"A personal falling out. You see, they went socializing to celebrate setting up such a secure account." Abdur sighed. "Unfortunately, the man they went socializing with was the drug-money launderer. And it was during their socializing that one brother spoke too freely."

Understandable, I thought. It's natural to want to talk shop with someone in the same line of work.

"To his great personal pain, the second brother realized his loose-lipped compatriot could not be trusted to keep a secret, and so it was necessary to redress his foolish talkativeness."

"Ah."

"There was great sadness all around when he informed us of his loose-lipped compatriot's scuba diving accident. The loose-lipped foolish fellow must have forgotten he couldn't swim."

"Jet lag will do that."

"Bereft at being in the Seychelles without a fellow countryman, the second brother told us that he had devised a way of sending us the account number. The postal services and electronic airways are so dreadfully vulnerable these days. However, being ever vigilant, he conveyed his regret that perhaps his compatriot had suffered his unfortunate scuba mishap too late."

"Too late for what?"

"Perhaps during their socializing with the drug-money launderer, when the second brother had to leave their table for a personal necessity, his loose-lipped compatriot had let slip one of their secrets."

I nodded in commiseration. "And this second brother, how did he die? Fighting in the resistance?"

"He was found floating in the hotel swimming pool. He had an excellent memory. He could not have forgotten that he, too, was a nonswimmer. The evil money launderer must have committed the foul deed because he had learned a most important secret from the loose-lipped one—the destination of the account number. And so we search for the account number. You would have our eternal gratitude if you found it before the evil one."

"How would I recognize the number if I found it?" I asked, mindful of the fact that loose lips had already sunk two mujahedeen. "Is it on microfilm?"

"All I have is the second brother's last message on the subject before he was killed."

"Which was?"

"Translating to the American vernacular, his final message was, 'You can't miss it.'"

The next morning, propped up outside Irene's door was a long cardboard box mysteriously unmarked as to origin. Detectives Clancy and Freiday arrived with a portable x-ray machine. Aside from the staples in the carton, there was nothing metallic inside. Nothing like a bomb trigger mechanism. We brought the box inside, and Detective Clancy opened it.

"They're gorgeous!" Irene cried as she unwrapped spray after spray of purple, pink, white, and yellow orchids from their excelsior tissue covering. An entire Colombian rain forest had been denuded of its flora. Detective Freiday lifted a ruffled spray up to her face and breathed in the minty-cinnamon perfume. Detective Clancy was watching Detective Freiday with a wistful air.

I felt a pang of jealousy for the anonymous sender who could afford such a floral extravaganza. Despite the worrisome state of my finances, I wished I was the one who had sent them to Irene.

Irene was reading a note tucked in at the bottom of the box. Detective Clancy asked Irene for a plastic baggie. He unfolded tweezers from his Swiss Army knife and used them to put the note into the baggie, saying to Irene, "It seems you have a secret admirer." Irene and Freiday went off to fill vases with water.

Seems, Madam, I thought, seizing the baggie with its hateful contents. Nay, not seems. I read the note:

> Lovely Lady,
> I know of your difficulties. Please accept this poor gift as my way of revealing what is in my heart. Since I first saw you I have worshipped your angelic loveliness from a respectful distance. Even now I see your image before me. Only on the face of the Madonna have I seen the glow of such purity. Should you desire to leave this country for a more pleasant climate, I offer you my services. I will contact you for your reply when I am able. Present circumstances make it necessary that I remain—
> Your Anonymous Admirer

My discomfiture was acute. The note's purple passion put me in mind of one of those paintings on velvet. Like cheap music and trashy movies, one ignores their insidious power at one's peril. I was going to break the head of the caballero responsible.

I looked up and saw Detective Clancy's condoling face. He had guessed my train of thought. "At least this time it's not a bomb," he temporized.

Damn your impudence, sir, I thought.

"Any idea who could have sent them?" he asked.

I thought of Biswanger. I still hadn't retaliated for the Thousand Happinesses Limited shipment, so it wasn't his turn yet. Also, he wouldn't involve Irene like this.

"No," I replied. "Your partner sure got a kick out of it. I couldn't help but notice," I observed venomously, "you two have a really *close* working relationship."

To my surprise, instead of telling me I was out of line and to mind my own business, Clancy sighed. "You and everyone else. She's been hinting pretty strongly it's time we got married." He lowered his voice. "Her biological clock."

I nodded. "But you're not ready yet?"

"It's not that. I'd ask her today, only. . . we couldn't be partners anymore. Departmental rules. As things stand now, we spend twelve, fourteen hours a day together, sometimes more. And that's not counting off-hours. When we're on night duty, we always can get away for a few hours in the afternoons." He trailed off, self-conscious. "Married, I wouldn't see her half as much." There was another embarrassed silence. Then, in a small voice, he said, "It's the name change."

"She wants to keep hers?" I asked.

"No. She says she wants my name."

I didn't understand what was bothering him. I said,

"Clancy is a perfectly honorable name. Mrs. . . . " Then I remember. Irene's first hearing in the district court. When Detective Freiday had taken the stand, she identified herself as Detective Nancy Freiday. I said it aloud. "Mrs. Nancy Clancy."

Clancy winced.

"Ask her," I said firmly.

"I don't know if our careers could withstand the strain."

"Ask her."

"What about our pending investigations? Our stakeouts? Our joint reports?"

"Love will find a way."

Irene and Detective Freiday returned with vases filled with the flowers. "I've been telling Nancy about your mousse shakes," Irene said. "She'd like to try one."

"Irene said you wouldn't mind," Detective Freiday said coyly.

In the interests of good police-community relations, I went downstairs and whipped up three brandied chocolate shakes with my Thousand Happinesses Limited shake machine.

Back upstairs, Irene, Detective Clancy, and Detective Freiday had a taste-testing party. After a chorus of ecstatic mmm-mmm's, there was general agreement that I was on to something.

"You ought to market that shake maker," said Detective Clancy.

"That's what I've been telling him," said Irene.

Detective Freiday said, "I don't suppose you could knock one up for me? I'd really love to have one."

"My liability insurance doesn't allow it," I said virtuously. "Also, my business manager is very strict about patent licensing."

"I swear, I wouldn't show it to anyone."

"Sorry."

"I've got a V.P. at Hudson's who's looking for something like this," said Irene, "but George won't even let *me* see his invention."

"I haven't worked out all the kinks," I said quickly.

"Anything new on the car bomb?"

"Not yet," said Clancy.

"By the way," I said, taking out a squat drinking glass with dried Bloody Mary on the inside. "Would you check if the fingerprints on this match the ones you found on Irene's bureau from the first break-in?"

"Who's are they?" Clancy said.

"Reynolds's."

When Clancy and Freiday had departed I said, "What was all that about?"

Irene calmly went about rearranging the flowers. "Ethan wanted a focus-group reaction. Now I've got one for him. If it's a go, they'll market it as Mousse-Maker Deluxe."

"Two homicide cops qualify as a focus group?"

"They're in the right age bracket, and they're going to set up a household, " she said. "Just the right socioeconomic stratum Hudson's is interested in."

Demographics aside, something far more important dawned on me. "Ethan sent those flowers!"

"Not in a million years."

"I bet he wears custom monogrammed shirts that don't have pockets, and has a maroon handkerchief poking out of his jacket," I said. "He calls the place he exercises a fitness center instead of a gym, he's into warm, caring relationships, and to show you he's into commitment, he told you his cholesterol and triglyceride levels. Am I right?"'

"You have no shame, do you?"

"I knew I was right."

"Mums are his style," Irene said. "Six roses at the most."

Biswanger and I met for lunch at the Real Seafood Company on Main; Biswanger was treating.

"I'll start with the oysters and a lager," he said to our waiter, "while I'm making up my mind."

"The same," I said, and as soon as the waiter had departed, I leaned forward. "I've come up with a strategy."

Biswanger looked up from his menu and raised his eyebrows. "*You* have a strategy?"

"And why shouldn't I?" I asked, my resentment rising.

Biswanger put down the menu. "George," he said with great tolerance and condescension, "I am your business manager. I have been doing your accounts and your taxes ever since you started bringing in enough to make them worth doing. I *know* what kind of strategic planner you are."

"We should investigate Charles Finch," I said.

Biswanger made a prayerful tent with his fingers and pressed them against his chin. He stared up at the full-sized boat that hung by cables from the ceiling, like one of the biplanes at the Smithsonian. I waited for him to comment. He continued starting at the boat.

"Well?" I said impatiently.

Finally, with all the gravity of a judge about to deliver an opinion that will be reviewed by appellate courts all the way up to the Supreme Court, he said, "Should I go with the broiled salmon, or the Cajun redfish?"

I felt the blood rush to my face. "Did you ask me to lunch just to be a smartass, or are you going to hear me out?"

"I'd rather do both," Biswanger said grandly.

A sense of impending futility loomed before me. "You're doing it to me again, you son of a bitch."

The waiter arrived with two metal platters of oysters.

Biswanger's eyes lit up. "Oh, good," he said, his concentration now fixed on the briny delicacies, to the convenient exclusion of my righteous indignation and everything else on the planet.

"He's doing it to me again," I said to the waiter.

"And long may he continue," the waiter said amiably.

"Whose side are you on?" I snapped.

"Whoever does the tipping."

Biswanger was tucking his napkin over his tie. "I'd like some of that Louisiana hot sauce."

The waiter hurried off and returned with two hot sauce bottles.

Biswanger gave the rest of his order. "Hearts of endive salad. Then the stuffed pompano," he said, squeezing lemon on his oysters, "with those little boiled potatoes with dill."

I ordered the Seven Seas linguine.

"Linguine?" Biswanger said disdainfully. "For God's sake, George. Live a little."

"The linguine," I repeated to the waiter through clenched teeth. "And a sharp steak knife."

"For *linguine*, sir?" the waiter inquired.

"For him."

The waiter departed.

"Today is my birthday," Biswanger said placidly, shaking on hot sauce. "Allow me my small pleasures. Now unclench your teeth and tell me why we should investigate Charles." He downed an oyster, smacked his lips, and raised his beer mug. "Cheers."

Between sipping beer and slurping down oysters, I told him about my meeting with Abdur Rahman.

"According to Abdur," I concluded, "it's either Reynolds or Charles. So I can't rely on Reynolds..."

"Your P.I."

"I can't rely on Reynolds to look into Charles, because if Reynolds is actually the one, he could implicate Charles with phony evidence that would fool the police."

"He can do that?" Biswanger asked.

"He works for the State Department.

Biswanger nodded knowingly.

"That's where you come in," I said.

"I was wondering when I'd be dragged into this."

"If *you* look into Charles, and he comes out clean, it must be Reynolds. The logical process of elimination."

"Might not Charles object if he finds out he's being investigated, and it turns out he's blameless?"

"I just want you to look into his business enterprises. Not his seraglio on the river. Although, come to think of it. . ."

"I already did."

"Did what?" I asked.

"I've looked into Charles Finch's business registrations."

I stared at Biswanger with surprise.

"You seem surprised," Biswanger observed. "Irene is up for murder. Someone framed her, then tried to kill her. Surely you don't think I've been standing by while you played detective with Reynolds."

I surely had, and now I felt an uncomfortable flush of shame. I said, "I thought you saw this as something of a joke."

"I look upon most affairs of the world as a joke," Biswanger said. "That doesn't mean I don't take them seriously."

"You could have fooled me."

"I'm not solemn about taking them seriously."

"What about my affairs?" I asked urgently.

"What about them?"

"You take *them* seriously, don't you?"

"We're talking about Irene."

"Irene is my affair," I said with a surge of protective pride, thinking of our recent reconciliation. "I don't know what I'd do if anything happened to her." I drained the rest of my lager.

"In that case," said Biswanger, "you'd do well to curb your obsessive jealousy and possessiveness."

I could scarcely believe my ears. "Jealous?" I sputtered, getting lager up my nose. I coughed. "Who are you to call me that?"

"Your business manager who sees his client going down the tubes."

"All right. Exactly what am I obsessively possessive about?"

"About Irene. Her friends."

The waiter put down two more lagers and said, "Listen to him. He knows what he's talking about."

"I will not be publicly psychoanalyzed over oysters," I snapped. The waiter glided off. "What did you find out about Charles?"

Biswanger wiped his fingers, reached into his jacket, and took out a folded sheaf of papers stapled together.

I flipped through them. At the top of each sheet was a business name, followed by an advertising blurb from the yellow pages and columns of financial data.

(1) Murdock's Hair, Nail, and Skin Grooming Salon for men and women: "Let us design your very own personal style."

(2) Golden Goose Foster Pet-Care Service: "Pet sitting for when you can't take your best friends with you."

(3) The Mink-Covered Seat: bathroom specialties.

(4) Chic à BonBon: chocolates for the decadent.

(5) Van Vane's Studio: the best of U.S. and European ultra fashion. "We don't follow trends. We anticipate them."

(6) Alternative Statement: "Secretarial typing service."

(7) Earth Mother Restaurant: "Try our soup. It couldn't hurt."

Biswanger said, "Charles is registered as their local manager. He doesn't own any of them. They're owned by holding companies."

I was overjoyed. Charles, that smirking self-satisfied S.O.B., wasn't what he pretended. I flipped through the papers. "Where's Cuddly-Wuddles?"

"Cuddly-Wuddles animal farm and veterinary hospital is the one enterprise Charles is associated with that isn't part of any holding company."

"He really owns it?" I asked, disappointed.

"Charles is a legitimate partner in Cuddly-Wuddles. The holding companies," Biswanger said, returning to the main subject, "all funnel into one holding company. Arbor Investors. Another thing these seven businesses have in common is that they all make large cash deposits into various local banks."

"A perfect setup for money laundering," I said.

"Perhaps."

"How can you say perhaps when it's obvious their cash deposits are drug money that is being funneled into Arbor Investors. We have the list of their whole operation right here!"

"George, George, you're confusing the laundry bins with the laundry itself."

"What the hell does that mean?"

"In a money-laundering operation, local businesses are merely bins. They just take in the illegal cash. Where the money goes from there is the tricky part. You have to move it through several front corporations and combine it with other accounts. You have to make wire transfers to overseas subsidiaries of U.S. banks and recirculate the credit ring-around-the-rosy so it loses its original identity. Import-export firms and currency-exchange houses are favorites. It's big, George. U.S. banks have liabilities to Panama, the Bahamas, the Caymans, the Netherlands Antilles, Mexico, Venezuela. An honest bank can be used to innocently warehouse money in correspondent accounts of other institutions; it can act as a currency broker for other banks. Currency has no pedigree."

Thinking of Abdur Rahman's special fund that the money launderer was after, I asked, "Does Arbor Investors bank in the Seychelles?"

"I didn't see any evidence they did."

"But they could."

"I suppose. George, I don't have the resources of the Treasury Department. You must allow the possibility that Arbor Investors is legitimate."

"Or they could be the detergent of choice," I said.

When the check came, Biswanger took out his credit card and his driver's license, because the restaurant gave birthday discounts.

10

THE PEOPLE V. IRENE Spinoza was on the circuit criminal court docket for Monday of next week to begin impaneling a jury. Today was Tuesday. Irene and I had a three o'clock meeting with Grunion to discuss his strategy for jury selection. Irene had told me that since Grunion was never in his office on time, she'd be there around three-fifteen. It was now two-fifty. I was looking forward to hearing Grunion's strategy with all the enthusiasm I have for root canals (even though my dentist is a great guy and a closet intellectual with superior insights). I dawdled along State Street. While I browsed under Border's outside canopy at the tables of discount books, I pondered the recent disappointing news from Detective Clancy.

Reynolds's fingerprints from his Bloody Mary glass had not matched those found on Irene's underwear drawer. The police already had a set of Charles Finch's fingerprints—since the beginning of the investigation he'd been cooperative to a fault—but his prints hadn't matched either. Therefore, neither Charles nor Reynolds had rummaged through Irene's drawer and stolen her lace teddy last Saturday. Okay, what did that prove? Charles was still a front man for Arbor Investors. I was betting he was the drug-money launderer that Wusthof was after. Also up in the air was the question of who had sent Irene those orchids with the turgid love note. Clancy and Freiday had checked florists and wholesale flower distributors without success; however, Irene had been flattered to hear that the orchids in the box wholesaled for around two thousand dollars.

It was more likely, I thought, that two different people had broken into Irene's place on Saturday: the killer who had planted the drugs and later planted the bomb in her car, and an underwear fetishist. Perhaps the fetishist had been spurred on by newspaper reports of Irene's things found in Miles Dixon's apartment. But that added up to three unknown people: the killer, the underwear fetishist, and the flower-giver. I didn't like the notion of that many men crowding Irene. Putting the killer aside for the moment, it occurred to me that the underwear fancier and the flower-giver could be one and the same. The mash note he had enclosed with the flowers read as though it had been inspired by third-hand knowledge, no doubt derived from Irene's photograph in the papers. Those expensive, ostentatious flowers were but symptoms of a pathetic, involuted passion.

Though I was not current on the latest research on psychosexual predilections of the criminal mind, I saw no flaw in this scenario.

Then why didn't I feel better? Why did I still feel homicidal impulses for the phantom of the underwear drawer? The gall of him sending flowers afterward was beyond belief.

I crossed from State to the corner of Liberty. Was it possible there was a smidgen of truth to Biswanger's accusation? Was I obsessively jealous and possessive?

It was midsummer and they were showing fall clothing in Jacobson's windows. Grunion, Grunion, Littlefield and Grunion loomed in my immediate future like the IRS, though without the IRS's charm. I became aware of the reflection in the window of Morton Blue standing beside me.

"Will you look at that?" he said cheerfully."Fan-fucking-tastic!"

"The suit?" I said, coming out of my reverie.

"The girl coming around the corner of Discount Records."

"I've got a meeting with Irene's lawyer," I said, explaining my lapse. "Mort," I said, "I had lunch with Biswanger the other day. He said something about me that's been bothering me."

"Don't worry about it."

"How can you say don't worry when you don't know what he said?" I said. Then the monstrous implication hit me. "Biswanger discussed me with you!"

"I haven't seen him since the party at Charlie Finch's." He gave me a puzzled look. "What the hell's wrong with you?"

"Biswanger said I was obsessively jealous and possessive about Irene."

"She's coming this way!" Mort cried, his voice throbbing with excitement.

The girl from the record shop bounced by in a tank top and silken jogging shorts, tossing her hair and letting Mort know by the faint smile on her face that she appreciated his appreciation.

"Look at them," Mort groaned, his eyes shining with boundless lust. "Thank God for the U of M undergraduates. Every year a new crop."

I'd once heard a philosophy professor say the same thing, referring to the fact that they afforded him a nice way to make a living without heavy lifting.

I said, "Do you think there's any truth to what Biswanger said?"

"About what?"

"About me, being jealous and possessive about Irene."

"Yes," Mort said without hesitation.

The breezy certainty of his reply hit me like a wrecking ball. "Would you care to explain that?"

Mort shrugged. "Sure. You're paranoid."

Was there something in the air, I wondered, that made people want to psychoanalyze me and give unwanted advice? First Biswanger and the restaurant waiter, now Mort.

"Irene's going to trial next week," I said. "Are you saying I shouldn't be worried about that?"

"I'm talking about Irene, not her trial. You demand bona fides when you should have the sense not to."

"That doesn't make me paranoid," I protested.

"You hired a private detective, didn't you?"

"*After* the murder!"

"Which only proves my point. You didn't trust her."

"You'd hire one too if you had to contend with drug-money launderers and a second-story man who planted drugs in Irene's bathroom and a bomb in her car," I cried, as events of the past weeks suddenly closed in. "There's an underwear fetishist who thinks he's in love with Irene. My P.I. thinks he's Thomas Jefferson, and my rug merchant is a front for... I'm not sure who he's fronting for, exactly, but you wouldn't want to get on their bad side." I raised my clenched fist in an agony of despair for what lay ahead. "And now I have to go listen to Irene's idiot lawyer, who I personally would like to strangle in his crib."

"Boy, you're touchy today."

"It's been absolute hell."

"Lighten up, George," Mort warned, "or you'll never achieve the success you crave."

Now I wasn't a success! "The millions who have bought

Hotel Rompé might not agree with you," I countered coldly.
"Frankly, I can't figure how you ever came up with *Hotel Rompé.*"

Irate, I rounded on him. "Fun and games are my business. I design toys. I eat, sleep, and breathe lighthearted diversion. I am one fun guy, you insensitive jerk."

"I don't see much of a future for you," Mort continued gravely, "Except possibly politics, and that's for people who can't do anything else and have no sense of humor. Knowing you, you'd want to be a successful politician." Folding his arms and cocking his head, he looked at me, as if sizing me up for a poster. "Can you honestly say that you have the necessary cunning and impervious stupidity? Oh, quick," he said urgently. "Turn around."

I turned. Across the street a statuesque blonde was strolling out of Leidy's china shop on legs that didn't stop. Tanned and lithe with promise, she was right out of a Bob Fosse musical.

"Do you think she's wearing anything underneath?" Mort asked seriously. Before I could render an opinion he said, "Boy, oh, boy. I can hardly wait for the art fair."

If there was a logical thread to our conversation, it had snapped. Mort was clearly out of his skull, because experienced Ann Arborites avoid going into town during the Ann Arbor Art Fair. It is a kind of purgatory scheduled for a week in July when all air movement ceases, save for the rising shimmer above the burning asphalt, and sensible people head for the parks or air conditioning. On Monday and Tuesday streets are closed off to traffic, covered display booths are erected, and merchants exhume their old inventories. Wednesday through Saturday millions of visitors are crammed cheek by jowl in the narrow, stifling alleyways between the sale tables and the art booths. They wind dazedly through town in an enforced chain-gang shuffle, pumping up the local economy. The exhibits are juried beforehand, though on what aesthetic basis is anyone's guess, and the number of permits is fixed. The fee an artist pays for a permit for booth space is high because the sale return on the three-day real estate rental can be awesome. Those who can't get permits to exhibit fulminate about racism, sexism, aesthetic fascism, fascistic aestheticism, and middle classism. Art has little to do with it.

"I may be paranoid, but you're crazy," I said. "It's hotter and more crowded than a Middle Eastern bazaar, and there's nowhere to park."

"The hotter the better," Mort said with lazy concupiscence. "That's when you see women at their finest."

It was after three. There was the pressing matter of *The People v. Irene Spinoza*. I said, "I've got to go."

"You want to know something else, George?" Mort called after me. "You used to be a lot more fun."

I continued down Liberty in a black mood. While Irene was slipping into the jaws of the criminal justice system, my friends had become an affliction beyond human endurance.

I entered the Liberty Building. All right. I was jealous and possessive about Irene. Though not, I decided upon further fair-minded reflection, obsessively so. Feeling better from this insight, I stepped from the elevator on to the thirteenth floor. It was still unfinished, except for the lone walled-in area that was Grunion's office. I went directly to the men's room.

Within the marble sanctum Grunion was practicing another version of his closing speech to the jury.

"The prosecution has suggested that Ms. Spinoza killed Miles Dixon as the result of a lover's quarrel," Grunion boomed at the bank of lavatory mirrors in a voice that had grown plummier and considerably louder since our previous encounter. "But, ladies and gentlemen, consider the other side of the coin. Is it fair to convict Ms. Spinoza just because she is an attractive woman—some would say provocative in her dress and manner—without also considering the late Miles Dixon's qualifications in that area?"

Grunion stopped to jot some changes on his note pad.

I was transfixed by what I'd just heard. In one fell swoop, he had implied that (a)Irene was a tart; (b)she had been embroiled in a sordid affair with Miles; and (c)Miles had gotten what he deserved. Let loose before a jury, Grunion would be more lethal than atomic waste.

Grunion looked up. "Gosh, is it time for our meeting already?"

I nodded.

"I'm honing the finer points," he explained, putting his notes into his briefcase. "Time sure flies when you're having fun."

"Ri-i-ight," I said.

Irene was waiting in Grunion's office chatting with a man and woman, whom Grunion introduced to me as Leslie Tweed and Deirdre Dumbarton. Or Lee and Dee, as the two chummily insisted we call them. They were Grunion's juror profilers. Lee Tweed was a social psychologist. Dee Dumbarton was a sociologist specializing in survey psychology. It was explained to me that Grunion, by using the fruits of their analytical labors, would be able to select the optimum jury for Irene at next week's voir dire.

We sat around Grunion's massive desk. With his furniture taking up most of the small office, it was a tight fit for Grunion, Irene, Lee, Dee, and me.

Lee and Dee began laying out survey forms and computer printouts.

"How did you two get into this area?" Irene asked.

"It started from our research in conflict resolution at the Academy of Mental Hygiene and Public Policy," said Lee. "Our grant ran out. We put out feelers to city hall, but they refused to take up the slack."

"One guy," said Dee, shaking her head, "told us to run for elected office if we thought we were so smart."

Lee raised an admonitory finger. "He told us to *get off our high horses* and run for office," he reminded her.

Both broke into the superior chuckles of the cognoscenti.

"Which just goes to show how much the public needs to be educated," said Dee.

"Then it occurred to us," continued Lee, "that the legal system afforded fertile ground to apply our theories."

My heart skipped a beat. "Theories?"

"They're thoroughly tested and validated," Lee assured me, squinting at a chart.

"Thoroughly," added Dee. "I myself am heartened by the fact that we can so easily reduce history, economics, law, and the U.S. Constitution to statistical models based upon coin flips."

They got down to business.

"We made neighborhood site visits from the names and addresses on the jury list," Lee explained, "to get demographic and attitudinal data. Here we've broken them down by their housing type. Single-family detached, duplex, condo, or apartment."

"Rental or owned," said Dee.

"Rich, middle class, or poor," said Lee.

"Here they're broken down by their occupations and their children."

"And the occupations of their children, and their friends, and their friends' children."

"And their friends' friends."

"With adjunct indicators like watchdogs and bumper stickers."

"To indicate their fear of crime and their political sympathies."

"From which data," Lee went on, "we coded, analyzed, and derived composite profiler scores of each potential member of the jury panel."

"In order," said Dee, "to predict their values on the basis of normalized categorical scores."

"We derived four value constructs for each person."

"Which are..."

"... authoritarianism..."

"... economic orthodoxy..."

"... cosmopolitanism..."

"... and racial tolerance."

I was becoming dizzy from looking back and forth between them.

"Why?" I asked.

"Why what?" asked Lee. Or maybe it was Dee.

"Why," I said slowly, "do we need to know what kind of a house a juror lives in?"

"I would have thought that was obvious," said Lee. "A single, detached homeowner might be prejudiced against someone who lives in a condo."

Irene, who had been listening along with me in a dazed trance, asked, "Is all this really necessary?"

"It got Angela Davis off the hook in California," said Lee.

"This is Michigan and I'm not Angela Davis," Irene pointed out.

"Every case has a political angle," said Lee.

"If you look hard enough," added Dee. "Forewarned is forearmed."

"But I'm innocent," Irene said.

"Excuse me?" said Lee.

"I'm not guilty," Irene reiterated.

"I don't understand."

"I didn't kill Miles Dixon."

"If you don't cooperate," said Dee, "you only make our job that much harder."

Against my better judgment, I looked to Grunion. "How do you intend to use this?"

"I'm using a minimax strategy," he said. He waited expectantly for someone to ask him what that meant. When no one did he said, "That means we assume the maximum loss. We assume you'll be found guilty."

Fright was in Irene's eyes. "You really think I won't be acquitted?"

"It's the most conservative strategy I can think of," Grunion said proudly. "It becomes a simple matter of tailoring our effort to minimize the effects of this worst of all possible outcomes. Minimax!"

Lee and Dee jumped in.

"To that end," said Lee, "we have advised Mr. Grunion to select jurors who fall into two antagonistic groups..."

"... so the two groups will polarize," added Dee, "during their deliberations."

"What does that get you?" I asked.

"A hung jury."

"That's good?"

"Absolutely," said Grunion. "With a hung jury, we get a second trial."

"We haven't had the first one yet!" I cried.

"The first trial will be good practice for the second trial," Grunion said with bland confidence, like a doctor reassuring a fretful patient. "Then I'll know what to expect in the way

of Wusthof's line of argument, unless he changes it."
Irene was looking slightly ill.
"How much is this costing?" I asked wearily.
"Mr. Grunion has our bill. . . " said Lee.
". . . based on our initial estimated project costs. . . " said Dee.
". . . but there will be an addendum. . . "
". . . which we will send him."
"And then," said Grunion, smiling benignly at Irene and me, "I send it all to you."

11

It was with a sense of impending doom that I departed from Grunion's strategy session. I walked beside Irene along Fifth toward Huron, my mind boggling at Leslie Tweed and Deirdre Dumbarton. Until this afternoon, it would not have occurred to me that two such nihilistic, meddlesome fugitives from the fringes of academe could flourish in anything other than appointed committee positions. But in fact they were loose in the criminal justice system. I prayed that some quick-witted officer of the court would stop the pestilential pair before trial-by-jury became irrevocably corrupted by social engineering.

"Irene," I said urgently, turning to look into her lovely eyes with total sincerity, and hence forewarning her that I was about to say something disagreeable, "I know you're your own person, and that it's your murder trial and Grunion is your lawyer. But I have to tell you, if you don't replace him, you're going to be up shit creek."

"I agree."

"What good is a famous law firm," I surged on in full oratorical passion, "if you get stuck with an incompetent who couldn't find his way out of the mailroom with a map and a guide dog?" I coasted to a stop as what she'd said sank in. "You agree?"

"I'm going to see one of the senior partners and lay it on the line: either someone takes charge over Grunion, or I switch to another firm."

"Darling," I cried, "does that mean you think Grunion is a jerk?"

"Is he ever!"

It is the little things we agree upon that knit together our raveled social contract. Irene and I were in front of the Ann Arbor Theater marquee. I embraced her with an ardor straight from my heart, and was rewarded with unmistakable signs of reciprocated passion. Perhaps it was our spiritual exhaustion: Irene, burdened by thoughts of her impending trial; and me, appalled at the prospect of life without her. We were two scared people reaching out for reassurance in a cruel world peopled by jury consultants, State Department double agents, and double-dealing rug dealers.

Our lubricious kissing was interrupted by light applause. We separated and discovered that we were surrounded by people streaming out of the theater from the three o'clock show.

"Go to it, Jack," a young man said gleefully. The girl he was with poked his upper arm and hissed that he should mind his own business. "Well, why not?" he protested as she tugged him along. "They're better than what we just saw."

Irene and I walked briskly on. At the corner of Fifth and Huron, desire reasserted itself over embarrassment and our eyes locked again. We fairly sprinted back to our condo building.

"What are you thinking right now?" Irene asked inside the ascending elevator in a throaty whisper that set my every nerve ending vibrating.

"At this moment," I blurted in a rush reckless, tumultuous honesty, "more than anything in the world I want to fuck your brains out."

"Me too."

We staggered through my doorway—it was too far to go up to her place—and careened off the Thousand Happinesses Limited carton that still stood inside. Natasha was wagging her tail in joyful greeting; I gave her a perfunctory pat, hauled her off to the bedroom, and locked her in. I raced back to Irene in the living room, only to realize that Irene and I should be in the bedroom and Natasha locked outside the door. I'd gotten it turned around, but Irene didn't seem to notice and I didn't care.

"Sorry I used that filthy word in the elevator," I panted as I frantically fought past Irene's buttons, snaps, and hook-eyes, popping some of them out of the fabric.

"It's a filthy situation," she panted back, and assisted my trembling hands.

Lust overwhelmed all further small talk.

Afterward as we lay sated on the rug, I looked up at the ceiling and, seeing Irene's fresh footprints, fell into a reflective, sentimental mood. Her pelvic muscles were in superb condition. Though surfeited from our sexual congressional banquet, I indulged in a few after-dinner mints.

"You know," I murmured between lazy kisses in strategic and sundry places on Irene's damp, glowing body, "I can't remember why we ever split up."

She yawned. "I remember."

I had intended my remark as an appreciative observation, neither wanting nor expecting a reply. "What does it matter now?" I said. "We're happy."

"Only because I divorced you when we still had a good chance of staying together."

"That makes no sense," I said.

"I divorced you to keep you, Georgie."

Curiosity overcoming prudence, I said, "Come again?"

"Early on in our marriage I realized that your possessiveness and obsessive jealousy would be our ruination. I decided to divorce you as soon as possible, so that we could reconcile and be happy as soon as possible. It's a lucky thing for you that you had me by your side to divorce you."

"I didn't feel lucky at the time."

"Just think of all the years and years of misery you won't have because of me."

"I hadn't looked at it that way."

"Take my word for it. A lesser woman would have stuck by you."

"I suppose I should be grateful."

"Consider yourself fortunate among men."

Goggle-eyed at Irene's idiosyncratic method of marital therapy, I looked for a place to sit down, only to find that I was already stretched out on the rug with my head propped up on one elbow. Any vestigial belief that I could plumb Irene's mystery had flown out the window.

"Except," she went on, "our reconciliation hasn't exactly gone the way I expected."

"You mean it's not the balmy romantic path you'd hoped for?" Her remarks had left me feeling bruised and touchy.

"It's been wonderfully balmy and wonderfully romantic," she reassured me, drawing closer. "Everything I'd hoped for, and more. I just hadn't planned on Miles Dixon being killed."

"It took us all by surprise."

She clung to me. "Oh, Georgie, I don't want to get on the stand and answer Wusthof's questions again. Do you think we could find who the real murderer is before Monday?"

I protectively embraced both Irene and her question. "Monday, jury selection begins," I said, thinking aloud, "which gives us at least an extra day before the trial begins."

"So we have till Tuesday."

"Give or take a day. Wait a minute!" I said, recalling the afternoon's meeting with Leslie Tweed and Deirdre Dumbarton. "We're forgetting Lee and Dee. Since Grunion is following their advice, all of next week will be devoted to jury selection."

"You really think it will take the entire week?"

"In this case," I said with absolute confidence, "we can rely on Grunion to come through for us."

"Then I won't fire him until after jury selection."

"Let's hope you won't have to."

I let Natasha out of the bedroom. She was miffed at having been so unceremoniously locked away from us. She gave me a frosty looked, climbed up into my swivel workchair, and sat with her back to me. I turned on the television. Channel 56 still had the auction going.

I whipped up a large rum mocha shake for Irene and, to make amends, poured some into a bowl for Natasha. Irene was still calling my shakes "mousses," saying they had that special mouth feel the French call "embrouillage." I wasn't about to dispute her terminology, but she was also still bugging me to demonstrate my prototype "mousse-maker"—the Lotus Flex-a-Pleaser multispeed vibrating massager I had grabbed from the Thousand Happinesses Limited carton and modified—to Ethan. That damned carton still stood in my living room. I *had* to get rid of it. It was just too damned large and heavy. When I'd called the Ann Arbor Solid Waste Department, they asked me for my name and address to set a date for a special pickup. I wasn't about to apply. I had briefly considered renting a pickup truck and smuggling the carton to the city dump at three o'clock in the morning, but with my luck the police would happen by. They were vigilant at the landfill site for industrial felons who might try to sneak in and dump dangerous chemicals. My Thousand Happinesses Limited carton was no less a hot potato.

"Georgie," Irene crooned, licking mousse from her spoon in a manner that put me in mind of the sultan's favorite in a harem.

"Mmm-hmm," I replied.

"You know that secret bank-account number Abdur is looking for?"

"Mmm-hmm."

"Well, I was looking through Miles's copy of *Signs and Symbols in Oriental Rugs*, and I think I know where the bank-account information is hidden."

"In the book?"

"No, silly. It's woven into a rug that Abdur imported."

"Wouldn't Abdur have noticed it?"

"Not if he wasn't looking for it. It's been right under his nose all along. That's why Miles ordered the book. To read the code. I'll show you how it works. Where's your afghan?"

From my workroom I got the afghan, still fringed with Natasha's silky hair. I was getting used to it that way.

Irene opened the book and showed me how words and even numbers could be woven into rug designs. We lay shoulder to shoulder on my afghan rug and pored over its fanciful designs, comparing them with the color photographs in the book. It was a pleasant way to wind up an extremely pleasant afternoon, excluding, of course, our meeting with Lee, Dee, and Grunion. Irene found some numbers woven into my rug. They were easily recognizable because, she pointed out, we use the Arabic numeral system.

She also found some script with the numbers.
"No doubt an Islamic prayer," I said knowingly.
"It's in English."
"Isn't it awful," I observed, "how cultural traditions are corrupted by pressures of the marketplace? I bet it wasn't even woven in Afghanistan."
Irene read it aloud. "Pacific Bank of the Commonwealth, Seychelles, U.K."
Our heads turned and we stared at each other in simultaneous enlightenment. Our prayers had been answered.
Not only had my rug been right under Abdur's nose, but since he sold it to me it had been right under my nose, Irene's nose, her knitting needles, Natasha's nose, Miles Dixon's nose, Charles Finch's nose, Reynolds's nose, the police's noses, and the noses of everyone who had been to my party the night Miles Dixon was killed. There didn't seem to be a nose that my rug, at some time, had not been under.
Irene said, "Now what?"
"We *don't* tell Grunion," I said immediately. "Jury selection is coming up, and we wouldn't want to throw him off his form. We'd better get Biswanger in on this." I got up to phone him.
Irene looked surprised. "The three of us together?"
"Sure," I said, tapping out his number.
"Like I'm one of the guys?"
Amazed, I said, "Sure."

"We can't tell Abdur Rahman," Biswanger said on Wednesday, the next day, having immediately assumed our problem as his own. "Or else Irene will lose the one advantage she has to smoke out the murderer."
Irene and I nodded. We were convened at the usual conference facility Biswanger and I used: a table outside

Zingerman's. Biswanger was nibbling Hutchin-Smith's Blue Cheshire cheese on Jacob's Cream Crackers, having forgone his usual monster sandwich-combo out of some odd notion of delicacy toward Irene at our confab. Irene, however, had ordered a hot brisket, turkey breast, cheddar cheese, tomato, with spicy-brown mustard sandwich (No. 15, *Bill's Two over prime*), with a side order of coleslaw, potato pancakes, and a Soho natural soda to keep it all organic. I was enjoying a molinari salami, smoked mozzarella, extra-virgin olive oil, dried tomato, roasted red peppers, basil-meatball combination on sourdough.

"Nor," Biswanger continued, "should you tell those two police detectives."

"Freiday and Clancy," Irene reminded him.

"They are duty-bound to turn the bank-account information over to Wusthof as evidence. Wusthof will think Irene is trying to plea bargain her way out. At this juncture, we must be very careful." Biswanger looked at me. "We can't tell your State Department man, Reynolds."

"Stuart Adams," I added helpfully.

"Adams?" Biswanger repeated. "Why have you been calling him Reynolds, and before that, Delmore?"

"Because we're on a first-name basis," I said testily.

"Make up your mind, George. Is he Reynolds Adams, Stuart Adams, or Delmore Adams?"

"He's Reynolds Stuart Adams."

"No Delmore in there?"

"Not anymore. He's got a thing about secret identities. He thinks he's descended from Thomas Jefferson," I added, showing Biswanger I hadn't been wasting my time with Reynolds. "He's also a backer of Afghan mujahedeen, and he's humping Miles Dixon's former lady friend."

Popping a Tunisian olive, Biswanger chewed it along with

this new information. "We can't tell Reynolds Stuart Adams for two reasons: he's a suspect and he's here to finish Miles Dixon's mission. If he didn't kill Miles, he would turn the money over to the State Department. If he were the guilty party, he'd take the next flight to the Seychelles to get the money for himself. Though, come to think of it, even if he didn't kill Miles, he'd still go after the money for himself."

"How does that follow?" Irene asked.

"Nobody leaves the State Department with just the savings from their salary," Biswanger reminded her.

"Of course."

"Either way, you'd be left high and dry facing the same murder charge."

"How about *we* go to the Seychelles," I suggested, "and transfer the money to another account for safekeeping."

"It's safe where it is," said Biswanger, "as long as no one else knows the number." He was eyeing my pickle. "Are you going to eat your pickle?"

"Yes," I growled, warning him off.

"You haven't touched it."

"I haven't finished my sandwich."

"You're practically finished."

"I like my pickle at room temperature."

"We're outside."

"I want it for my collection," I said wildly. "I chloroform them and mount them in a display case. Now quit bugging me."

"I was just asking," Biswanger said meekly.

"You're making sure I feel self-conscious so I won't enjoy my pickle. Goddamn it, I refuse to feel guilty. Now let's get back to finding the murderer."

Biswanger waited two beats. "You're sure you won't change your mind?"

I appealed to Irene as my witness. "See what he does?"

"Then I'll have it," she said, and executed a two-finger snatch of my pickle that had Biswanger and me gaping. She gave me a sweet look and added, "Unless you really want it?"

I rose from the table and marched back into Zingerman's. I waited patiently in line, and asked for twenty-five kosher dills. I had to repeat my request to the astonished clerk not to wrap them—they were for here. Outside again, I stacked up twelve of the enormous pickles before Irene and twelve before Biswanger. Irene and Biswanger remained impassive throughout the ceremony. I returned to my chair with the twenty-fifth pickle, which I had modestly reserved for myself.

Biswanger critically appraised his cord of pickles. He said, "Only *one* dozen?"

"Have one of mine," Irene generously offered.

"I'd rather have one of his."

We peaceably munched our pickles.

"So how do we smoke out the murderer if we can't tell anyone about the Seychelles bank-account?" I asked as we strolled up North Fourth past the Farmer's market toward the Wildflower Bakery. Biswanger had promised Emily he'd pick up some all-natural, unrefined, honey-bran-sesame-soy scones. Irene was walking between us. Her eyes were alight with conspiracy and intrigue.

"We can't reveal the account number, but we can tell *about* it," she said.

Biswanger and I inclined our heads toward her, like book ends.

"We can tell Reynolds and Charles each separately," said Irene, "that Miles Dixon had some important information about a bank-account hidden in his apartment that we think can clear me. We tell them Grunion needs it for my defense, but we can't get at it because the police still have the apartment sealed. The murderer puts two and two together, and realizes it must be the Seychelles bank-account number. Then we stake out the apartment and see who tries to break in."

"Reynolds is my P.I.," I pointed out. "He might suggest that he break in and get it for us. After all, he told us himself that he excelled in picks and locks."

"Fine."

"But when he breaks in, he won't find anything."

"He will if we plant a false bank-account number in Miles Dixon's apartment *before* we tell him and Charles. Then we see who breaks in, and what they do with the false bank-account number."

"All the murderer has to do is wire the Seychelles bank and he'll find out there is no such account."

Irene thought a moment. "We'll open a real account in the Seychelles bank with, say a hundred dollars in it."

"Why a hundred dollars?" I asked.

"Whatever the minimum is," Irene said impatiently. "We'll give the bank strict instructions not to disclose the amount in the account, unless the request is made with the proper signature."

"Whose signature?" I asked. "The two mujahedeen who set up the original account are dead."

"Abdur Rahman's signature, of course," Irene said.

A warning alarm went off in the back of my head. "I don't think we should bring Abdur into this scheme."

"I'll forge Abdur's signature, and we'll send it when we set up the account."

"As your personal business attorney," Biswanger interjected, "I must point out that you're getting into a gray area here."

Both Irene and I turned toward him in puzzlement. Since her entire scheme was gray smoke and funhouse mirrors, why worry about one little forgery? In unison we said, "So?"

In a petulant tone Biswanger said, "I want to forge the signature."

Here I had to put my foot down. "I'm the toy designer. *I'll* forge Abdur's signature."

That settled, we continued our stroll down the red-brick sidewalk, past a new boutique that had sprouted like a mushroom and would decay back into the mercantile litter just as quickly. I said, "Suppose Charles is the murderer, but Reynolds breaks in, strictly as my P.I., before Charles. When Charles breaks in, the planted bank-account information will be missing."

Irene had an answer for that one, too. "Then we open two accounts in the Seychelles bank and plant the two numbers in two different places in the apartment. One account for Reynolds and one for Charles."

It was getting complicated.

"Uh, excuse me," said Biswanger. "In order to plant these two bank-account numbers in Miles's apartment, *we* have to break in past the police seal. Do either of you have a set of burglary tools?"

"Very funny," I muttered. But his objection still stood. "How do we break in without the police knowing about it?"

"We get Reynolds to do it." Irene replied brightly.

I frowned. "We get Reynolds to break in and plant the information that we want him to break in for, assuming he's the murderer?"

"No, silly. First we ask Reynolds to break in for another reason."

"Like what?"

"To find something to help my case, of course."
"Maybe we will."
"Don't confuse the issue," Irene said impatiently. "We accompany Reynolds on the first break-in, and that's when we plant the two bank-account numbers."
"It now totals two hundred dollars," I pointed out.
Irene waved off my objection. "Then later, after the first break-in, that's when we confide in Charles and Reynolds separately that we've found out about the bank-account stuff from Abdur and ask them what we should do about it."
My mind boggled trying to encompass Irene's logic. I said, "So if Reynolds is the murderer, he'll break in a second time for the bank-account stuff that we planted when he broke in the first time with us, only he won't tell us about the second break-in."
"Exactly. And if Charles is one, he'll break in."
"You know, it's crazy, but it just might work," said Biswanger, sounding like an old movie.
"It's crazy," I said.
"It *will* work," said Irene.
Biswanger's bulk, stuffed with Zingerman's finest, was vibrating with excitement. "I've always wanted to go on a stakeout."
I recalled Abdur Rahman's cautionary talk about the three travelers, the story he'd told that afternoon with Reynolds and Charles present. One traveler was good and the other one evil. And I was still the ignoramus in between. My sole consolation was that now I had Abdur's precious bank-account number, though turning it against the money-laundering murderer was turning into a real chore. Several chores, in fact.
I said, "Can't we plant the two accounts someplace else,

and avoid all the break-ins?"

"Then we wouldn't have any reason to complain to Charles and Reynolds that we can't get it," said Irene.

Damn, I thought. "Let's assume everything works out as you say: We get Reynolds to break in the first time and we plant the two false account numbers; then the murderer breaks in to the apartment. Eventually he's going to find out that the bank-account number is a setup. He's going to feel very put out."

"Surely more than *put out*," Biswanger interjected.

"How about vindictive?"

Biswanger nodded sagely. "Yes. Whoever the murderer turns out to be, *vindictive* will definitely describe his emotional state."

"And," I said, picking up the thread of my argument, "he'll know we're the ones responsible for sending him on a wild-goose chase to the Seychelles."

Biswanger said, "As soon as we know who the murderer is, for our own protection we'll tell Wusthof. We'll trade the murderer and the real bank-account number to Wusthof in exchange for dropping charges against Irene."

"Assuming everything goes according to plan," I said. "And assuming Wusthof will believe evidence of the truth."

"Sometimes, Georgie," said Irene, "you can be annoyingly pessimistic."

We went into the bakery. While Biswanger and Irene bought scones and muffins, I pondered the fact that a vindictive, drug money-laundering murderer is not a nice person to have on your back.

12

THURSDAY, BISWANGER SET UP two decoy bank accounts in the Pacific Bank of the Commonwealth, Seychelles, U.K. They turned out to be very expensive decoys.

The bank assessed special fees for handling secret accounts, in addition to their currency-conversion fees and management fees tacked onto the minimum balance, which from my position was hardly minimum. Irene and I had to put up a big hunk of money, with Biswanger putting up a third.

While I raged about being ripped off, Biswanger logically pointed out that we needed the Pacific Bank of the Commonwealth more than they needed us. The bank's attitude was understandable, said Biswanger. With all that drug money and dictator money and CIA money keeping them busy, law-abiding middle-class people like ourselves had better make it worth their while. My attitude was, comes the revolution, I'll be leading the charge against those smug bastards. I told Biswanger to transfer the required amount from the real secret account into our two new accounts. Temporarily. We'd transfer it back afterwards. Why should we have to compete, I argued, with the currency chicanery of South American juntas? The money was already there in the real secret account. Use some of it. But Biswanger vetoed the idea, on the grounds that Wusthof would look suspiciously at any transactions Irene and I made with the real secret account. It would negate the purpose of our operation, which was to show who knew of the account and so had a motive to kill Miles when Miles stumbled on the secret himself. We had to keep a strictly hands-off policy. Caeser's wife, and all that.

My feeling was, to hell with Caeser's wife. What had Calpurnia ever done for me? My financial state was past critical. It was on life-support, what with Irene's bail, legal fees, Lee and Dee's fees, and now the two Seychelles bank accounts. I began to think seriously about going along with Irene's idea of marketing my "mousse-maker." After all, Irene *had* said there was a huge upscale market for mousse. And Ms. Leung *had* stated in her letter of transmittal that Thousand Happinesses Limited was looking for a stateside distributor. I decided to go ahead with it and let the chips fall where they may. The question was, how many Lotus Flex-a-Pleaser multispeed vibrators could Thousand Happinesses Limited crank out to my specifications?

Meanwhile, the first break-in to Miles Dixon's apartment was imminent. Friday at midnight.

Irene and I drove into the guest lot of Riverside Towers at a quarter to twelve. Of course, there was a full moon in a clear sky. Nice and bright for anyone to see us. Per Reynolds's instructions, Irene and I had dressed for a party, so we would not be out of place at Riverside Towers on a Friday night. The two decoy bank-account numbers were on slips of paper on Irene's person. Once inside the apartment, I'd distract Reynolds while she secreted them away.

We waited in the car for Reynolds, listening to a *Golden*

Days of Radio broadcast on WAAM. It was a *Fibber McGee and Molly* episode. While Fibber rummaged through his famous overstuffed closet, I had second thoughts about stashing our decoy bank-account numbers in the apartment. What if a police detective found them? What if the detective decided to make a personal reconnaissance in the Seychelles? There went our sizable investment.

I thought midnight a trifle dramatic, but since Reynolds had readily agreed to get us into Miles Dixon's apartment, I didn't complain. Irene had simply told him she wanted to look for anything that might help her defense. Her request made sense. The police had already been through the place; Wusthof had helped himself to the choice bits of evidence planted there by the real murderer. It was only fair Irene had a look around.

Reynolds's Porsche pulled up beside our car. We got out.

Reynolds had a camera bag slung over his shoulder and carried a picnic cooler. Clever disguises for his special break-in equipment.

"You're looking sharp," Irene said, complimenting Reynolds on his Ralph Lauren jacket.

"And you, dear lady, put me in mind of Lauren Hutton," he replied with his Virginia gentleman flourish.

I said, "I half expected Perdita to be with you."

"Perdita is spending quality time with her husband."

I noted his camera bag. "Are burglary tools in there?"

"My camera is in there. Since we can't remove anything, I'll photograph whatever you think your lawyer can use."

"The cooler?" I asked.

"Snacks," said Reynolds.

"How thoughtful," said Irene.

"I find searching makes one peckish. We'll want a break in midsearch. Now remember, we're on our way to a party."

We sashayed into the building, ha-ha-ing and ho-ho-ing all the way.

On Miles's floor, Irene and I stood lookout down the hall. Reynolds, ignoring the sign in front of Miles's door that said *DO NOT CROSS. POLICE ORDERS*, stepped with catlike stealth over the yellow barrier tape.

"What are you doing over there?" Reynolds asked.

"Standing lookout."

"Come on. This won't take long."

Such hubris, I thought. But then, he had excelled in pick and locks.

Still catlike, Reynolds dexterously reached into his jacket pocket and withdrew a small leather case. I could only imagine what feats of U.S. Government miniaturization had gone into Reynolds's break-in tools. Selecting a metallic object that looked for all the world like a key, he inserted it into the lock. He turned it. The door opened.

It *was* a key.

Withdrawing the key, Reynolds went back for his picnic cooler. He carried it inside. "Come on in."

Irene and I stepped over the yellow tape and followed Reynolds into an omnium-gatherum of the American West. The chairs were leather, the Chesterfield sofa was leather, and between bookcases lined with Zane Greys and Louis L'Amours, the walls were covered in antelope suede with tintype photos of Indians, cowboys, saloons, and Teddy Roosevelt when he was a Rough Rider. There were antlers over a fake stone fireplace, a bronze bronco on the mantle, crossed Indian peace pipes, and gleaming silver spurs. On display in a glass tabletop were eight-inch lengths of varieties of barbed wire.

Miles Dixon had been living apart from his wife and had indulged his fantasy of riding the purple sage. Not to mention Perdita Cunliffe.

Irene was watching my reaction. "Well?" she said.

Having seen Irene's decorating skills, there remained not the slightest doubt in my mind that she'd had no hand in Miles Dixon's personal accoutrements. Looking deep into her eyes I said, "Darling, I'll never doubt you again."

Reynolds pocketed the apartment key.

I said, "You've been here before."

"After Miles was killed. Of course, the police don't know that."

"You made up your own key from the lock?" I asked reverently.

"Miles sent me an extra key when he contacted me to back him up."

Oh, how to the self-deluded does the obvious appear obscure. I said, "Then you've already searched here."

"Thoroughly. I didn't find anything. Maybe you will."

The plan Irene and I had so carefully devised was evaporating into the universal either. Reynolds had searched every nook and cranny. How could we hide the two account numbers so he'd find them in a place he hadn't already looked, when only he knew where he'd already looked?

It became a repetition of:

"Did you look here?"

"Yes."

"Here?"

"Yes, but go ahead. You've got a fresh perspective."

Reynolds's *yes*'s fell like stones into a muddy puddle of futility. Where would we stash the two phony bank accounts? Miles's apartment was the most thoroughly searched apartment on earth. Even if Reynolds said no to a place, we couldn't put one of the accounts in that place, because he'd know we looked there. I stopped asking. Irene, though, gave no sign of sharing my concern. Reynolds obligingly took photographs as we moved from room to room. We reached the calico bedroom, and once again I had to re-evaluate my opinion of Miles Dixon, for mounted on a three-foot post was a cowboy saddle with a pillion attached to the back for an extra rider.

After an hour of this charade, we stopped and dug into the picnic cooler. Reynolds was right about searching giving one an appetite.

"What a waste of time," I said to Irene as I drove along Huron River Drive back home. "And money."

Irene, who had acted very chipper when we bid bon soir to Reynolds, now gave me a questioning look. "What are you talking about?"

"You don't have to pretend anymore for my sake," I said, and sighed. Our best-laid plan had failed. We'd just have to add it to our loss column. "Tomorrow I'll tell Biswanger to close out the two accounts. I doubt the Pacific Bank of the Commonwealth pays anything near the competitive rate," I added in sardonic afterthought.

"Georgie, if we close down the accounts, the murderer will find out the number he finds is to a nonexistent account."

I had to admire Irene's never-say-die attitude. Ever the optimist, she was cooking up another scheme for planting the two account numbers somewhere else.

"Darling," I said gently. "Miles's apartment was the most logical place to put the numbers. You said so yourself."

"So what's the problem?"

"For one thing, you couldn't hide them there."

"But I did."

"Oh, no! We'll have to go back and get those numbers out."

"Why, Georgie?"

"Darling," I said, struggling to remain gentle and forgiving, "Reynolds has been over that place with a fine-toothed comb. At least twice, counting this evening. He's got his own key, for God's sake! Where could you possibly put the account numbers that he hasn't looked?"

"In the doorlocks, of course."

Of course. Where does one hide something in plain sight when one of the intended finders was an A student in picks and locks? In a doorlock, of course.

"I thought you saw me do it."

"I didn't. How did you do it?"

"I just slid each slip of paper behind the knob faceplates of the bedroom and bathroom locks. Everyone agrees that Miles let the killer inside—the police found no sign of forced entry. And I'm sure the murderer—whoever he is—made a copy of Miles's key so he could return and search some more if he had to. With everyone having a copy of Miles's key, everyone has put doorlocks out of mind. It's so logical, Georgie, I'm surprised you didn't think of it, too.

"Well, I didn't."

"Georgie," she cajoled, "look how bright the moon is. Isn't the moon bright?"

"It's bright, all right."

"And isn't it romantic, driving on Huron Drive along the Huron River in the moonlight?"

The moon was very bright indeed through the trees. Driving on Huron Drive in the moonlight *was* rather romantic, actually. Tomorrow—Saturday—we'd start casting the bait: we'd tell Reynolds and Charles about the accounts and see what each one did. Monday, jury selection would begin. I prayed Irene wouldn't have to finish the trial.

I turned on the radio to *The Larry King Show*. Larry was

interviewing a political reformer who had written a book. Its main thesis was that campaign money from special interests corrupted politicians, and this was a Bad Thing for democracy. How original. How thought-provoking. I turned to WAAM, and was astonished to hear Grunion's voice. It was a rebroadcast of yesterday's *Ted Heisel Show*.

". . . no such thing as a hopeless defense," Grunion was saying. "Only noncreative lawyers."

I listened in a stunned trance.

"I can't comment directly on Ms. Spinoza's case," Grunion went on, "but may I just say generally, I like to think of it as an opportunity to raise people's consciousness about the problem in society of the 'other woman.'"

"That does it," I said sternly. "I'm going to clean and oil my gun, and then I'm going to the men's room on the thirteenth floor of the Liberty Building and blast that blithering glory-grabber to judicial oblivion."

"You don't own a gun," Irene reminded me.

"Then I'll buy one and oil it. What's the matter with people, Irene?" I complained. "How can they buy that load of farmer's helper?"

"I thought he sounded rather good."

"But he suffers from acute anemia of the reasoning faculty."

"Be fair, Georgie. It's only a local radio show, and we've had more time to know him."

"What's next?" I cried. "Mayor Grunion? *Senator* Grunion? God, what a thought!"

"It wouldn't be the first time."

It was after three when we got back. Irene didn't want to go to her place, so she wound up in my place. Again. While her place upstairs functioned as a beautifully decorated parlor for clients, she was doing a lot of her living down one floor with me. I liked our new arrangement just fine.

Natasha raised her head from my afghan, blinked at us, and thudded back into slumberland. Irene and I were both too wound up to sleep. There was nothing on television. I noted that Channel 56 still had its interminable auction going.

Logically, there was only one activity for us to relax with.

Afterward, we flipped a coin. It came up heads. Irene would tell Reynolds, and I would tell Charles Finch; however, upon further reflection, Irene pointed out that since both Charles and Reynolds had been to Marderosian's Ruggery with me to see Abdur, it would sound more plausible to Reynolds if the bank-account story came from me. I should tell both Charles and Reynolds. When I pointed out we could simply reverse how the coin came up, so that she tell Charles, she pointed out that Charles had to be told under the pretense of seeing him about a veterinary problem concerning Natasha. I had legal custody of Natasha, so it was logical I tell him. And besides, Irene said, she had a Saturday-morning hair appointment and then a meeting with Ethan, the Hudson's V.P., about my mousse-maker, which could take all day. And Charles didn't have Sunday hours, so when was she supposed to tell him?

Irene's logic being what it was, it fell to me to tell Reynolds and Charles.

Saturday morning, I took Natasha in for a checkup at Charles's animal hospital, having invented a story about her listlessness and poor eating. After expressing concern about the trial coming up, Charles said he could squeeze Natasha in that same morning. I was worried that one look at Natasha might generate some skepticism about her "poor eating," but I figured Charles would be more interested in my story about Miles.

"Stop feeding her junk," Charles admonished me as he probed Natasha's well-padded middle. "She's twenty percent over her proper bodyweight."

"She's big-boned," I said defensively.

"If her bones get any heavier, she'll need a barn and a saddle. Walk her more."

"I walk her a lot. People stop to admire her and they slip her bits of whatever they're eating."

"Put a muzzle on her."

"I tried that," I said, avoiding Natasha's eye as I recalled the shameful experience. "It made people feel sorry for her and want to feed her. I got dirty looks, and she sucked it up through her muzzle anyway."

During this exchange, Natasha sat placidly on the table of the medicinal-smelling examination room, unbothered by the unhappy doggy whines and cat meows filtering in from adjoining rooms. Her quiescent indifference spoke volumes. She seemed to be saying, Can I help it if I was born gorgeous? Can I help it if I'm naturally the center of adulatory attention wherever I go?

"Pets reflect their owners' habits," Charles continued, in the manner of a prep-school headmaster. "Show me an overweight dog, and I'll show you. . . " He was staring at me with furrowed brow. He tweaked his mustache. "I say, George, how have *you* been feeling?"

Although there was a fifty-fifty chance Charles had stabbed Miles, planted drugs in Irene's bathroom, and installed a bomb in her car, for the moment he was a medical man who saw something worrisome about me. "What's wrong?" I asked, my voice rising an octave.

"You've lost weight since I last saw you."

I shrugged. What could I say? That my obsessive-compulsive sex life with Irene had displaced my obsessive-compulsive snacking? Perhaps Natasha was putting it on because she felt she had to take up my slack.

"I expect you've been worried about Irene," Charles said with unexpected sympathy.

"Listen, Charles," I said in a low, confiding voice. "I'm worried about something Irene remembers Miles telling her." Preparatory to taking Charles into my confidence, I paused dramatically to look up and down the hall for eavesdroppers before shutting the door. "Miles said he'd found this bank account. He said it was going to blow the lid off."

"Off what?"

"He didn't say. Irene's guess is, embezzlement at the university. That's where he worked, right?"

"Right."

"Apparently, he had a premonition someone was on to him. He told Irene if anything happened to him, she'd find the answer to everything behind his bathroom doorknob."

While I pretended ignorance of the implications of my cock-and-bull story, I observed Charles for his reaction.

He flicked his mustache with his knuckle again, though whether out of secret satisfaction for my spilling the beans, or out of his habitual amusement at my predicaments was unclear. He said, "A bathroom doorknob is an odd place to hide the answer to everything."

"Miles was an odd person," I acknowledged, and could have added, But not half as odd as Reynolds. "The police have sealed off the apartment, so we can't sneak in and find out if what's behind the doorknob will help or hurt Irene's case. Just the fact Irene knows something is there could be used against her."

Charles stroked his mustache. "Hmmm," he mused. "Should you tell the police and take potluck, or should you let sleeping dogs lie? Tricky one, that."

"What do you think?"
"Hmmmmmmmmm."
"Well?"
"I think you should ask Grunion, your lawyer."

Later Saturday morning, I called Reynolds and told him a freely adapted version of the truth. Since we found nothing in Miles's apartment last night, I told him, this morning I went to see Abdur Rahman on the hope of another lead. And miracle of miracles, after hearing of our valiant search, Abdur's conscience got the better of him. He admitted there was a Seychelles bank-account number that Miles had found and secreted in a doorlock. Miles's murder and the police's presence had deterred Abdur from attempting to break in and look for it. Reynolds agreed to our doing another search together next week, after Irene conferred with Grunion.

We took turns staking out Miles Dixon's apartment. Biswanger and I alternated Saturday afternoon while Irene had her meeting with Ethan, then she put in a shift Saturday night. Emily took Sunday morning. Biswanger volunteered for Monday morning, when Irene and I would be in court.

I discovered that stakeouts are boring.

13

NINE O'CLOCK MONDAY MORNING, July 3rd, the Hon. Samuel Geary was presiding in Court Room Number Five in the Washtenaw County Building at Main and Huron, which was a convenient ten-minute walk down Huron from my condo. One of the advantages of downtown living. Tomorrow was July 4th, so Irene would have an extra day before the actual trial began, in addition to the days Grunion would take up with jury selection.

The Ypsilanti District Court had been brisk, courteous efficiency. Circuit Court was high church. Court Room Number Five was windowless and soundproofed against outside traffic noise, with a twenty-foot-high ceiling, the enormous Great Seal of the State of Michigan high above the judge's bench, and gold-eagled U.S. and Michigan flags flanking the bench. I sat with Charles Finch in the first row of the packed spectator area, just behind the polished wooden barrier separating us from the court. Irene's trial had all the requisite elements of scandal; there wasn't an empty seat in the house. One woman who was obviously a descendent of Madame LaFarge had brought her knitting. Biswanger wasn't with us because he was watching Miles Dixon's apartment. I was scheduled to spell him at noon. I noted that Reynolds was not present. I wondered if Biswanger would see him going into Riverside Towers.

The court officer glided in, and a chapel hush fell over the crowd. He asked us to rise. After three beats, the door to the right of the judge's bench opened, then another beat and Judge Samuel Geary entered. In keeping with the lofty atmosphere, he was at least six-four. He climbed the steps and took his place.

Judge Geary had white hair, tired baggy eyes, and hay fever. He rubbed his nose and fiddled with his pen while he went through the litany of asking the prospective jurors to his right whether they knew any members of the prosecutor's office, or defending counsel, and whether they had family members or friends in the police force. None did. When in his soft, avuncular voice he asked if any of them had been assaulted with a weapon, or had a friend or close relative assaulted or murdered, a woman raised her hand. She was into quiltmaking, and just wouldn't feel comfortable in the murder trial where the weapon was a pair of sewing scissors. She was thanked and excused.

Judge Geary took out a large white handkerchief and blew his nose, then said to the people in the jury box, "I'm going to give you a breakdown of this case from the information file. It is claimed that the defendant, Irene Spinoza, on the night of June 9th of this year was with Miles Dixon at his Riverside Towers apartment residence. It is further claimed that on June 9th she stabbed Miles Dixon with a pair of scissors and caused his death."

While Judge Geary briefed the potential jurors, my gaze was drawn again toward the right side of the room to the defense table. Irene was a picture of wan loveliness. If only she were being defended by Charles Laughton, Spencer Tracy, or Gregory Peck. Instead, she was flanked by Grunion, whose shoeshine and new haircut went nicely with his perdurable look of earnest bafflement. At the prosecutor's table, Wusthof was going over his notes. No doubt he had honed them to an edge one could shave with.

Sharing the front row with Charles and me were reporters scribbling notes on steno pads. Everyone had been searched at the courtroom door by sheriff's deputies with metal detectors. That indignity had caused my undershorts to ride up; as I twisted round to surreptitiously tug at them, I spotted two familiar faces among the crowd.

Abdur Rahman sat two rows back. He smiled and waved at me. I waved back. A reporter for the Ypsilanti Press, seeing our exchange, got up and headed toward Abdur to wangle an interview. Earlier, I'd responded to the reporter's request for an interview with a curt "no." As ex-husband of the accused, I was getting a reputation of not cooperating with the media. An aggressive TV camera crew had asked me, in so many words, how it felt to have been cuckolded by Miles, and I told them in so many words to fuck off, thus precluding the possibility of the soundtrack of our on-the-street interview being included in the six and eleven o'clock news segment about Irene's trial. Flushed with this victory over vandalish video news, I had toyed with the idea of affecting a stout hickory cane and spiked boots. But still they importuned Irene. They had ambushed her when she was in the act either of entering or leaving our condo building, her car, the county court building, or committing the foolish indiscretion of walking on a public street in broad daylight.

The other person I spotted behind me in the courtroom crowd was Charles's business associate, Rafael, whom I recognized from when our paths had crossed at Charles's brainstorming party, when Terri had guided me through Charles's house and Rafael had been on his way to do some

VIP-ing—Very Important Phoning. Now Rafael was sitting all the way back in the last row. Maybe he had arrived late. Maybe he was shy. Or maybe he didn't want to be seen.

Curiouser and curiouser.

The voir dire proceeding had begun. Wusthof was at the podium opposite the jury, making his opening statement.

"I have no intent to pry into your personal life or embarrass you in any way. However, my duty as prosecuting attorney requires that I make inquiries, and I hope you will bear with me."

Wusthof was perfect. Low-key, courteous, and professional. Would that Grunion were the same. After Wusthof questioned and found acceptable a man of about fifty-five who wore a plaid shirt and zip jacket, it was Grunion's turn.

"If you are chosen in this case," said Grunion, "do you know of any reason you could not sit as an impartial juror?"

The man sucked on a tooth. "If it's a short trial."

"Why?"

The man leaned forward and mumbled something to Grunion.

Judge Geary said, "Please speak up, sir, so the court can hear your answer."

The man mumbled again.

Grunion, acting as translator, said, "Hemorrhoids, Judge."

I was reminded afresh that whatever path Grunion trod, disaster awaited over the next hillock. My attention was diverted by Detective Clancy's voice whispering to me from the side aisle.

"Mr. Spinoza."

Both he and Detective Nancy Freiday were motioning me over. I got up and excused my way across the feet of a gaggle of reporters.

Freiday held her hand out for my inspection. I whispered

a discreet "Wow!" at the engagement ring.

"We owe it all to you," she whispered.

"You were right," Detective Clancy whispered. "Love will find a way."

I blushed, for I am not immune to a compliment when it is well deserved. Two reporters close to us had pricked up their ears.

"And I hope you won't hold it personally against us," Detective Clancy added, "when Mr. Wusthof calls us to give our evidence."

"We're all professionals," I said.

Detective Freiday whispered, "We're registered at Schlanderer's for silver, and Leidy's for place settings."

She and Clancy departed from the courtroom. The two reporters jumped up as if joined at the hip and hurried out after them. I was proving a fountainhead of newsworthy leads. I tried an experiment. At random I picked out a woman in a polka-dot blouse. I nodded and mouthed "hello" to her. She nodded warily back, wondering if she ought to know me. Another reporter in the front row got up and started picking her way over knees and feet to get to the polka-dot woman.

I thought, this could become habit-forming.

Now there was more room on the front bench. Charles and I spread out and got comfortable.

I was not comfortable for long. Grunion was questioning another juror. A middle-aged woman. She was a salt-of-the-earth type who seemed sympathetic to Irene.

"Madam," said Grunion, "had you heard of this case before you came here for jury duty?"

"Yes."

"Did you read anything about this case in the papers?"

"It was hard to miss."

"What do you mean, 'hard to miss?'"

"It was on the front page."

"Have you formed an opinion from the news media, television, and radio that would be a burden for the defense to overcome?"

"The reverse, actually. I don't think she did it. Anyone could have taken her scissors and used them."

Grunion hooked his thumbs into his vest. "The reverse, you say? When is the first time you got the opinion of the defendant's innocence fixed in your mind?"

"When I saw the story on the Channel 7 *Action News*."

"Don't you, in fact, mean the *Eyewitness News?*"

"It might have been."

"The *Action News* Team is Channel 4, Madam! And is it not also a fact that you carried that opinion until about a week ago, when you became a prospective juror in this case?"

"Well, yes. I figured you should have an open mind when you're doing jury duty."

"In what way do you have an open mind?"

The woman did a double take. "What?"

"What has come into your own thinking that has given you this fixed opinion you have that this is an open-and-shut case?"

The woman stared at Grunion as if he had landed from Mars. The corner of her mouth twitched. "Young man, I still think she's innocent. It's you they ought to lock up."

"Then would I be accurate in saying that you *do* harbor hostile feelings toward the defense in this case?"

"That's the only thing you got right so far, sonny."

"Your Honor," Grunion said, his voice tinged with regret, "this witness is unacceptable for cause."

My experience with Grunion should have prepared me for the horror I was witnessing. *Grunion had just impeached a witness who thought Irene was innocent.* Grunion was following the advice of Lee and Dee to the letter. He was doing a bang-up job of creating a polarized jury. The trouble was, they were all being polarized against *him*. Grunion's curse was that he knew some of the form, but hadn't the foggiest notion of the substance.

I looked at the defense table to see how Irene was taking it. We exchanged pained looks. It couldn't get any worse. It just couldn't.

It did. Grunion's questions to successive jurors were of the same damaging ineptitude.

Viz:

Grunion asked a fat, beetle-browed man, "Do you have any religious or moral scruples against imprisonment as a punishment for adultery?"

"I thought the defendant was divorced."

"So she is. Where did you learn of that nonmarital fact of her?"

"Judge Geary told us."

"And would you have objections to that?"

"Being divorced? No. Three quarters of Ann Arbor is either in the process of getting or has gotten a divorce."

"Where did you learn that fact?"

"I'm a demographer for the local branch of state Social Services."

"You pride yourself on having facts like that at your fingertips?"

At this point, Judge Geary admonished Grunion, in so many words, to put a cork in it, because his questions to the juror had no probative value.

And viz:

Grunion asked an architect, "Have you been a victim of a crime similar to that charged here?"

"I was never stabbed with a scissors, if that's what you mean."

"Then you would not necessarily have a special sympathy for the victim."

"I didn't know him, but I'm sorry he's dead."

"But how do you feel about it?"

"Getting stabbed?"

"Yes."

"Well, I know I wouldn't like it."

"Is this a deep-seated conviction on your part, one to which you have given a lot of thought?"

The architect gave Grunion a puzzled stare that was becoming depressingly familiar.

And viz:

Grunion said to a Ms. Nusstorten, "I see that you put your occupation as accountant."

"For twenty-three years."

"Do you have any hostile feelings toward persons whose lifestyles differ considerably from your own?"

"Like Life Styles of the Rich and Famous? I guess everyone is a little jealous."

"If you decided that a verdict of not guilty for Ms. Spinoza might cost Michigan taxpayers hundreds of thousands of dollars, would you still find her not guilty?"

"I don't see how that follows."

"Ms. Nusstorten, isn't it within the realm of possibility that, should Ms. Spinoza be found not guilty of the death of Miles Dixon, the family of Miles Dixon might institute a *civil* action for damages? Mr. Dixon worked for the university. A tax-supported institution. And under our victim's compensation law.... You're an accountant. You know who would pay."

"I hadn't thought of it that way."

And viz:

To a Mr. Oswald, Grunion said, "If it appears from the evidence that Ms. Spinoza was exercising the lawful right of self-defense, would you vote for an acquittal, even though you find that the defendant struck the first blow?"

"If the guy was coming at her... sure. You gotta protect yourself."

Will no one stop him! my soul screamed. He's as good as telling them Irene killed Miles. The trial had yet to begin, and already the damage was unrecoverable. I was seeing the fruits of all those hours Grunion had labored before the mirror in the vineyard of the men's room on the thirteenth floor of the Liberty Building, fertilized with Lee and Dee's advice.

Charles leaned toward me and murmured, "Your Mr. Grunion certainly seems bent on giving you your money's worth." There were no signs of malice in his expression, only serene, twinkling good humor.

A suffocating pain clamped my chest. I sucked in air. At the edges of my vision red pinpricks winked like fireflies. I made a noise that came out as "Gack."

"Did you say something?" Charles inquired.

"I need air."

I needed more than air. I needed the safety margin of distance between me and Grunion, or else I risked enlivening the court proceedings by vaulting over the barrier and rendering Grunion into barristerial confetti.

I stumbled across many pairs of feet toward the outside aisle. An outcry penetrated the maelstrom of my consciousness, and I deduced that I had inadvertently stepped on someone's instep. I weaved drunkenly past the armed deputies into the blessed coolness and sanity of the nondescript corridor. Down at the far end was a water fountain.

The meager jet was nicely refrigerated to toothaching cold. When I finished slurping, I turned around and there was Rafael.

"It is not going well for Irene," he said solemnly.

"Did you follow me out here just to tell me that?"

"Mr. Spinoza, I would like to have a word with you about Irene. Please."

"You have something that will help her case?"

"I can't tell you here. It is a personal matter."

Something in Rafael's maniacally fixed gaze warned me to put him off.

I smiled back. "Gee, you've caught me at a bad time. The trial and all. Call my answering machine and we'll do lunch."

Rafael took hold of my right upper arm in an iron grip, so that we stood side by side, facing away from the deputies down the hall, as if in friendly conference. "Please," he repeated.

"I have to go back," I said, trying to pull away, but was given pause by the very solid gun that Rafael jammed into my right rib cage.

And then I knew Charles Finch was the one. He'd been sitting right beside me in court to put me off my guard, while his henchman waited. But why should Charles want me out of the way? And where the hell was Reynolds when I needed him?

"I insist," Rafael murmured. "For our convenience, I have parked my car on this side of the building on Ann Street."

As he expertly hustled me into the stairwell, I got a last look over my shoulder at the armed deputies down the hall, who were chatting among themselves at the Court Room Number Five doors, ever vigilant for weapons on the persons of citizens who might wish to observe the judicial process.

Rafael's Lincoln Continental was parked right across the street in front of the storefront lawyers' offices. I was amazed he'd found the spot on a weekday morning!

He unlocked the driver's door and said, "I apologize for this, but you must believe my sincerity."

"Oh, I do, I do," I assured him.

He motioned me to get in and slide over to the passenger side. I did, then he got in. Reading my mind, he said, "The doorlock will not open manually."

I'm being kidnapped at gunpoint, I thought, right from the Washtenaw County Building that at this moment is crawling with armed cops.

"How did you get the gun past the guards?" I asked, as if by way of conversation.

"I hid it in the men's room."

"Clever."

"It was nothing."

Rafael turned on the ignition. I waited for him to pull away from the curb, but he turned on the air conditioning and just sat there. He appeared ill at ease. The seconds ticked by. I grew impatient. What kind of kidnapping was this, anyway? Maybe he was having second thoughts!

I took an oblique approach. "How much is Charles Finch paying you to do this?"

"Charles knows nothing of this."

"*You* killed Miles Dixon?"

"I did not kill Mr. Dixon," Rafael said, pronouncing it Deek-*saun*. "Though in all sincerity I am not sorry he is gone."

"Uh, what did you have against him?" I asked.

"I did not know Mr. Dixon personally. I only know that it was fated that he should die so that Irene and I could be together."

I have always subscribed to the Random Nut Theory of Events. I said, "Did you break into Irene's condo and search her underwear drawer?"

Rafael's solemn demeanor was belied by the perspiration that broke out on his face. He nervously clasped his hands together, and discovering he still held the gun, he put it in his pocket and reclasped his hands. He cleared his throat. "She has stolen my heart."

"And then you sent her those flowers."

"A poor gift to accompany my declaration of my honorable intentions," he said, waving it off. The maniacal gleam returned to his eye. "You cannot save her, Mr. Spinoza," he cried, grabbing my lapel and gesturing wildly with his other hand. "You saw this morning what is in store for her. Only I can take her away to a new life."

Shoving his hand from my jacket, I pressed back against the passenger door. "The court doesn't look kindly on people who skip bail. And we put up a lot of money to get it."

"That is of no consequence."

"Maybe not to you..."

"She will be my queen of heaven in Medellin."

"Medellin?"

"On an Andean plateau on my native Colombia, gateway to South America!" He straightened up and his chest swelled alarmingly. "Where can it be—this land of Eldorado?" he declaimed in full oratorical voice. "Over the mountains of the moon, down the valley of the shadow, ride, boldly ride, the shade replied, if you seek for Eldorado!" When he finished he let his head fall dramatically, as if he expected me to applaud. "Your own Edgar Allen Poe understood."

"Uh, excuse me, Rafael, but there's this thing we have called extradition."

"Medellin is a land of eternal spring."

"I think it extends even to lands of eternal spring."

"But no one will know Irene is there. She will be my Madonna. My queen of heaven."

Rafael had written that purple note, all right.

"Mr. Spinoza, let us face facts. You are deeply in debt. I can provide Irene with escape to a life worthy of her special qualities. To demonstrate my sincerity, here are the particulars of the account I have set up for her." From the glove compartment he withdrew a legal-looking document and gave it to me.

It said *Banco Internacional* at the top. I saw Irene's name, with some impressive peso figures. Bank accounts were multiplying around me like rabbits. The secret one in the Seychelles, plus our two decoys, and now this one in Colombia. I wondered what the rate was for exchanging Colombian pesos into U.S. dollars.

Rafael anticipated my question. "The current rate is three hundred pesos to a U.S. dollar."

Even after dividing by three and moving the decimal over two places, Irene had a tidy nest egg in Colombia. I said, "Colombia is known for its drug traffic. Where did you get all that money for Irene's bank account?"

"I resent that, sir. Just because I am from Colombia does not automatically mean I must be a drug trafficker. We are a cultured people. Our capital, Bogota, is known as the Athens of South America."

Yeah, yeah, I thought. And Medellin is the land of eternal spring. I was locked in a car with the Colombian Chamber of Commerce.

"You want what is best for Irene," he cajoled. "Therefore, you are honor-bound to convey this to her, along with my message that I am ready to take her to a new life."

"I'll show this to Irene, with your compliments."

"Thank you, sir."

Our business concluded, I asked, "Is the kidnapping over?"

Rafael pushed a button on the dashboard and all the doorlocks clicked up.

When I returned to the court, Judge Geary had recessed for lunch. The spectators and reporters were gone. Irene and Grunion were gone, and not even Charles had waited for me. Where oh where was Irene?

The court officer came up to me in the hall and asked me how I was feeling, since he'd noticed my hasty exit from the courtroom earlier. I told him fine. He informed met that since the court had other business scheduled and people had holiday plans, Judge Geary had said there was no reason to convene the veniremen this afternoon. Irene's case would be taken up again the morning of July 5th. Jolly decent of the judge, I thought. The court officer told me Irene had left in the company of Grunion and Charles. Then he asked if I knew where Detectives Friday and Clancy were registered for their wedding pattern? I told him Schlanderer's and Leidy, thanked him for his courtesy, and departed.

I did not feel fine. I was feeling testy about being kidnapped at gunpoint from the circuit court with cops all around. Also, with the Banco Internacional statement in my pocket I was feeling envy for Rafael's wherewithal, plus guilt that I couldn't provide Irene with that kind of security.

It was twelve-fifteen. I was overdue to take over the stakeout from Biswanger at Miles Dixon's apartment. I stopped by my place to get Natasha, and continued on to Riverside Towers.

"This is a disaster!" Biswanger said after I'd told him about Rafael kidnapping me.

"I did get away," I said, pointing out the obvious, since I was sitting right beside him in his car. We were in the outside parking lot of Riverside Towers with a clear view of the entrances. "Though it was touch and go for a while."

"Not that," Biswanger said dismissively. "This!" He rattled the Banco Internacional statement Rafael had given me to give to Irene. "If news of this ever gets to Wusthof... that Irene has a Colombian bank account with this much in it..." He looked again at the bank statement and narrowed his eyes. "This could be his way of pressuring us into giving him the Afghan bank-account number."

"Rafael doesn't know about the Seychelles account. He's got this crazy fixation about Irene being his queen of heaven in the land of eternal spring."

"His what?"

"He's the underwear fetishist. He sent Irene those flowers with the crazy note."

"Irene is going to have to tell him she's not interested, and to dissolve the bank account."

"He'll take it hard," I said, remembering Rafael's automatic in my side. "You know how sensitive those underwear fetishists are."

"No, I don't."

"Take my word for it. This one is."

It was my turn to watch Riverside Towers. I got out of Biswanger's car to rejoin Natasha, who sat inside my car with the air conditioning running and the radio tuned to the Canadian classical music station. She hadn't wanted to get out into the heat. We had a long afternoon head of us.

As I walked over to my car, another car roared into the parking lot and sideswiped a row of clipped yews. I jumped out of the way, and a second later the car screeched to a halt where I had been standing. Its door flew open and Perdita Cunliffe flew out.

"He's disappeared!" she cried.

"Who?" I asked, picking myself up from a bed of Boston ivy.

"Reynolds. You've got to help me find him."

Biswanger walked over to her and calmly asked, "How did you know we were here?"

"I couldn't get Mr. Spinoza at his number this morning. Then I remembered the trial started today, so I called your office, and they wouldn't help, so I got your home and your wife told me where you were after I told her about Reynolds."

I said, "I thought it was supposed to be secret about you and Reynolds."

"That's history. I've left my husband for Reynolds. You've got to help me find him," she wailed.

"How long has Reynolds been missing?" Biswanger asked.

"Since Saturday. Friday, I told him I was leaving my husband, so I was free to be with him always. Then Saturday afternoon I couldn't get him on the phone. Sunday, he wasn't at his house for our..." She paused, then said delicately, "... our Afghan culture seminar. It was locked up and his car was gone. He wasn't there this morning either."

Biswanger looked significantly at me. Saturday morning was when I had told Reynolds about one of the decoy bank accounts hidden in the doorknob. Had Reynolds gotten into Miles Dixon's apartment without our seeing him? It was possible. He was probably on a flight to the Seychelles. Or, maybe he'd gotten cold feet about Perdita. My money was on the decoy Seychelles bank account. Actually, my money was *in* the decoy Seychelles bank account.

Perdita saw our reaction and said, "He got scared about commitment and ran off, didn't he?"

"I don't think that's the reason he's gone," I said truthfully. "Let's go search the house he rented."

14

Biswanger, Perdita, and I got into our cars and drove to Reynolds's rented house on Geddes. I didn't know what I expected to find. I thought an airline-ticket carbon of the next Seychelles flight out of Detroit International would be dandy. The Pacific Bank of the Commonwealth had strict orders to notify us if anyone inquired about either of the two decoy accounts. I wanted more evidence before we went to Wusthof with our story. We needed more detective work. Unfortunately, my P.I. wasn't the one to do it because he was the one who needed tracking. Maybe Clancy and Freiday could find the time between making wedding plans.

We all parked in the shady gravel driveway in front of the detached garage. It had a cupola skylight with a finial on top. A pigeon perched on the cupola and began cooing.

"You were here Sunday and this morning," I said to Perdita. "And both times he was gone?"

She slapped at a bug. "Yes."

I walked over to the garage. Natasha followed me. Its paneled door was padlocked.

"He never parked in there," Perdita said.

I was amazed, because Reynolds drove a Porsche and car theft was a growing industry around Ann Arbor. "Not even at night?"

"Never."

"Why not?"

"Pigeons. He kept his Porsche outside under a tarp. It had an alarm system."

"But if he had a tarp, he still could have parked it inside."

"Then he'd have to clean pigeon doo off the cover. Reynolds was very neat. The only thing he kept in the garage was the garbage cans."

I nodded. "Because of aesthetics."

"No. Raccoons."

"He locked the garage before he left," I observed. "Not much of a lock, though. No wonder he didn't bother putting the Porsche in."

Perdita walked up and examined the hinge latch. "I hadn't noticed. That lock was never there before. There isn't anything in there worth stealing."

"Except the garbage cans," said Biswanger.

I went to my car, opened the trunk, and took out the jack handle.

"George!" Biswanger said in alarm. "What are you doing?"

I slipped the jack handle between the padlock and the hinge latch. "Private property will have to take a back seat to a murder investigation," I declared, and popped off the padlock. I raised the garage door.

Reynolds's Porsche was inside. The tarp was covered with pigeon droppings. I guessed about two days' worth. Natasha ventured in and sniffed at the tarp.

"I don't understand," said Perdita.

"Everyone notices a Porsche," said Biswanger sagely. "Reynolds didn't want to be spotted driving away."

We walked around the house. It was locked drum tight. Doors and windows. We stood on the back porch and pondered our next move. It had a nice view of the river. Since

I'd been there last, nice homey touches had been added. Hanging plants, and colorful embroidered cushions on the swing seat. New curtains hung in the kitchen window.

"You really fixed up the place," I said to Perdita.

She sat in the swing seat, staring off into the leafy distance. "You'd think the bastard could at least have left a note." She squared her shoulders, got up, and removed her jacket. "Please hold this," she said. "May I?" she asked politely, taking my jack handle. She swung it against the kitchen window. Glass exploded inside. She reached in, unlatched the sash, and opened it. After brushing away broken glass, she hitched up her skirt, revealing the fineness of her thighs, and climbed inside with surprising agility. She unlocked the back door.

Ignoring the broken glass, it was clear that Reynolds had kept up with his household chores. The kitchen counter was spotless. The dishwasher had a washed load inside. He had made sure no annoying smells would attract the curious. Natasha barked, wanting to be let in, too. I found the dustpan and brush in the broom closet and swept up the broken glass, then let Natasha in. Since her sensitive nose had detected the drugs planted in Irene's bathroom, I figured she might find something useful.

I went into the living room. Reynolds's computer was still there. I thought it odd that he would leave behind his precious genealogical records about his descendency from Thomas Jefferson, then I realized he just had to take his floppies. The computer itself didn't matter. Curious, I looked at the titles in the bookcase. They were mostly on Afghanistan, its culture and people and their political struggle. The Steelcase file cabinets were industrial grade with heavy bar-locks in place. No jack handle was going to get them off. I checked the wastepaper basket. Empty.

So was the one in the downstairs bathroom, the one in the bedroom upstairs, and the plastic one in the bathroom off the bedroom. One thing the upstairs had was closet space. Two walk-in closets, with built-in sweater drawers, tie racks, and shoe cubbyholes. And it was all filled.

There were about twenty suits; dozens of ties and scarfs; a huge selection of shirts, ranging from conservative oxfords to wild Italian silk prints. There was even a linen summer suit, the kind the late, great Colonel Sanders wore. There were cotton shaker sweaters, geometrics, and cashmeres. As for jackets and slacks, there was everything. They ranged from businessmen's M-Club to alpine loden; from doctors' golfwear to torn stone-washed denim. There were two highboy dressers. I pulled open the drawers of one of them. There were gray hooded sweats, rugbies, nylon joggers, knit polos, mesh T's, and windjammers. There were black dress socks, formal kneehighs, argyles, ankle-length weekenders, blue-banded athletics, and hiking ragknits.

There were enough costume changes for a repertory company. Or one chameleon government operative. The only way Reynolds could transport his wardrobe, should he ever send for it, would be in a eighteen-wheel moving van full of steamer trunks.

I opened the top drawer of the other dresser. It was filled with Perdita's stuff, a wonderland of nighties, panties, and other ladies' garments that could have come from the Thousand Happinesses Limited line.

Natasha was staring at me from the bedroom doorway.

My God, I thought, I'm turning into Rafael.

I closed the dresser drawers, then went to the bedside phone and called Irene. I got her answering machine. I tried Grunion's office. The secretary said Mr. Grunion was in a meeting with his uncle and, no, Ms. Spinoza had not returned with Mr. Grunion after the morning's voir dire. I frowned. Where the hell was she? I called her Hudson's office—no go. On the slimmest of hopes, I called Charles Finch's home, and recognized the voice of the young woman who answered—lithesome Terri of the bikini. Charles hadn't been home since leaving in the morning to give moral support at Irene's trial, she said. Rafael was there, making some overseas calls; did I have any message for him? I told her thanks, but I had no message for Rafael. I hung up the phone. Charles and Irene were having lunch somewhere without me. I had a sinister mental picture of Charles flicking his damnable mustache while he gave Irene moral support.

Natasha and I went back downstairs.

Perdita and Biswanger were in the kitchen. Biswanger had decided to search for evidence in the refrigerator. His mouth was full and he had the door open and was examining a flat loaf of chocolate-colored whole-grain bread.

Perdita paced around, distracted. "It's authentic Afghan bread made from Afghan wheat," she said. She sat down and absent-mindedly ruffled Natasha's fur. "He told me it was possible I was descended from the Byrds of West Virginia. We were going to Princess County to investigate original sources together."

Biswanger broke off a piece of the bread and tried it. "Mmm-mmm, good." He put a slice of salami on it. Even better. "And what's this?" he asked taking out something that looked like a hunk of plaster.

"Dried milk curd," she said. "You soak it in hot water and get Qurt. You can make a stew out of it with veggies and lamb."

Listening to the two of them I thought, what the hell is this? The Betty Crocker Recipe Exchange? The next thing I

expected was the Pillsbury dough boy to come bouncing in.
I heard a key in the front doorlock. Uh-oh, I thought. There's an alarm system and its summoned the cops.
Instead of the Pillsbury dough boy, Reynolds came staggering in. He was unshaven, disheveled, and his shoes were covered with dust.
Natasha bounded over to him, wagging her tail.
"Hello, Natasha," he said in a surprised, hoarse voice, and collapsed onto the sofa.
"Darling," Perdita cried, rushing to him. "What happened? Where have you been?"
"I was kidnapped."
"You poor baby," she said, raining kisses on him.
"Rafael?" I asked.
"Charles Finch," Reynolds croaked. "Would someone get me something cold to drink?"

Since late Saturday, Reynolds had been locked up at the Cuddly-Wuddles boarding kennels.
"Charles asked me to meet him for a drink at the Campus Inn on the pretext of doing a deal," said Reynolds, recounting his tale from a reclining position on the sofa. Perdita had bathed his fevered brow, gotten him into a robe, and pumped him full of ginger ale and orange juice. "Charles said since we were both after the same thing, we should pool our resources. I knew he was lying. Unfortunately, by the time I found out the reason for the meeting was to get me out of the way, it was too late. He put something in my drink. A veterinarian has easy access to heavy tranquilizers, you know. When I regained consciousness, I was on a concrete slab in a chain-link enclosure. I heard dogs barking, and I realized where Charles had taken me. The drug screwed up my coordination, so even though I am a graduate of picks

and locks, I was not able to escape until this morning. Charles had taken my wallet and keys, and there I was, stranded in open country between Chelsea and Ann Arbor. It took a while getting a hitch back. Fortunately, on M 14 a fellow stopped his Mercedes and gave me a ride."

"With you looking like that?" Perdita exclaimed.

"He still remembered the sixties."

"How did you get a key to the front door?" Biswanger asked.

"I keep a spare buried on the premises. How did you get in?"

"Kitchen window," said Perdita. "When you disappeared like that, we thought something might have happened to you."

"And here I find you all waiting for me." He petted Natasha. "It's very gratifying to be missed."

Since Reynolds's harrowing escape from Cuddly-Wuddles had given him a sentimental regard for us, none of us—Perdita, Biswanger, nor I—mentioned our previous suspicions that had brought us to his house. It was now obvious beyond a doubt that Reynolds was the good traveler that Abdur Rahman had talked about.

Reynolds gazed at Perdita. "An experience like this gives one time to re-evaluate one's priorities about one's career and one's significant others."

The twin lights of hope and desire danced again in her eyes. "And Princess County?"

"I have a leave coming up."

Biswanger said to me, "This makes Charles the one."

Something clicked in my head. Charles had kidnapped Reynolds to get him out of the way. Out of the way to do. . . what? I didn't like the logical implication. I called Irene's number again.

Nothing. Just her answering machine. Then it occurred to me that there might be a message on *my* answering machine. I called my own number, and used my beeper to signal my answering machine to replay its messages back over the line. I listened to Emily Biswanger telling me Perdita was looking for me; then an excited Ms. Linda Leung calling from the Thousand Happinesses Limited Sales and Distribution office in Singapore, saying she'd call back around eight tonight, U.S. Central Standard Time; then a Shearson-Lehman-Hutton hustler inviting me for a talk about my financial future. (Hah!) And then, Charles Finch's voice. He said simply, "Call this number."

"Son of a bitch," I muttered.

"George," Biswanger said sharply. "Who are you calling now?"

"Charles."

"I don't think that's wise."

"Irene left the court with Charles this morning, and I haven't been able to locate her since. He left me a message to call him at a number I don't recognize. It's not his home and it's not his vet hospital. I think he's kidnapped Irene."

Reynolds got up from the sofa and put his hand down on the telephone cradle, interrupting my call. "First, let me turn on the recorder."

Reynolds went to his desk and did something with his computer keyboard. I heard electronic noises. Then he unlocked a file cabinet and took out three telephone headsets. Reynolds seemed to have everything the well-equipped field operative needed. Maybe Reynolds thought he was descended from Thomas Jefferson; and maybe he also saw himself as an Afghan rebel leader. All right, so maybe he was crazy. But it was nice he was on our side. After hooking up the three headsets so that he, Biswanger, and Perdita could listen in, Reynolds gave me the okay sign.

Natasha pawed his leg and said, "Wuff."

"What is it, girl?" Reynolds asked.

"Wuff."

"If you don't give her a headset, too," I explained, "she'll keep making a fuss."

Reynolds got out a fourth headset, adjusted it to Natasha's doggy cranium, lifted her ears, and put it on her. She settled down on the floor to listen.

"You'd better hook it up," I said.

"How can she know the difference?"

"She'll know."

Reynolds hooked up Natasha's headset.

I called the number again. I waited with sweating palms while it rang. Where oh where was Irene?

"Hello?" said Charles.

"Where's Irene," I demanded.

"I see you've figured it out. Good for you, old chap."

"If you harm one hair on her head..."

Reynolds made signs for me to cool it.

"Only a fool makes threats when he can't back them up," Charles said coolly. "I want the rug."

"What rug?"

"Come now, George. You think I was fooled by that pitiful story about a mysterious bank-account number in a doorknob? Really! It told me you knew there *was* a bank account. The rug is no good to you, because you don't know the code, or you'd have gotten the money by now."

I realized that Irene had told Charles a whopper. It was keeping her alive and buying time. "All right," I said, trying to sound defeated. "But why didn't you just steal the rug from my place this morning and leave Irene alone? You'd already broken into her place to plant those drugs."

"Oh, I didn't do that. I sent Rafael. He's the expert on break-ins."

Even though Rafael had kidnapped me, I was disappointed to learn he had not acted like a gentleman. "And then you sent him to plant the bomb in Irene's car."

"No, I did that. Rafael refused."

I felt better about Rafael.

"Odd, that," Charles mused. "If I didn't know better, I'd say Rafael was growing sentimental. I certainly couldn't send him to your place for the rug, now could I. He'd know it was valuable, and take it for himself and keep it until he found out why."

"The rug is out being cleaned," I said.

"Bullshit, George. Oh, by the way, I have that Reynolds character tucked away for safekeeping, so don't get any ideas about heroics."

Reynolds whispered to Perdita and Biswanger, "He doesn't know I escaped!"

"Perhaps I should check in on him," Charles said idly, "and see that he is watered and all that. Hee hee hee hee." Charles cackled at what he thought was his own private joke, since he assumed Reynolds was still locked in the kennel.

Winking at Reynolds, I said into the phone, "I don't give a damn about Reynolds. Is Irene okay?"

"Pretty as a picture. Though not at all pleased with her accommodations. Hee hee hee hee."

"Then Reynolds can rot."

"That's the spirit."

"I want to speak with Irene."

"You'll see her when you bring me the rug."

"Where?"

"I'll tell you where to deliver it when I'm ready. Expect my call around midnight."

"Why midnight?" I asked, remembering that was when Charles had killed Miles Dixon.

"Why not midnight?"

"I was hoping Irene and I could have an early dinner and catch a movie."

"Bravo, George. I must say, George old boy, this conversation is a revelation. Too bad our friendship has to end like this."

"What about Irene's murder charge? Her trial resumes day after tomorrow."

"So it does. Ah, but not to worry. You've got *Grunion*."

"You swine!"

"Hee hee hee hee."

"You're twirling your mustache, aren't you!" I shouted into the telephone.

"Hee hee hee hee."

The line went dead.

"I'll kill him," I fumed.

"First we have to find him," Biswanger said gravely, removing his headset.

Reynolds was at his computer again. "Charles wouldn't have given the number to you unless it's a public phone," he said, tapping away at the keyboard, "or unlisted . . . it's unlisted. The address. . . there we are. The address is Cuddly-Wuddles Drive in Chelsea."

"You do that very well," said Biswanger.

Reynolds shrugged modestly. "A link to the telephone company's electronic directory." He leaned back and stared at the ceiling. "Cuddly-Wuddles Drive," he repeated. "Now why is that address familiar?"

"Because it's the Cuddly-Wuddles boarding kennels!" I said.

I was overwhelmed with need for Irene. My fear for her

was a piercing pain in the area of the heart. How could I save her? How could I hang onto Charles to prove he was the one who killed Miles Dixon?

"I can't let that bastard escape and leave Irene high and dry," I declared. "I'm going to Cuddly-Wuddles to see if she's there."

"Shouldn't we enlist Clancy and Freiday," said Biswanger. "We have a tape of your conversation with Charles."

"They'll have to get a warrant. Can you hear them telling Wusthof, 'We think the murder suspect is being held prisoner at a dog kennel of a family friend because he wants their afghan rug.' And Wusthof says, 'For Christ's sake, tomorrow's the fourth, and you want me to go to the judge with that? She's skipped bail. Go check it out.'"

"And they'll check it out," said Biswanger.

"Sure. They drive up in their patrol car to Cuddly-Wuddles, and say, 'Excuse us, but did you happen to see Ms. Irene Spinoza?'"

"I still think we should have professionals in on this," said Biswanger.

"Sir," said Reynolds. "I *am* a professional."

"Who got drugged and locked in a dog kennel," Biswanger reminded him.

"And escaped," Reynolds reminded Biswanger in turn.

"We're going there," I said forcefully, "only we'll be there before midnight."

"What if Charles calls when we're there," asked Biswanger the pessimist.

Amateurs, I thought. "Haven't you heard of call forwarding? We'll use the radio phone."

"Bring the rug just in case," said Biswanger. "And don't breathe a word to Emily, or she won't let me go."

"My lips are sealed," said Reynolds.

15

It was half past six when I pulled into my reserved bay and discovered Rafael's car parked in the adjacent bay, with Rafael waiting inside. Thinking, Now what? I put Natasha on her leash and got out of the car. Rafael got out of his car. In two and a half hours Biswanger and Reynolds were coming by with the van for our assault on Cuddly-Wuddles. Preparatory to zero hour, I wanted to go up and soak in a hot tub instead of wasting time dealing with Rafael's contorted obsessions about Irene.

Rafael walked stiffly over to me. On his face was a dangerous mixture of taut expectancy and sincerity.

Without even a preliminary hello he said, "What does Irene say to my proposal?"

"I haven't had a chance to present it to her."

"The trial recessed this afternoon. You have had ample time."

"I haven't seen her since then. Now if you'll excuse me, my time is not ample."

Rafael leveled his automatic. "Do not try to play me for a fool, Mr. Spinoza."

Not again, I thought. I was dealing with a man who judged the fall of a leaf with regard to its possible effect on his dignity. "I have not seen Irene since our conversation this morning."

"You will take me to Irene."

I had a busy night ahead and was losing patience with the hopeful Latin lover. "If you must know, she's been kidnapped by Charles Finch. Now put the gun away."

"Again you try to play me for a fool. You will take me..."

"Bloody hell," I muttered.

Rafael looked shocked. "There is no reason for profanity."

"And there is no reason to continue this idiotic conversation." Praying that Natasha would not roll over to have her belly rubbed, I jerked her leash and said, "She is a trained attack dog. I am going up to my home. Good-bye."

"Do not play me for a—EEE-AAAH!"

To my astonishment, Natasha had opened wide her considerable mouth as if to yawn, and clamped her considerable teeth around Rafael's gun forearm. She did not waste energy growling or snarling. A practitioner of the philosophy of minimum force, she just held tight while Rafael yelled blue murder. Only when the gun skittered across the floor into a dark recess of the parking bay did she release him and run into the bay after the gun. She pranced back with it in her mouth. I patted her head and took it from her.

"Good girl."

"Wuff."

Along the length of the barrel, chiselled into the metal, it said *Kirikkale Tufek Fb. Cap 9 mm*. I shivered.

Rafael was curled up into a ball on the concrete, clutching his arm. "I'm bleeding! Get an ambulance!" he cried.

I didn't see any blood. "You shouldn't pull guns on people. Take off your jacket and we'll have a look."

"Keep her away from me. Ouch. I'll do it."

With much grimacing and ouching, Rafael gingerly pulled

off his suit-jacket and rolled up his shirt-sleeve. The marks on his forearm were bruises rather than puncture wounds. Natasha had a very accurate touch. Nevertheless, Rafael was distraught, I supposed as much from the assault on his dignity as physical discomfort.

"Why do you doubt my sincerity?" he said sorrowfully. Keeping a cautionary eye on Natasha, with his uninjured hand he reached into the breast-pocket of his folded suit-jacket and withdrew a black velvet jewelry box. He opened it. The diamond on the heavy pendant was very large. "See?" he said.

"Wow," I said.

"And look." He opened the trunk of his car. Inside was yet another box of orchids, and a wooden crate of exotic fruits nestled in tissue paper. "From the cloud forests of Colombia."

"Wow."

"A small token of what awaits Irene in Medellin. Now do you believe in my sincerity?"

"Rafael, will you get it through your thick skull that Charles has kidnapped Irene?"

I took him up to my place to bandage his arm.

"Ouch, ouch, ouch," he said as I swabbed on alcohol.

"Natasha's had all her shots," I assured him.

"Would a cup of revivifying coffee be possible? Colombian, if you have it."

I made coffee and heated some coffee cake.

"Explain, please," said Rafael, "why Charles should kidnap Irene? She is no threat to his business enterprises."

At that moment, I realized three things. First, that Rafael was the go-between for the drug-money people and Charles Finch's laundering operation. Second, that Rafael knew nothing about the Afghan bank account. And third, that having Irene up for the murder suited Rafael as well as Charles, because it might force her to be his queen of heaven in Medellin.

I said, "Charles wants my afghan rug. He kidnapped Irene to force me to give it to him. As soon as he gets the rug, he's going to leave the country."

Rafael looked skeptical. "I know Charles is a dedicated collector, but that is extreme."

"It's a very special rug. Look, tonight some friends and I are going to rescue Irene. When she's safe and sound, you can make your offer to her yourself. Okay?"

"Okay. I'll be at Charles's house on the river. May I have my gun back?"

I didn't want Rafael screwing anything up. "After Irene is safe and sound. I have to know something. How do you get all the stuff?"

"Pardon?"

"The big box of flowers you left for Irene the last time. The stuff in your car. I give a lot of business parties. Who is your importer?"

"I don't have one. I smuggled it on a plane of drug shipments."

"I thought you said you resented people assuming you were into drugs just because you are Colombian."

"I do resent it. In my case, it happens to be true."

My curiosity knew no bounds. "In the course of your business, have you ever killed anyone?"

"Killed? No. Though once I shot a man I found with my wife. He recovered. The courts were of course on my side."

"You are divorced?"

Rafael looked shocked. "My religion does not permit that. I am a family man, Mr. Spinoza. My wife and my five beautiful children live in Bogota."

My mind boggled. "And Irene will be your queen of heaven in Medellin?"

"I am observing all the proper forms. Irene will live like a queen."

"Irene will be interested to hear all about that. How did an educated man like yourself get involved in money laundering?"

"It is *because* of my education. I studied accountancy here at the university's business school."

I shouldn't have been surprised. "Papa Doc" Duvalier of Haiti had been a graduate of the University of Michigan School of Public Health.

After Rafael departed, I was able to devote all my energies to worrying about Irene's rescue. I had to put all extraneous matters out of mind. I got into a hot tub. The telephone rang.

I picked up my Rolex and saw it was three minutes after eight. Reynolds and Biswanger weren't due until nine. Had there been a hitch? I put on my terry robe and took the call on my workroom extension.

It was Linda Leung of Thousand Happinesses Limited, calling again from Singapore as she'd said she would. I listened politely while she rhapsodized over my offer to market the Lotus Flex-a-Pleaser I'd redesigned as a mousse-maker. My design specifications, she chirped, were pure genius. Biswanger's terms were entirely satisfactory. She assured me the Thousand Happinesses Limited factories were prepared to manufacture however many mousse-makers I should require.

I listened politely, assuring her I had complete faith in their quality-control procedures, thanked her for her support, hung up, and thought, *Irene, Irene.*

I had to relax. To lull my mind, I returned to the tub and started reading the Ann Arbor *News*:

Court to Rehear Challenge to Rule-Change Ban

The Federal appeals court, which last February struck down the U.S. Army's ban on a rule allowing the continuance of a ban on inquiries into rule-setting procedures, nullified that ruling today and agreed to a rehearing.

No date has been set for the rehearing before the 11-member panel of the 25-judge court. Said a spokesperson for the Army: "The hearing may be rendered moot because we have been unable to find the original rule-setting procedure referred to in the inquiry."

And another important story:

Director Takes Honors

The renowned director Stanislaus Richter has been named this year's recipient of the Luciano Fabiano award for his contribution to cinema. The award is the highlight of the annual conferral of the Fabiano prizes.

Coincidentally, Luciano Fabiano was named as the recipient of the Stanislaus Richter Award at last month's Richter festival in Belize, as best producer for *Persona Non Grata*, which he co-produced with Richter.

The world is going mad, I thought, and so will I until I get Irene back.

The telephone rang again.

"Charles here," the hated voice announced jauntily. "Time to make the exchange."

"Now? You said midnight."

"So I did. You sound cranky, George. You didn't have anything planned between now and midnight, did you?"

The bastard was jerking me around so I wouldn't have

time to plan anything. "I was taking a bath," I said idiotically.

"Well, dry behind your ears, put on your Sunday best, and bring the rug to Cuddly-Wuddles Drive."

Cuddly-Wuddles Drive! Despite the last-minute shuffle, I was elated for the confirmation that Charles was holding Irene at the boarding kennel. I'd last been there two years ago. I played dumb and asked, "Where the hell is Cuddly-Wuddles Drive? Down by the dinky dell?"

"Off the I 94 Chelsea exit going north on M 52. You'll recognize it when you get there. Hee hee hee."

"Irene better be okay."

Charles hung up. I immediately phoned Reynolds. His *hello* sounded cranky.

"I was taking a bath," Reynolds said.

"Forget the bath," I said. "Forget Biswanger and forget the van. Charles just called from Cuddly-Wuddles. He wants me to leave now to make the exchange. Get in your Porsche and get here as fast as you can. You're going to get us to Cuddly-Wuddles before Charles expects me to arrive."

I quickly dressed in jeans, a pullover, and jogging shoes. I rolled up the rug and tied it with sisal twine, then dragged it out to the elevator with Natasha in tow.

Reynolds's Porsche vroomed into the garage and eased to a stop like an F 14 in a hangar.

Reynolds climbed out and helped me stuff the afghan rug behind the two seats. It was our insurance should anything go wrong. I noticed he was wearing racing gloves. The only place for Natasha was back there on top of the rug. I told her, "Come on girl, we're going for a ride to find Irene," and she clambered in without coaxing. She curled up on top of the rug roll with her long legs folded like a carpenter's rule. Her body blocked the rear window and her head projected forward between the two seat headrests. Fortunately, the side mirrors gave a panoramic rear view.

As Reynolds drove down Huron he went through a proud litany about his Porsche. There were six transmission ratios and he was using the second one. It had a broad powerband: low-engine-speed city driving was strong, he said, because of the staged turbocharger system. Once we got on the freeway, the second turbo would cut in at 4300 rpm, then I'd really see something.

Although the houses along Huron were whizzing by, the Porsche gave the impression of idling down a runway to position itself for takeoff. Natasha stared intently through the windshield and panted, looking for all the world like a car enthusiast anticipating an awesome ride.

As we went up the I 94 East onramp, Reynolds shifted with a quick fluid motion, and I heard the power of the Grand Prix come to life under the hood. I double-checked my seat belt.

It was exhilarating and terrifying. Trees were a blur. Road signs were flash cards. Other vehicles on the highway were stationary obstacles to be anticipated and whipped around. The odometer was a blur of advancing numbers. I didn't dare look at the speedometer. I'm doing this for Irene, I reminded myself as my heart hammered through my chest.

"There's usually a radar speed trap at the next overpass," I warned Reynolds as we streaked through the overpass, and in the next instant had lost it in the gathering twilight behind us.

Reynolds pointed to a red blinking light on the dashboard. "I've got the jammer on."

"A fuzzbuster?"

"No, a jammer. Like they use on jets to foil enemy radar beacons."

"Oh, *that* kind of jammer."

"Naturally, this one has more limited power, range, and capability, but it does the job."

I was impressed and heartened that our defense budget hadn't gone entirely down the rat hole. I screwed up my courage and searched among the dials for the speedometer, but my attention was drawn to two trucks ahead. The road hogs were occupying both lanes in typical behemoth arrogance. Cars were bunched up behind them. We were nearly upon them when I realized Reynolds was not braking.

Oh shit! my every cell cried in instinctive anticipation of my imminent annihilation. Natasha's warm panting was a roaring cataract in my left ear. In my final seconds I thought of Irene. I tried, my Love. I tried.

Reynolds tracked onto the shoulder. As we skinned by the trucks the Porsche experienced not the slightest sway nor disturbance from their wake. We sent gravel rooster-tailing high into the air, raining against their windshields. Both trucks blasted their horns.

I gave a hysterical laugh.

"Notice," said Reynolds with blithe confidence as he swung us back onto the highway, "how the control coupling on the four-wheel drive distributes power to the wheels in response to their dynamic loading."

"What will they think of next," I said.

"And note the absence of aerodynamic lift. Though I wish the seats had more lumbar support."

"There's always something," I said philosophically.

Behind us the outraged truck horns faded into the retreating horizon. I shed no tears for the damage their windshields had sustained. It was small justice for the times that uncovered asphalt carriers had sent tarry stones dinging against my car.

"I think we have a problem," said Reynolds.

And there's always something else, I thought. "What?"

"That loud thumping. Can't you hear it? Funny. My tire monitor shows no loss of pressure."

The thumping sounded familiar. I turned around, and relaxed. "That's Natasha wagging her tail."

Earlier that afternoon at Reynolds's house, Reynolds and I had drawn upon our respective memories and made a diagram of the Cuddly-Wuddles kennel layout. I had a rather good idea of the place because two years ago Irene and I had to fly to England on business concerning our *Hotel Rompé* licenses and we had boarded Natasha there for a week. When we dropped Natasha off, Charles had given us the grand tour. The kennel was laid out like a giant *H*. One leg of the *H* was the front office where the public brought and picked up their animals. The crossbar was dog housing and included a central kitchen, grooming, storage, janitorial, and an isolation room for ill animals. The other leg of the *H* was more dog housing. Chain-link runs jutted out from both sides of the housing buildings. There was even air conditioning for large heavy-coated breeds. Barbed wire topped the chain-link fence surrounding the building's perimeter to keep out thieves. To keep the four-legged inmates in, there were chain-link fences around and on the top of each outdoor exercise run. The gates slid rather than swung open to prevent any energetic animal from charging at the gate and bashing it wide open when the staff unlocked it. Cuddly-Wuddles also had an elaborate intercom system.

I hadn't realized before that a dog boarding kennel is built along the lines of a prison camp. Now as we drove along, I took out Rafael's automatic from my pocket. I was prepared to use it if I had to.

"What have you got there?" Reynolds asked.

"Natasha took it off Rafael this afternoon," I said. "I thought I'd hang onto it."

Reynolds took the pistol with his right hand and, keeping one eye on the road, examined it. "Hmm. It's a copy of the German Walther Model PP. Of Turkish manufacture."

"How can you tell?"

"It says so right here." Reynolds indicated the words chiseled on the barrel: *Kirikkale Tufek Fb. Cap 9 mm.* Still using only his right hand, he checked the clip in the grip. "It's empty," he observed.

"What!" Rafael had kidnapped me and menaced me with an empty gun. Not only that, it wasn't even an original. It was a Turkish knock-off. "May I use your phone?"

Reynolds obliged by detaching it from his jet console.

I called Charles Finch's house on the river. Terri answered, and I asked to speak to Rafael. He was delighted to hear from me. Was the news from Irene favorable?

"I haven't found her yet," I replied frostily. "Are you aware that your gun is loaded with an empty clip?"

"Of course. I never put bullets in it when I am in your country."

"Why not?"

"Surely that is obvious, Mr. Spinoza. I am a foreign national. A Colombian. I do not want to risk being apprehended carrying a loaded weapon." In the background Terri called playfully to Rafael. "Is that the only reason you called?" he asked me.

"Yes."

"I was in the hot tub. Please have the courtesy not to call again tonight unless it concerns Irene."

"When we get there," I said to Reynolds, "the locks and the guns are your department."

"We're there," said Reynolds, gliding up the Chelsea exit

ramp. He came smoothly to a stop at the stop sign, then turned north onto M 52. We had made record time. We glided by Chelsea Village Motors, and I saw by the banner that it was Ford Truck Bonanza Days.

16

CUDDLY-WUDDLES WAS IN A wooded area just outside of town before M 52 became Chelsea's Main Street. Reynolds parked off the shoulder inside the entrance of Cuddly-Wuddles Drive, and we got out. We were about half an hour earlier than Charles could reasonably expect me to arrive. Natasha shook herself and went into the long grass to relieve herself.

The sun had set and the air had a lingering red glow. The kennel was a few hundred yards ahead. There were fireworks explosions in the distance, which promptly set off a round of barking. Tonight was July 3rd. I could imagine what Cuddly-Wuddles was going to sound like on the fourth. Natasha returned to us at the car. She sniffed the damp evening air, turning her head fiercely this way and that, and I was reminded that Afghans had been hunting dogs of royalty. Did she detect the presence of Irene on the grounds? Was Charles near by? Was the smarmy bastard with Irene at this moment, guarding her till he thought I would arrive.

I hunkered down beside Natasha. "Where's Irene?"

Natasha became motionless except for her twitching nose. She held this alert stance, fairly vibrating with determination as she deployed her olfactory radar.

"That's it, girl. Find Irene."

Natasha charged up the drive, leaving me holding her unattached lease. I scrambled after her.

She went past the brightly lit entrance of the front office. Dogs were barking again. Dozens and dozens of them. So much for stealth and surprise. They were better than an electronic alarm system. I kept running, but by the time I reached the office entrance, I had lost sight of her. I had also lost Reynolds.

Standing in the open doorway beside a sign that said *Cuddly-Wuddles Boarding House* was a young woman in shorts and a halter top. Down at her feet a cat poked its head out.

"May I help you?"

Between huffs and puffs I said, "My dog seems to have gotten away."

She looked at the leash I was holding. "That often happens with new boarders. You take 'em out of the car, they smell the other dogs and take off."

The girl was vaguely familiar, but I couldn't place her. The kennel dogs were still barking. Unlike an alarm system, they couldn't be switched off. I looked farther up the drive. Beyond the exercise paddocks was another building. I asked, "What's up there?"

"Our new north wing. Don't worry. Your dog can't get out except where you came in. What breed?"

"Afghan."

"They cover ground fast all right." The girl was staring at me with a disturbing intensity. "Is this your first visit to us?"

I thought fast. "Actually, I'm leaving town the day after tomorrow. Natasha is very sensitive. She had a checkup Saturday, and Charles suggested I accustom her to the place first, before I check her in. The yellow pages said you have a twenty-four-hour intake, and I had time, so I brought her here tonight to see how she'd react. I'd better go after her."

"Aren't you George Spinoza? Irene Spinoza's ex?"

"Yes," I said reluctantly.

"Oh, wow." The girl's stare relaxed. "I *thought* I recognized you. *Hotel Rompé* is my absolute favorite game. Me and Steve—he's my boyfriend—we play it after his shift." She giggled. "It really gets him going."

"That's nice."

"I recognized you from the TV news," she went on, apparently starved for someone to talk to. "Are you really standing by your ex-wife through the dark and stormy night of her personal hell?"

"Yes."

"Then why are you leaving town the day after tomorrow?"

"To pursue a new lead for Irene's case. I leave no stone unturned, nor spare any expense. If you'll excuse me. . . "

"Oh, wow. I wish Steve was here to hear you say that."

Her *oh, wow* was very familiar; I was sure I knew her from somewhere. "Have we met?" I asked.

"You met my sister, Terri. I'm Gerri. We're twins. Not identical, though. Terri told me about that party Dr. Finch gave. Oh,wo-o-ow. Talk about your coincidences. Dr. Finch is here tonight."

"That's some coincidence all right," I said, keeping my voice down because the door was open.

"Dr. Finch isn't ordinarily here, but tonight he's staying so the night staff can go to the pre-Fourth of July celebration. Is he some kind of boss, or what?"

"He's one in a million."

"I was about to leave when you showed up."

"Don't let me stop you. I'll go find Natasha."

Another series of fireworks explosions went off somewhere in town. There followed a chorus of sharp yelps, barks, and yowls from inside the kennel that echoed off the concrete runs and rebounded in multiple stereo. Gerri turned around and hollered into the kennel, "All right, you guys. Stop acting stupid."

Amazingly, the barking decreased a few decibels to merely deafening. I had to get away and join Natasha and Reynolds to find Irene. "I've held you up long enough," I said, moving off.

"Why don't you leave Natasha here tonight, so you won't have to drive here again to drop her off?"

"Gee, I don't know about tonight. Loud noises make her jumpy."

"The new north wing has soundproofing. It's state-of-the-art. Outside and inside runs. Dr. Finch hasn't opened it to boarders yet. . . "

"Darn."

". . . but seeing as you're a close personal friend, I'm sure he will. I'll tell him you're here." Gerri turned to go inside.

"No!" I said, too abruptly, for she gave me a puzzled look. I smiled. "I wouldn't want Charles to open an entire state-of-the-art kennel for one dog on my account. Please don't bother."

"It's no bother. Really."

"But you were just leaving," I reminded her.

"Dr. Finch would never forgive me. Come inside. It'll only take a moment to call him on the intercom."

I was up against implacable midwestern kindliness. Pointing at a right angle from the direction of the north wing, I said, "I think Natasha went that way. I'll go find her and bring her here."

"Don't you want to say hi on our new state-of-the-art intercom?" Gerri called after me.

"Charles and I will say hi later."

Gerri went inside, and I ran up the drive toward the new soundproofed kennel where Natasha had gone. A three-quarter moon lighted my way. Obviously, Irene was locked inside. There wasn't much time. Where the hell was Reynolds?

The north building had to be the very latest in self-contained kennel construction: one and a half stories, accommodating double-decked pens. The pens connected via guillotine doors to the outside runs. Awning windows were placed high on the walls, just underneath the eaves of the long gabled roof. The architect must have said, no dog is going to escape from *this* place.

I called to Natasha, hoping her sensitive hearing would pick me out from the damned barking. A small spot of light waved at one end of the building, and I heard Reynolds.

"Yo, George."

I went over. Reynolds was crouched at the door. Natasha stood beside him, panting expectantly. He held a small penlight between his teeth with the light focused on the double sliding-bolt locks he was working on. He seemed frustrated.

"Id day-ging doo long," he groused.

"What?"

He unlocked his jaws and removed the flashlight. "It's taking too long."

"But you escaped from here before."

"From an outside run. It had a simple padlock."

"Then let's go *in* through an outside run."

Reynolds clapped his hand to his forehead and stood up.

The three of us hurried around the corner to the dog runs that jutted out from the building. They were also enclosed in chain-link fence, sides and top. In less than a minute Reynolds had the padlock off one of them and was sliding open the gate. Where the run abutted the building wall there was a dog-sized guillotine door to the interior pen. I raised the door; Reynolds got down on his hands and knees and crawled into the building. Natasha and I waited outside in the run. There were metallic noises as Reynolds worked on the inside pen.

Finally Reynolds poked his head out the guillotine door. "It's open." He disappeared back inside.

I held up the guillotine door, let Natasha in, and followed her. I felt smooth, fiberglass under my hands and knees. Guided by Reynolds's penlight, I crawled through the pen to the interior door he had opened, and out onto a cold, hard surface. I stood up.

My eyes adjusted in the moonlight filtering down from the high windows. We were in a long corridor that ran the length of the building. Lining it on both sides were rows of double-decker cages, like a doll house Alcatraz. Natasha bounded off. Her toenails scrabbled on glazed tile as she disappeared into the ghostly half-shadows.

I heard Natasha's bark echo from the far end. And then the excited voice of Irene.

"Natasha! What are you doing here?"

"Irene!" I called."

"Georgie?"

"It's me," I said, and took off, expecting Charles Finch to step out from the shadows at any moment.

I found Natasha standing with her front paws up against a second-tier pen. Irene was padlocked inside.

Irene curled her fingers through the chain links and said, "Georgie, sweetheart?"

"Yes, darling?"

"Get me the hell *out* of here."

While Irene and I exchanged kisses through the chain

links and Natasha slurped us both, Reynolds expedited the lock. I lifted Irene down to the floor and held her, loving her more than my own life.

"Darling, are you all right?" I asked for the twelfth time.

"Do you have anything with sugar in it?"

I had a mashed Mounds bar in my pocket. Reynolds had breath mints, and oddly, a plastic bag of dried apricots, apples, and dates. Irene eagerly took it all. Clearly, she was famished. My wrath roiled, and I silently cursed the person of Charles Finch—disembowelment was too good for the smarmy bastard.

I said, "We have to hurry. By now Gerri's told Charles I'm here."

At the mention of Charles Finch, Irene let loose a stream of blue language, the gist of which was that disembowelment was definitely too good for the smarmy bastard. "He must have slipped something into my drink when we were waiting for you at the restaurant," Irene said as we hurried down the corridor to the other pen through which Reynolds, Natasha, and I had gained entry. "It made me like a zombie. When I came out of it, locked in there, I was scared. Then I got tired of being scared and I got mad. I also was mad at myself for trusting the S.O.B. Why didn't I believe George, I kept thinking. George never liked him." Irene was half babbling, delirious in regaining her freedom. "I never lost faith, George. I knew you'd come for me. Who's Gerri?"

"Terri's twin sister. Terri is Charles's little friend at his river house."

"I remember."

"Gerri doesn't know what's been going on. Well, only what she sees on TV. As far as she's concerned, Charles is a prince among men."

"And Terri?"

"I think she's put two and two together and is going to wind up with Rafael. Charles's business partner. Actually, he's an accountant. He's been giving Charles the drug money to launder. It's a long story. Rafael is the one who sent you all those flowers. He's hot for you."

"Oh, him."

"You know about Rafael?"

"Only that I sensed something from him that afternoon at the brainstorming party before you arrived."

"He's got a wife and five kids in Colombia."

One by one, we crawled through the pen to the outside run and out the sliding gate. We weren't out of the woods yet. In fact, we were going into the woods for cover. Charles Finch had killed Miles Dixon; he could kill again. A breeze had risen. Natasha trotted ahead, leading us through the undergrowth. We kept out of sight of the drive and skirted the front office, which was still brightly lit. We went around an asphalted area where Charles's Jaguar was in a spot marked *Reserved for Director*. But there was no sign of Charles. Was he in the north wing discovering that, despite all his vile duplicity and contrivances, his hostage had escaped? If so, I hoped he was having an epitaxic fit.

The moonlit drive was clear where we had left Reynolds's Porsche parked on the shoulder. Natasha stopped. She refused to go farther.

"Charles must be around," Irene whispered.

I didn't see him, but that didn't mean anything. I signaled Irene and Reynolds to stay back.

"Where are you going?" Irene whispered.

"To smoke him out, if he's here."

"George, don't be crazy."

"We can't stay here all night," I replied, and fastened the leash onto Natasha.

Natasha clamped onto the leg of my jeans and pulled me back.

"It's okay, girl," I said.

Apparently she didn't think so, for she refused to budge.

"Then I'll do it alone. Cover me," I said to Reynolds.

"With what?"

"Your gun, of course."

"What gun?"

"You're kidding."

"No, I'm not."

"But you're CIA," I said in stunned disbelief.

"I'm State Department."

"For Chrissake, Reynolds. This is no time to split hairs. You're a federal agent."

"I still don't have a gun on me."

I had left Rafael's empty gun inside the Porsche because I'd assumed Reynolds had a loaded one. I rounded on him. "I wonder what Thomas Jefferson would have to say about this?"

"I must ask you not to patronize me. It is against department policy and a violation of professional ethics to kill potential witnesses, unless they're witnesses against us."

"Okay. What would an Afghan freedom fighter do in this situation?"

Reynolds thought a moment. "Ask for a truce, then when negotiations were under way, butcher his enemy the first chance he got, strip the body of all valuables, and leave the mutilated corpse for his other enemies to find."

I was getting nowhere fast. *We* were getting nowhere fast. I walked onto the drive. I continued walking toward the Porsche in full view of anyone who might care to see me. Yoo-hoo, Charles, I thought. It's me, George. If I ignored the barking and the fireworks explosions and the loud flub-dubbing of my heart, it was a lovely night. I waited. No Charles. I jumped up and down and waved my arms like a semaphore. No Charles. I went back to Irene and Reynolds.

"Okay?"

Reynolds was unlocking the Porsche door, when I realized Natasha wasn't with us. Charles strolled into view from outside the Cuddly-Wuddles entrance where he'd been waiting for us. His gun was trained on Reynolds.

"Stand clear of the car," he ordered.

Reynolds moved away from the open door.

"I see you found Irene without my help. Very resourceful."

Irene fixed a vengeful eye on him. "You stink on ice."

"The discommodation was necessary, my dear. Hee hee hee. I've sent Gerri on her way, so we can get on with our transaction. It was very wise of you to bring the rug, George. This splendid machine will be more than adequate replacement for my Jag, though I will miss it. Mr. Adams, you seem to have put the keys in your left pocket."

I realized Charles had waited till he was sure of getting the Porsche keys.

"Be good enough to toss the keys to me," Charles ordered. "Slowly."

Reynolds slowly took out his keys and dangled them at arm's length. "George, Irene," he said. "Go in opposite directions. Now!"

Irene darted off like a rabbit into the dark vegetation. I scrambled to the other side of the drive. I flopped onto my belly beneath the branches of a bush. Bits of grass stuck to my face and palms. I knew Charles had no compunctions against shooting Reynolds right then and there. I cautiously raised my head.

Charles's gun was wavering slightly back and forth. He steadied again on Reynolds. "Very commendable," he sneered. "But it doesn't change anything. The keys."

With a flick of his wrist, Reynolds flung the keys into a high arc. In the seconds that Charles reflexively followed their trajectory off the road into darkness, Reynolds sprinted in the opposite direction. He was rolling like a gymnast into high weeds as Charles brought his attention back to him. Reynolds disappeared into the night.

Charles fired after him. The percussions cracked the sky.

I pressed myself down into the ground. Please, God, I prayed. Please don't let Reynolds get hit. I don't care about the rug. Charles can have the lousy money in the Seychelles. I just want Irene.

A long minute passed while I listened to Charles tramping in the undergrowth in the general area where Reynolds had tossed the Porsche keys. I doubted that two gunshots would attract attention on a night alive with fireworks. Frustrated, Charles gave up the search with a curse. The next thing I heard was the sound of the Porsche door being opened. Then from inside the car came grunts, some metallic scraping noises, a loud beeping alarm sound, and more curses. The noises stopped.

Reynolds had equipped his Porsche with security systems. I doubted it was susceptible to being hot-wired. Cautiously, I raised my head again for a look.

Charles seemed to have reached the same conclusion. He was facing backward on the driver's seat, struggling to get my afghan rug out from behind the seats. It had been a chore for both Reynolds and me to maneuver the rug in, and during our trip to Cuddly-Wuddles, Natasha's weight had wedged the rug firmly in place. Charles spitefully smashed his gun into the rear window. It didn't help.

I heard branches rustling close by. The wind? A nocturnal animal? I felt a wet nose against the back of my neck. I rolled over to find Natasha panting in my face. Irene was tiptoeing toward me. Natasha had led her to me.

"Good girl," I whispered, feeling a newer, deeper appreciation of her canine wisdom. I got a slurp.

Irene crouched down and crept under the bush next to me. "Darling," she whispered with her lips touching my ear, "are you okay?"

I placed my mouth against her ear and breathed, "Tiptop."

Irene whispered, "I'm afraid Reynolds isn't tiptop."

"Oh, no!" I whispered. I had a vision of Reynolds lying in the dark, manfully stifling his moans from his gunshot wounds. "How bad is he?"

"He threw his back out from that tumble."

Inadequate lumbar support in the Porsche seat, I thought ruefully, recalling our wild ride to Cuddly-Wuddles.

Irene whispered, "He's going back to the kennel office to call the local cops."

"Charles can easily escape before they get here. We have to disable his Jag."

Leaving Charles to struggle with the rug, we stealthily got out from under the bush and began sneaking back toward the main kennel with Natasha. To my previous prayer for Reynolds's health, our safety, etc., I now appended an update: as a reward for his efforts to dislodge my afghan rug, Charles should incur a double hernia.

We went straight to the Jaguar. Irene lost no time in breaking the driver's window, unlocking the door, pulling the hood-lock lever, then going around and lifting the hood. The mad fires of vengeance flickered in her face as she surveyed the luxury engine.

"Uh, Darling," I said. "Don't do anything we can't put right in a hurry."

"Why not?"

"Reynolds threw away the Porsche keys. The Jag is our only ready transportation out of here."

Irene had to satisfy herself with removing the distributor cap. Natasha was sniffing the wind. She nudged me and gave me a warning, "Wuff."

This time I believed her. We hurried to the kennel building entrance where I'd encountered Gerri.

The front reception area had a broad counter dividing the waiting area from the clerical area. There were glass-fronted cases with pet supplies, and a tall case displaying dog-show trophies. A life-sized ceramic Pekinese stood on a table with brochures and magazines.

In a low voice I called, "Reynolds? Yoo-hoo."

There was a chorus of barking, through which I heard Reynolds yell, "Over here!" It sounded as though he was in the same room.

"Where?" I asked frantically.

"Behind the transom."

I went through the spring-loaded door section, and found Reynolds lying supine on the floor with an office phone beside him. He was holding his right bent knee up against his chest.

From his odd position he greeted me with, "Charles disconnected the PBX and the outside lines. We'll have to call out on my car phone."

"If he's left it in one piece," I said gloomily. Reynolds remained on the floor, so I asked, "Why are you lying on the floor like that?"

"My back is in a spasm. If I lie like this, I can usually stretch it out in about fifteen minutes."

"We don't have fifteen minutes. Can you make it to the Jag?"

Reynolds changed legs, bent his left knee and then held it

with clasped hands against his chest. He straightened it out and tried to get up. His face contorted into something resembling a bent canvas shoe.

"No," he gasped.

"We don't have two minutes," Irene said, hurrying from the front entrance. "I spotted Charles. He's dragging the rug with him."

The no-good rotter had gotten it out of the Porsche. He hadn't wanted to take the chance of us getting it before he drove his Jag to the Porsche, so he was taking the rug to the Jag. When Charles discovered the Jag wasn't going anywhere without its distributor, he'd come after us.

I ran to the other side of the transom to the trophy case and selected a nice heavy one, a massive cup sporting two dog heads for handles that pointed nose upward, like snooty ship prows facing away from each other. I grasped it by the column attaching it to the base and tried a practice swing. It had a good heft. It wasn't a gun, but it was better than nothing.

"George," Irene said, "what do we do about Reynolds?"

Reynolds couldn't move, and we had to get out of there. Fast. I had an idea.

If Charles could drag the rug, we could drag Reynolds. I grabbed a square plastic cushion from a chair, and went back to Reynolds. I knelt down and put the cushion under his head.

"Thanks," he said. "The floor is awfully hard."

"Keep it behind your head; it's going to be a bumpy trip," I said. I placed the trophy cup on his stomach, got up, and took hold of his left ankle. "Irene?"

She took hold of his right leg.

Together, Irene and I dragged him feet first from the reception room through the door into the kennel quarters.

The atmosphere was decidedly doggy, though not unpleasant, and certainly not as odoriferous as the upper seating of the Michigan Theater after a show. It was enchanting to Natasha. She pranced along, sniffing and saying hi to her caged counterparts.

We hauled Reynolds by his feet down the center walkway by the pens of dogs, who seemed fascinated with the spectacle of a man being slid past them on the floor with a dog-show trophy on his middle. The cushion protected his head from bumps and abrasions.

"Sorry to do this to your back," I shouted to Reynolds over the barking.

"On the contrary," Reynolds shouted back. "The stretch on my spine feels great. I spent two days in traction once. This is much better."

We were in the middle of the crossbar of the *H*-shaped kennel building. We came to a door marked *Grooming*. I looked inside. There was a table with clippers and shampoos, and a big bathtub. Stacked against the wall was a pile of clean mats for the dogs' cages. I thought about hiding Reynolds in the tub and putting mats over him, but since when did they pile mats in the tub? Charles would spot that ruse in a second. We dragged Reynolds onward to the kitchen and food-storage area.

There were shelves of canned dog food, mineral supplements, vitamins, medicines labeled with dogs' names and pen numbers, and stacks of stainless-steel bowls. Large stainless-steel bins were marked *Dry-small*, *Dry-medium*, *Dry-large*, and *Semi-Moist*. I opened the semi-moist bin. It was filled with packets of semi-moist dog food. Dry-small was full of small-sized dry-bulk kibble. Dry-medium was half full. Dry-large was nearly empty—enough space to hide Reynolds inside.

Reynolds groaned as Irene and I levered him up over the top and down into the dry-large bin.

From the front reception area there came a roar of outrage that cut through the barking: "What did you do to my Jag!"

"Never mind his Jag," Reynolds commented from the open bin. "What's he done to my Porsche?"

I shut the bin, grabbed the trophy, and Irene and I hightailed it toward the far wing, the second leg of the *H*.

17

The dogs were just as noisy in the far part of the *H*-building as in the other wings. The barking was making my ears ring. Charles was looking for us in the other wing. It was only a matter of time. The trophy I had brought from the front office was becoming heavier by the minute. Irene and I went in opposite directions to try the two exit doors. We returned to the middle and informed each other that the doors were locked.

I said, "We can't keep running. We have to do something."

"Especially since we're in a dead end," Irene observed.

I switched the trophy to my left hand. "Where's the distributor cap?"

"When we hid Reynolds, I hid it in the semi-moist."

"We need a plan," I declared.

"Let's kill the lights, so Charles can't use us for target practice while you think of one."

"Good idea."

"No, wait—we don't have a screwdriver," Irene said with sagging morale. "I don't even have a nail clipper on me. Charles took all my stuff."

"We'll use dog tags."

A miniature male schnauzer was looking up amorously

from his pen at Natasha. I put down the trophy and unlatched the door. The little guy launched himself at me in a paroxysm of joy. Free at last! Free at last! And a great big exotic Afghan to frolic with!

I slipped off his collar chain, and closed the pen. "Sorry, fella."

The light switches were at three locations. Two were at the locked exit doors we had checked. The third was in the middle where we had entered from the central connecting wing. Using the schnauzer's metal license and address tags, Irene and I removed the switch cover plates.

"Disconnect the line wire first," I called to her over the barking. "The top one."

"I know, I know," she called back. "I remodeled my place, remember? Don't forget to put the plate back on when you're done."

"I know, I know," I replied.

While we worked on the light switches, I assessed our situation. Charles had a gun. He had disconnected the kennel phone lines. He was not about to reconnect them and phone for Rafael to transport him and my rug out of Chelsea. He was going to shoot us to get the distributor cap to his Jag. The awning windows were high and escapeproof. The only way out was through a dog pen into an outside run, but the outside sliding gate would be padlocked, and with Reynolds unavailable in the kibble bin, we had no one to pick the lock for us.

With the last switch disconnected, the kennel wing was plunged into gloom. I opened an empty pen and hurried Natasha inside. Irene followed me into the pen. There was standing height, but we remained huddled together on the floor. I sat on some hard kibble, dry-medium by the feel of it. I got up and brushed it away. Since leaving the court at noon with Charles, Irene had been drugged, kidnapped, cooped up in a dog pen, rescued, chased through the woods, chased back through a kennel, and was now cooped up again in the dark, albeit this time with me for company. I didn't know how much more she could take. Charles was right. It was only a matter of time for Irene. Even if we did escape from Cuddly-Wuddles, her trial was resuming July 5th.

Irene said, "I hope Reynolds is all right. Have you thought of a plan?"

"I'm working on it. How about you?"

"Working on it—He's here!"

Charles was silhouetted in the entryway from the central wing. He flicked the useless light switch. "You can't stop the inevitable," he shouted over the dogs. "Tell you what. I'll do you a deal. Give me what I need for my Jag, and I'll be out of your lives."

"But not forgotten," Irene muttered.

Charles began to walk cautiously along the pens and peer into their darkened interiors. Canine eyes reflected back at his gun. "Come on, George old boy," he shouted. "It's only a matter of time before I find you. Irene? Talk some sense into him before my patience runs out."

I put my arm around Irene. "Yeah. Talk some sense into me."

"I think we have him on the run," she said, forcing a smile. "Psychologically."

"No kidding. How can you tell?"

"He isn't going hee-hee-hee anymore."

"This is your last chance," Charles bellowed. "I'm running out of good will."

We let his offer expire.

The gunshot echoed deafeningly through the kennel. Irene and I jumped. The dogs went wild.

Natasha was sensibly keeping low to the ground. She crept on her belly toward the guillotine door. I opened it and she went through to the outside run. Irene said something, but I couldn't hear her above the din. I cupped my mouth against her ear. "Psychologically," I said, "we just about have him whipped. Would you care to join me for a walk on the veranda?" We crawled through the guillotine door and joined Natasha outside in the attached run.

A cooling breeze blew away the doggy atmosphere of the kennel. The barking level was now tolerable, but the fireworks booming around Chelsea more than made up for it. Irene slumped tiredly against the fence. She stroked Natasha, who plumped herself down beside her for moral support.

I tapped my fist against the metal trophy. If only it were a gun that could fire bullets over a distance rather than being limited to an arm's length swing. Damn it. As much as I hated Charles, we needed him alive and talking. I thought of Reynolds in the kitchen area, and it occurred to me that since the support rooms in the central wing didn't have exterior doors, one of them would be a good place to lock Charles inside. I'd have to threaten him, and shoot him nonfatally if he didn't cooperate. If the trophy were a gun. Which it wasn't. All right, then. What did I have with me to make a weapon?

I looked around the run. The metal chain link was all one piece, bolted with heavy U-clamps to the galvanized posts sunk in the concrete. I turned my attention back to the trophy. It was heavy. It had a peculiar shape. If I couldn't get close enough to Charles to club him, how about throwing it at him? Hitting the gun out of his hand? No, the trophy was too clumsy for accuracy unless I got up close, and then I might as well bash him. If I could lure him. . . the trophy was too big to hide. I turned it around in my hands. A useless hunk of metal.

I became aware of Irene and Natasha watching me pace back and forth.

"We can't let Charles get away," I said, pacing back and forth.

"That's the spirit," Irene said.

I poked my head inside the guillotine door. Charles was still stalking us in the dark, getting more p.o.'d by the minute at being thwarted by our tactics. Eventually he'd know we weren't in any of the pens, and figure out we had to be outside in a dog run.

I got up and resumed pacing. I needed to make a weapon. I was a toy designer with a degree in fine arts and a cognate in mechanical engineering. What toy weapons might be effective against a gun? Javelins. Bows and arrows. Air guns. Rubber balls. Darts. Nothing like that in here. Toy darts were now safe, harmless rubber. Rubber darts. Hah. Soon they'd be making jump ropes with safety nets. What ten year old jumped rope anymore? They painted their hair purple and addled their senses with rock lyrics. Take away their electronic amplification, and they'd be forced to learn how to speak in complete sentences. What had happened to childhood? Toy companies promoted dolls of storm troopers and robotic death machines, while child psychopaths sold dope out of abandoned HUD houses and fought gun battles with real guns. Too bad the criminals weren't restricted to rubber darts and slingshots.

Of course!

I picked up the trophy again and examined the two snooty dogs with their noses in the air. Then I took off my shoes.

"Georgie, what are you doing?"

"I got you into this mess," I declared, "and I'm going to

get you out of it."

"You didn't get me into this mess," Irene generously pointed out.

"Let me have your bra."

"Georgie, are you feeling all right?"

I removed my jeans. "I feel fine. Hurry, sweetheart. There's no time to lose." I pulled down my briefs and stepped out of them.

"George, this is not the time for a quickie. Well, not out here."

It *was* chilly. Sans underwear I got back into my jeans, put my shoes back on, and proceeded to test the waistband of my briefs. "Sweetheart," I said, "I need the stretch elastic in your bra. If I hook it up to this trophy cup, it will make a dandy, deadly slingshot."

"Will it have enough impact? What about recoil?" Irene asked, immediately taking the idea and considering the ramifications.

"Industrial strength," I assured her. "Charles is going to get a whammy he won't forget. The recoil energy is proportional to the ratio of the mass of the projectile to the mass of the trophy. Newton's third law. The trophy is big and heavy, so I won't break my wrist."

"What about ammunition?"

"Dog kibble," I replied.

I sharpened the edge of the dog tag against the concrete while Irene removed her blouse. She was wonderfully fetching in the moonlight. When I was thirteen, I'd been a pretty good shot with my Whammo. Now I was working with a handful of dry-medium kibble and a dog trophy cup. I trimmed elastic from my briefs and Irene's bra. Then a quick sortie back inside the pen for kibble, and I was ready to practice firing against the fence posts with various widths and lengths of elastic tied to the two dog-handles.

Boom went the fireworks. Whang went the metal posts. When my test firing exploded the kibble into dust and made the metal sing, I had my slingshot calibrated for battle. I blessed Rafael's underwear fetish for giving me the idea.

I crawled through the guillotine door into the pen. In the faint light I could make out Charles about ten yards away. His back was toward me, and from his body language I could see he was frustrated and trigger-happy. I opened the pen door and rested the base of the trophy on the bottom lip. With all the barking, I didn't have to worry about being quiet. Angling my slingshot upward, I drew back the elastic and sighted on the back of Charles's noggin'—I had to hit him high so he'd think I was standing back in the dark somewhere.

I let fly. . . and scored a direct hit. One! Charles hollered as if he'd stepped on a rake. As he was turning round, his hand automatically going to the new meteor crater in his scalp, I reloaded with another kibble chunk and. . . two! He caught the second hit on the side of his jaw, shocking him even more and. . . three! A searing hit on his gun arm, not giving him time to think as he clutched simultaneously at the side of his face and back of his head. He fired the gun wildly and hit the ceiling. And four! A slicing hit to his ribs. Holding his arms around his head to protect himself, he ran in a weaving, blind crouch toward the central connecting wing from where he'd pursued us.

I got up from the dog pen, and in snappy succession I scored hits five, six, and seven on Charles's retreating hind end. His yowling was in harmony with the diapason of the barking dogs. Some were leaping into the air, biting at the metal mesh of their pens. They seemed to be cheering me on, urging me to run Charles to ground. He disappeared around the corner into the central connecting cross-wing of the kennel.

Irene and I cautiously followed Natasha toward the central wing. I was out of ammunition. We checked into nearby pens. Gerri and her coworkers kept things very tidy. Natasha was sniffing at something where Charles had been. I bent down to have a look. A trail of wet spots.

"I drew first blood!" I chortled to Irene. "If the dry-medium packs that kind of wallop, imagine what the dry-large ammo will do."

"A larger size will give more recoil and less penetration," Irene said.

I peeked around the corner down the central wing. "I don't see him."

"He could have ducked in anywhere. Grooming. The kitchen area."

"Yeah," I conceded. I thought of Reynolds in the dry-large kibble bin with all that lovely ammo. "Even inside a dog pen."

"Not Charles," Irene stated. She reached around and hit the nearby light switch for the central wing, dousing the lights in the half nearest us. A few seconds later, the far half went dark. "That doofus," she said gleefully. "Now we know he's down at the far end. If I can make it to the kitchen area, I'll toss you all the ammo you need. Did you notice any extra-hard chunks? The kind for controlling canine tartar."

I was appalled. "If *you* can make it?"

"Is something bothering you?"

Our success thus far had made her reckless. "Charles still has the gun," I explained patiently. "I didn't come this far to lose you."

"And it's all right if I lose you? How can you be so selfish? Or have you forgotten already that I'm facing a murder trial."

"I'm faster," I retorted.

"Wanna bet? I'll present a smaller target."
"So what? It's dark."
"Charles can switch on the light any time. I'm going," she said.
"Absolutely not," I said.
"Georgie," she said, her manner now placating, "it gives me a warm, secure feeling to know how much you care." She took off into the central wing, running low to the ground. Natasha sprinted off, too.

I went after them.

The reports of two gunshots echoed throughout the kennel. I flung myself onto the ground. Once again the dogs assaulted my hearing. It was hard to tell where the shots had come from. I couldn't see Charles. I half crawled, half scrambled to the kitchen area.

From inside his bin, Reynolds was handing dry-large kibble to Irene.

"You're all right!" I cried in relief.

"Of course we are," Irene snorted.

"Didn't you hear the gunshots?"

"Shots? There's so much barking and fireworks. . . where's your slingshot?"

In my haste, I had left it behind. "Back there. Where's Natasha?"

"I thought she was with you."

"She followed you," I said.

I poked my head out of the kitchen. I became aware of a commotion filtering through barking. At the top of my voice, I shouted, "All right, you guys! Stop acting stupid." And for a few precious seconds, the dogs were cowed into a lull. The sound of Charles, yelling and cursing, came through loud and clear. "Hear that?" I said, turning back inside. "It's coming from Charles's end of the wing."

The three of us stared at one another, sharing the same ghastly thought. Grunting painfully, Reynolds heaved himself up and climbed out of the bin. "If he's harmed one hair on your doggie..."

I sprinted back for the slingshot, then the three of us went warily toward the ruckus at the far end of the central wing.

Charles was in the front office, yelling blue murder and doing a hopping dance, alternately clutching at his sore butt, his sore head, and his tattered arm while providing his own musical accompaniment of ow-wow-ow's, goddammits, and ouches. His arm was freshly tattered by Natasha.

"What the hell kind of a dog have you raised?" he shouted when he opened his clenched eyes and saw us. "Sneaking up like that. Doesn't she know enough to bark? O-o-o-h, this hurts."

I put my slingshot down, and Natasha deposited Charles's gun into my hand. I patted her. "Good girl."

"Wuff."

"Oh, sure," Charles retorted. "*Now* you bark. You overbred bitch. I should have drowned you when you were whelped."

Natasha curled her lip and sneezed at him.

"Keep her away from me!" he shrilled.

"Good girl," said Irene.

Reynolds arrived, holding himself in a stiff posture so as not to move his back. "I see Natasha has things under control," he said, and lay down flat on his back beside my afghan rug.

I turned to Charles. "How do we reconnect the phones?"

"Fuck you. And fuck *you*," he said to Natasha.

Natasha was too much of a lady to reply. She stood at the ready, should Charles try anything.

Irene and I conferred with Reynolds down by the rug. He checked Charles's gun. It was empty.

I said, "We have to hold him here till we can get the police." I glanced up at Charles. Though in considerable physical discomfort, he was already showing signs of plotting how to turn the situation to his advantage.

Irene had an idea. "Georgie, help me unroll the rug." We did so, then she said to Charles, "Lie down at that end."

"The hell I will."

"Oh, Natasha. . . " I called.

Charles fairly flung himself onto the rug.

Irene and I took hold of the edge and started pulling it over him.

"Hey! What do you think you're doing?" he cried.

"Hoisting you on your own petard," Irene said.

Irene and I rolled Charles up in the rug. He lay there with just his head sticking out, complaining bitterly and promising dire consequences.

"I'll sue. When I'm done, you won't have a penny to your names. Assault. Kidnapping."

Reynolds wriggled over till he was nose to nose with Charles. "Base-born infidel," he said into Charles's face. "Son of a dog, you dare make threats?"

Natasha looked at Reynolds with disappointed sadness.

Reynolds paused. "Excuse me. Uh, son of a . . . son of a. . ."

"Spawn of a back-alley goat?" Irene said helpfully.

"Yes. Thank you. Spawn of a back-alley goat," Reynolds resumed at Charles with renewed vigor, "your very footprints foul the air. You will know the vengeance of the mujahedeen."

"You and who else?" Charles shot back from his rug cocoon. "When my people. . . "

"Your people?" I interjected. "Who are they?"

"You know damn well. I've got connections..."

"You've got zilch," I said. "By now Rafael suspects you haven't played straight with him. What do you think he's telling his people. Face it, old boy. You've become a liability to them."

"You don't scare me."

"I don't have to. Who would you rather take your chances with? Your people? The mujahedeen? Or the county prosecutor."

"Wusthof? He doesn't plea bargain with drug dealers. He plays hardball. They grab all your assets in drug cases."

"True," I said. "It's a question of who gets you first. For Irene's sake and your own protection, you'd better go with Wusthof."

Reynolds said, "I suggest you read some history of how Afghans treat their enemies when they get their hands on them—either the British in the nineteenth century, or recent Russian experiences. Me, I prefer the nineteenth century. The Great Game of the British Empire. You know Kipling's advice about what to do when the Afghans are coming after you when you're wounded on the plain?"

"No, what?" Charles snapped back.

"Better a bullet in your brain."

I could see that despite his bravado, Charles was weighing his diminishing options: all his expensive possessions, stacked up against either being machine-gunned by drug lords, or having his gizzard cut out by an Afghan assassin.

I turned to Irene. "Sweetheart, whom should we call? Abdur Rahman or Rafael?"

"Let's call them both," said Irene, "and see who gets him first. I think it will be Rafael's bosses. They'll want to make an example of him."

"I'm partial to Abdur Rahman myself," I replied. "Charles always claimed he's a sporting man, so I'll take a page from his book. Just to make things interesting, I'll bet you lunch at the London Chop House that Abdur Rahman's people will get to Charles first."

"You're on, sweetheart."

Charles was staring up at me in disbelief.

I ignored him and turned to Reynolds. "Do you want in on the action? The Chop House has a terrific wine list."

"Sounds good to me," Reynolds said without hesitation. "You already know I'm for Abdur Rahman."

"You're all crazy," Charles cried.

"Hold it," said Irene. "Both of you are betting on Abdur Rahman, which means if I lose I'll have to buy you *both* lunch. I want fair odds. If I win—if Rafael's people get Charles—you two have to treat me to *two* lunches. The London Chop House, and the second lunch at a place of my choice, to be named later."

I nodded. "That's only fair."

"Agreed," said Reynolds, "and done! Can Abdur come along, after he's finished with Charles?"

"I don't see why not," I said. "Irene?"

"Wait," Charles cried.

"Sure," Irene replied cheerfully. "We'll split Abdur's tab among the three of us. Mark it up to entertainment."

"Absolutely," said Reynolds.

"Wa-a-ait," Charles hollered.

I looked blandly down at him. "Oh, did you want to say something?"

His mustache was damp and scraggly, and his hair clung to his forehead. "Call those two police detectives."

"Clancy and Freiday?"

"Yes. I want to make a statement."

"You'd better make it a detailed confession," I warned him, "and follow it up with lots of convincing evidence so that Wusthof asks the judge to dismiss Irene's case..."

"I will."

"... because if you don't, the rest of us will be settling a wager at the Chop House."

Charles swallowed hard. His face was the mottled coloration of Gorgonzola.

18

By WEDNESDAY, JULY 5TH, Charles Finch was giving an earful to Wusthof's office. On Thursday I asked Detectives Clancy and Freiday why Wusthof hadn't made a formal motion to Judge Geary to dismiss Irene's murder charges, to which Frieday replied, "There's a lot of politics going on."

"There's always politics going on," I complained.

"Basically," she instructed me, "Wusthof is anal retentive. He'll make the motion tomorrow."

Freiday was right. Friday morning Judge Geary heard Wusthof's motion. Grunion put up a brave front, but the prospect of having his case dismissed from under him seemed to dislocate his growing sense of self. Detroit area newspapers had the story that evening: "Irene Innocent? Did Dapper Dog Doctor Do It? Loot Laundering Supported Lavish Lifestyle."

On Monday, Judge Geary dismissed all charges against Irene. That evening the Ann Arbor *News* led off with "Spinoza-Dixon Love Triangle Four-sided. Local Veterinarian Involved. Drug Connection Confirmed." To which Irene's only comment was, "They never get it quite right, do they?"

Irene was a free woman, and I was broke.

"I missed all the excitement," Biswanger griped.
"What excitement is that?" I asked with studied innocence.
"You know damn well."
"He's been sulking ever since George didn't call him that night," Emily remarked to Irene. "All I've been hearing is 'George got his name in the papers,' and 'George got interviewed on *Live at Five*,' and 'They're calling George a hero.'"
"Cheer up," I chided Biswanger. "You'll go with me the next time Irene is kidnapped and held for ransom."
"Is that a promise?"
"Would I lie to you?"
With peace restored, Emily, Irene, Biswanger, and I settled back to enjoy our chauffeured limousine ride to the Berkshire Hilton, where Hudson's was hosting an invitation-only, black-tie mousse party to announce my Magic Mousse-Maker. Irene said the Hudson's distribution was going to bail me out financially.

Things were actually looking up. Focus groups had gone bonkers over the mousses. At Irene's direction the Hudson's marketing people had set up a blind taste-testing by French chefs. The chefs had rated mousses made with my machine right up there with the best from Michelin-starred restaurants. Predictably, certain French culture critics had had fits upon learning a Gallic stamp of gustatory approval had been put on American gadget-produced mousse. Crying deception and trickery, they railed against American co-option of the sacred French mousse. But the word was out. European buyers were clamoring for a piece of the Magic Mousse-Maker action, and Magic Mousse-Makers had been stolen by Japanese spies. In a corporation laboratory somewhere in Japan, engineers had reverse-engineered them.

Hudson's knew about this, and their lawyers were conferring with a powerful Michigan congressman and both Michigan senators to head off the expected Japanese knock-offs. Smarting as they were from the beating our electronics and automobile industries had taken from Japanese zealousness, they were on a hair trigger about theft of U.S. intellectual property.

On the positive side, Ms. Linda Leung of Thousand Happinesses Limited was ecstatic about the burgeoning market for the redesigned Lotus Flex-a-Pleaser. She said *her* spies had gotten hold of the Japanese prototype copies, and that mousses made with them didn't come near the sensual qualities of mousses made with the Magic Mousse-Maker. The Japanese copies, Ms. Leung had assured me, lacked the magical je ne sais quoi that only Thousand Happinesses Limited knew how to put into its products.

We got out of the limo feeling very soigné.

We were nearing the conference room when I heard, "Pssht. Irene. May I take your coat?"

It was eight o'clock in the evening and eighty humid degrees outside. No one was wearing a coat. Irene and I looked toward the coat check. Rafael was at the counter. The same Rafael our incorruptible county prosecutor had accused of smuggling in drug money for laundering. I told Emily and Biswanger to go on ahead.

"What are you doing here?" I exclaimed. I looked for evidence of his automatic, then I remembered he didn't carry it loaded. "You are not going to ruin my party. Go away."

Ignoring me, Rafael blurted to Irene, "Come with me to Medellin."

"I'm expected at the mousse party," she replied.

"I depart tonight."

"You're a fugitive," Irene pointed out.

Rafael's eyes blazed. "I was willing to go away with you when you were accused of murder."

"Try to understand," Irene said gently. "I'm back with George."

"This is your last chance to be my queen of heaven."

"The feds have seized Charles's house and cars. They've frozen his bank accounts. The police and the feds are looking for you. The last thing you need is a queen of heaven. I think you should go back to being an ordinary accountant."

"And what of beauty, gracious living, refinement of mind, and fashion?"

"They're fine," Irene said, "as long as people pick up after you."

"In Medellin you will have them."

"That's not what I heard. So many people are into drug gangsterism down there, it's hard to find a same-day dry cleaner."

Rafael sighed. "May I kiss you good-bye on your hand?"

I intervened. "Absolutely not."

"Just a quick one on her pinky. I swear."

I pre-emptively took hold of Irene's hand. "Rafael, go back to your wife and five beautiful children in Bogota."

Having concluded our business with Rafael, and having no coats to check, Irene and I went to the mousse party.

There were about two hundred people in the chandeliered room. A refrigerated buffet had been set up with mousse fixings to suit any fancy: ice creams, sherbets, creme anglaise, clotted cream, and Chantilly cream; dark, medium, and white chocolate; liqueurs, brandies, wines, and whiskies; flavors, essences, and extracts; honeys, syrups, and sugars; fruits fresh and preserved; nuts toasted, whole, and flaked. To accompany the mousses, there were macaroons, lace cookies, and meringues. There was even liquid nitrogen for quick-freezing.

Ethan, the Hudson's marketing vice president, introduced

the overseas representatives: Gunar Snikvalds, Cecily Etherington-Pratt, Ramanujan Srivishnu, Layiwola Dinka. . . their names flowed effortlessly off Ethan's tongue. Layiwola was from Nigeria; Cecily was British. It didn't really matter. They all had the poise and international accent that comes from attending expensive Swiss schools. I was captivated by their charm. I was dazzled by their polished manners. I reflected that when the party was over I would be unable to remember one from the other.

Ethan was called away to soothe the nerves of someone important who had gotten lost and was calling from a Saline gas station. Irene went off to circulate. A woman fairly wept from gratitude as she thanked me for providing her with a way to make decent dietetic mousse. She declared life worth living again.

"It is a great occasion for eye-brightening, George-jan," said Abdur Rahman. He was eating lemon mousse.

My sanguine attitude nose-dived despite Abdur's fulsome praise, because Grunion was standing beside him. Grunion was engaged with minty green mousse covered in shaved chocolate. I deduced that Irene, in her euphoria following dismissal of her murder charge, had sent Grunion an invitation.

"Did it work out okay with the rug account?" I asked Abdur delicately.

Abdur nodded. "Peachy fine."

"How've you been doing?" I asked Grunion.

"I've been promoted in the firm."

"To what?"

"The fourteenth floor." Grunion blinked at me a few times, then said, "You mean what am I *doing* now. My uncle said I pursued Irene's case with such enterprise and diligence in the short time I had, he's putting me into trusts and estates. No more trial work for me. I'll be traveling a lot, getting acquainted with our out-of-state clients, maybe going overseas."

Who would be there to tell Grunion the difference between Des Moines and Cedar Rapids? Between East Lansing and Grand Rapids? Ossining and Ishpeming? Abu Dhabi and Dubai?

"I really owe my promotion to you," Grunion said.

"Me?"

"Absolutely. Your pep talks when I was practicing my closing arguments. You gave me the confidence to make a maximum effort, and it paid off. My uncle noticed. I'll always remember what you did for me."

"And my people," said Abdur, "shout your praises for what you did for them. They call you The Man Who Makes Toys And Is The Likeable Fool of God."

I didn't know what to say.

Abdur Rahman was wreathed in smiles. "It must be wonderful to bring so much happiness to so many."

"I guess I can't help myself."

"One might as well plead with the sun to stop shining."

I was still pondering Abdur Rahman's words when I saw Reynolds, looking as if he'd been born to wear black tie, and Perdita with two of the overseas representatives. Reynolds strolled over with Perdita.

"How's your back?" I asked.

"Never better. I'll be leaving Ann Arbor."

"It won't be the same without you."

"They want me in D.C. I'm being promoted to a big job with lots of responsibility for my successful handling of the Dixon affair."

Reynolds's flexible adaptation of the truth was breathtaking. I also noted a more subtle change. No more Miles Dixon.

No more murder. Now it was The Dixon Affair.

"Of course," said Reynolds, "I can't divulge exactly what my job is. Though I will say it's big."

"How big?"

"Big big."

I was impressed. "That big, huh?"

"Bigger," said Reynolds. "They need experienced people with field operative experience who are experienced and knowledgeable about the Afghanistan connection. You yourself have priceless experience that could be of inestimable value for a position-planning paper. They've been hearing good things about you, George."

"They have? How?"

"From me. At present, I'm a knowledgeable source. Soon I'll be a power to be reckoned with. If you're agreeable, I'd like to keep you in mind as a consultant."

I figured my hunches were as good as theirs. "Count me in."

"But first I must ask you something, and please answer truthfully, or failing that, to the best of your knowledge. Would you object to being put up in a fancy hotel for weeks at a time, and attending lavish parties while your opinions are sought by State Department policy planners?"

"Only if I could take weekends off to see Irene."

"That goes without saying. Our weekends begin Thursday afternoon and end Tuesday morning."

"Then I'm your man."

"Splendid. You'll hear from me when I've got my bearings."

"How do you think you'll like living in Washington?" I asked Perdita.

"Who's going to Washington?"

"I thought you and Reynolds..."

"Heavens to Betsy," Perdita exclaimed, smiling pertly.

"I'm staying here with my husband."

"I thought you said you left your husband."

"I did. I just didn't tell him."

"Didn't he notice something was missing in his life?"

"I think he might have," Perdita said slowly, giving it some thought; then, gathering confidence, "He must have. Yes, this time, I'm sure he did."

Her fling with the State Department was over. I said, "I hope you find happiness."

"In life, every encounter should be a positive learning experience," Perdita explained.

With Perdita and her husband having such vague notions of each other's awareness, feelings, and presence, it was no wonder that she should be ineluctably drawn to exotic infatuations. She wanted her indigenous husband to *notice*.

Ethan pulled me aside. He was excited but not breathless. "Our lobbyist just informed us the bill has been reported out of the House-Senate conference committee. They didn't fuck it over like they do other bills. It's intact!"

"What bill?"

"Our trade bill to defend us against foreign usurpation of our Magic Mousse-Maker, of course."

"I didn't know we needed one."

"Good God, man! How else can we protect our Singapore manufacturer and our overseas distributors from unjust foreign competition with our American product?" Ethan pulled a telegram from his pocket and read from it. "Congratulations. . ." blah, blah, blah. . . "One of the finest pieces of special-interest legislation I've seen in twenty years of public service. Mood positive for passage on voice vote. Proposed name: The Spinoza International Trade Fairness Doctrine." Ethan beamed at me. "How does it feel, George?"

"How is it possible," I pleaded, "for my elected representatives to put my name on a bill I haven't read? Not even in executive summary."

"You're too modest for your own good, George. That's what I like best about you." Ethan's perfect executive composure was vibrating emanations of jubilation, triumph, and greed. "Oh, George, George," he cried, "we're going to make a shitload of money. I always had faith in you."

"Actually," I said, trying not to sound churlish, "it was Irene who had the faith."

"Her, too. Where is she?"

"Circulating."

Irene and I returned home around eleven-thirty. We were utterly moussed out. Irene went up to her place to change, and I went to mine to take Natasha out for her walk. I saw no earthly or spiritual reason for us to change our living arrangement, which was for Irene to entertain her business associates up in her condo—hers being so beautifully decorated—and to use mine solely for eating, sleeping, putting away the groceries, reading, balancing the checkbook, talking, making love, and watching television.

It was a warm summer night. While skateboarders careened by me in Liberty Plaza, I reflected that only a short week ago Irene had been on trial for murder. I had faced penury, suffered the loss of respect from my friends, and been plagued with self-doubt. Now senators were dedicating landmark legislation to me, and I was being sought for advice on foreign affairs. Visions of sugarplum mousses danced in my head.

When I returned with Natasha, Irene was still upstairs and my phone was ringing. "Now who can that be?" I asked Natasha. Perhaps one of those wonderful media people was calling about setting up an interview about my trade bill.

Irene was calling from upstairs.

"Aren't you coming down tonight, Josephine?" I asked playfully.

"I've locked myself in."

Bloody hell. It was those new locks she'd had installed. I said, "Lean against the door, then try turning the key."

"I don't have the key."

"How did you get in without a key?"

Irene explained that she *had* gotten in with a key. She had automatically put her keys in her evening bag with the business cards from the mousse party, then tossed the bag into a file-cabinet drawer and shut the drawer. Unfortunately, the file-cabinet keys were with her door keys—locked inside the file drawer.

"Can't you jimmy the file drawer open?" I asked.

"It's a heavy-duty Steelcase. I got it used. It was at Bendix before they were acquired and closed down their Plymouth Road aerospace division."

Bloody, bloody hell. The file cabinet that once held NASA Lunar Lander papers now held the keys to Irene's sliding bolt lock, and to my happiness.

"I'll call the locksmith tomorrow," Irene said.

"It would be terrible for our public image," I said.

"Our what?"

"Public image. We have to face facts, Irene. We're nearly famous. Even as we speak, landmark trade legislation is being passed because of us. I may become an informed source. How would it look, when we're nearly husband and wife again, if we were discovered living in separate domiciles?"

"Husband and wife. . . Georgie?"

"You had to divorce me. Now we have to get married again."

"We do?"

"For the good of our country's trade posture, Irene, and because I love you."

There was a sweet pause, then, "I'll marry you again Georgie. If you'll do me one favor."

"Name it."

"Get me the hell out of here."

I laid out bed sheets where stairs had once connected the two floors when our two condos were one, and moved my heavy parson's worktable to the middle of them. Then I got a crowbar.

Natasha watched me from her customary position in my swivel chair.

I climbed onto the table and started bashing away at the ceiling. Plaster blue-board rained down on me. I hacked onward.

When I was done, I was covered in white dust. My reward was Irene's lovely face framed in the hole in my ceiling. She dangled her legs down through it. I reached up and, holding her hips, guided her as she slowly slid down till we stood face to face on my parson's table. She had escaped from the seraglio.

We climbed down from the table.

Irene said, "I've got a surprise for you. Haven't you noticed anything different about your place?"

I looked around. My living room looked larger. Perhaps it was its new coating of plaster dust. Or had Irene started to redecorate it? Then I realized. The big Thousand Happinesses Limited carton was gone.

"What happened to the big carton of toy samples that was by the door?"

"Turn on Channel 56," Irene said, changing the subject.

"They've still got that nonstop twenty-four hour auction going to raise money. Uh, sweetheart, what happened to the carton?"

"That's my surprise. I donated it to the Channel 56 auction in your name. They're auctioning off everything in the carton."

"Irene, sweetheart," I croaked, "why did you do that?"

"You're going to need the tax deduction. Turn on the TV, Georgie. I want to see how they're doing."

It was the biggest-grossing fundraiser by a local affiliate in PBS history.

▽

Appendix

Hotel Rompé is a naughty board game for up to ten players. The game pieces are as follows:
Suspect Cards—chambermaid; bell hop; traveling salesperson; mysterious permanent lodger; newlyweds; four wild-card guests; the Reverend Silliphant; the house detective.
Naughty Secret Cards—are shuffled and dealt to the players.
Compromising Position Cards
Hotel Room Cards
Excuse/Alibi Cards—are shuffled and dealt out to the players.
Imposter/Phony-Identity Cards
Naughty Clue Cards—such as articles of clothing, which the accused must explain with a plausible excuse card.

As play progresses, it becomes necessary to make *Uneasy Alliances*. For example, if your piece lands in a room with another player, and a third player is in that room, any player can challenge the other two players by showing a naughty clue card and saying 'J'accuse!" The accused players in the room can either lose points, or else maintain their innocence. The two or more accused players must collude in an *Uneasy Alliance* in order to rebuff the accusing player. One of the accused players must show an Alibi card. If the accusing player calls the bluff, then all the accused players must show that their *Excuse/Alibi Cards* match, in which case the accuser forfeits points to them. You can also use an *Imposter/Phony-Identity Card* to double-cross someone who is in an *Uneasy Alliance* with you.

Blackmail—If you've figured out the *Naughty Secret* on the back of a player's card, you can exact blackmail, which can be in the form of money, or a future *Uneasy Alliance*. If two players decide to cooperate and lure someone into making an accusation about them, they must have a good idea about their respective excuse cards and *Naughty Secret Cards*.

Imitators have tried to get market share from *Hotel Rompé*. For example, a guy in Florida came up with *High Rise Condo*, which in turn inspired its own imitation, *Real Estate Ricochet*, so they canceled each other out. No others have been able to capture the pure delight that Victorian naughtiness provides, not even *Dirty Trickster* or *Hallelujah Bingo*.

THE END

1